D1551656

Flight

Other Emerson Moore Adventures by Bob Adamov

- *Rainbow's End* – released October 2002
- *Pierce the Veil* – released May 2004
- *When Rainbows Walk* – released June 2005
- *Promised Land* – released July 2006
- *The Other Side of Hell* – released June 2008
- *Tan Lines* – released June 2010
- *Sandustee* – released March 2013
- *Zenobia* – released May 2014
- *Missing* – released April 2015
- *Golden Torpedo* – released July 2017
- *Chincoteague Calm* – released April 2018

The Next Emerson Moore Adventure:
- *Assateague Dark*

Flight

Bob Adamov

PACKARD ISLAND PUBLISHING
Wooster ❀ Ohio
2019
www.packardislandpublishing.com

Copyright 2019 by Bob Adamov

All rights reserved.

No part of this book may be used or reproduced in any manner whatsoever without written permission from the author except in the case of brief quotations embodied in critical articles or reviews.

www.BobAdamov.com

This book is a work of fiction. Names, characters, places and incidents are either products of the author's imagination or are used fictitiously. Any resemblance to actual events, locales or persons, living or dead, is entirely coincidental.

First Edition • May 2019

ISBN: 978-0-9786184-8-3
(ISBN 10: 0-9786184-8-3)

Library of Congress number: 2019931255

Printed and bound in the United States of America.

Cover art by: Denis Lange
LANGE DESIGN
890 Williamsburg Court
Ashland, OH 44805
www.langedesign.biz

Printed by:
BOOKMASTERS, INC.
PO Box 388
Ashland, Ohio 44805
www.Bookmasters.com

Layout design by: David Wiesenberg
THE WOOSTER BOOK COMPANY
205 West Liberty Street
Wooster, OH 44691
www.woosterbook.com

Published by:
PACKARD ISLAND PUBLISHING
3025 Evergreen Drive
Wooster, Ohio
www.packardislandpublishing.com

Dedication

This book is dedicated to my dear friend and mentor JOHN EMERSON for whom Emerson Moore is named. John has passed on, but his legacy from helping others, lives on. This is also dedicated to my friend, HOWARD MYERS, who passed away. He was such a unique individual. Whenever we met for lunch, I'd take along a pen and paper because of his funny stories and one-liners.

They that wait upon the Lord shall renew their strength;
they shall mount up with wings as eagles;
they shall run, and not be weary;
and they shall walk, and not faint.

—Isaiah 40:31

Acknowledgements

For technical assistance, I'd like to express my appreciation to Chuck "Big Daddy" Meier in Cudjoe Key, one of the most interesting characters I've met during my book research. Thank you to Roe Terry for introducing me to Big Daddy and to Doctor Chris Ranney and Doctor Linda Wang for medical advice.

A special thanks to Joe and Ray Daschner for telling me about their unique Gremlin which made its way into this adventure.

I'd like to thank my team of editors: Cathy Adamov, John Wisse, Peggy Parker, Julia Wiesenberg of The Wooster Book Company, and Andrea Goss Knaub.

For more information, check these sites:
www. Bob Adamov.com
www. Visit Put-in-Bay.com
www. Miller Ferry.com

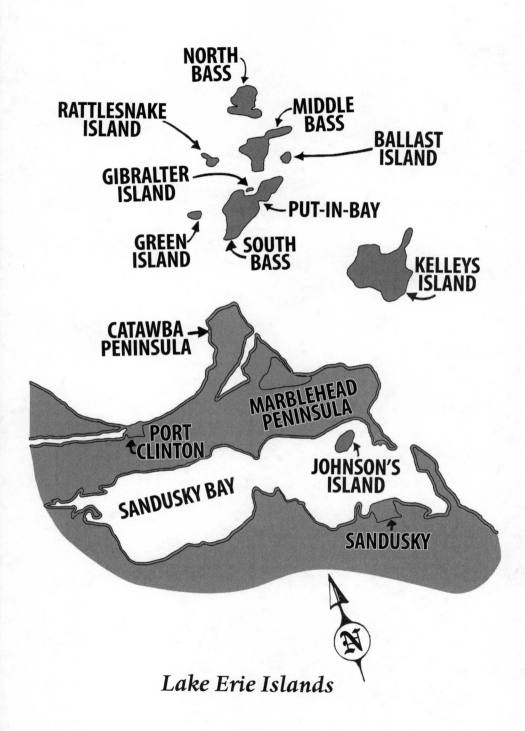

NORTH BASS

MIDDLE BASS

RATTLESNAKE ISLAND

BALLAST ISLAND

GIBRALTER ISLAND

PUT-IN-BAY

GREEN ISLAND

SOUTH BASS

KELLEYS ISLAND

CATAWBA PENINSULA

MARBLEHEAD PENINSULA

PORT CLINTON

JOHNSON'S ISLAND

SANDUSKY BAY

SANDUSKY

N

Lake Erie Islands

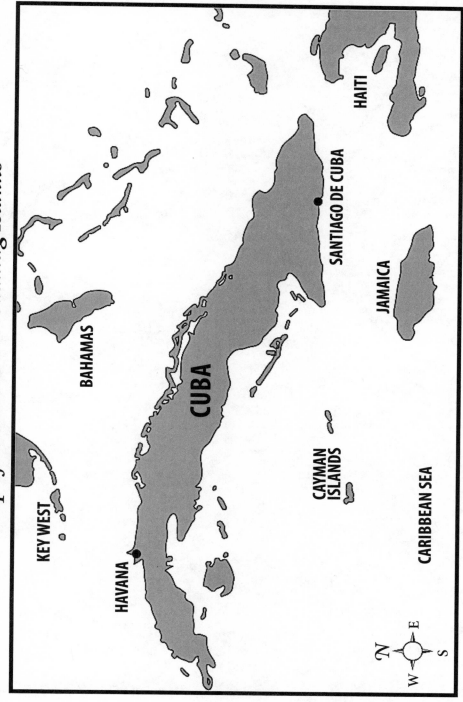

Map of Cuba and Surrounding Islands

Flight

CHAPTER 1

September 16, 1928
Florida East Coast Railway Station
St. Augustine, Florida

The heavy rain dragged down the thick black clouds overhead as it poured with a roar upon the city. The loud, threatening booms of thunder disrupted what had been a relatively quiet night. Warm rain struck the already wet surfaces of the sidewalks, streets and buildings, hitting them like bullets from above. The outer bands of the oncoming hurricane were responsible for the rain and dark black sky where just hours ago, it had been a clear blue, early fall day.

Beneath the overhang at the end of the train station, a muscular man stood ghostlike in the shadowy light from the street lamps, appearing when he wanted and then vanishing into eerie obscurity. The man, wearing a long, black raincoat and gray fedora with a black band, reeked of danger and held secrets as one would expect. His name was Joshua Van Duzer. He was the head of the Pinkerton Detective Agency contingent.

He reached inside his coat pocket and withdrew a crumpled pack of cigarettes. Extracting the last one, he threw the pack to the gutter where the water carried it away. Van Duzer watched it, thinking how the currents of life directed his path into dangerous situations. He stuck the cigarette in his mouth and pulled a match out of his pocket. Striking it, he cupped his hand around it as he lit his cigarette and inhaled. He held the match up in the dim light and examined it. A useful tool a few seconds ago had now lost its usefulness. He wondered how long it would be before he too was no longer useful.

Flicking the worn match into the street gutter, he watched as it washed away. Turning his head, his eyes tried to pierce the downpour for any signs of trouble. One never knew when it may arise. Van Duzer was always prepared.

The light caught his body and cast a shadow in the downpour. It was a good night for shadows. They somewhat shielded the activity on the train behind the station. Van Duzer scowled into the darkness as he inhaled. His mood mirrored the dark sky.

He had picked his vantage point carefully and could easily observe his agents at work as they loaded their precious cargo onto the train. It was also easy for him to step around the building to keep an eye out for any vehicles approaching the front of the station building. Rumors had been rampant about the train's cargo, and he expected trouble.

The noisy engine of an approaching car caught Van Duzer's attention. Clenching his cigarette tightly between his lips, he walked under the overhang to the front corner of the station. As he walked, he brought up his shotgun from under his raincoat and cradled it in his arms.

When he stepped around the corner, Van Duzer was

pleased to see five of his armed men stationed in front of the building. They each brandished their Thompson submachine guns and glared at the two 1927 black Ford sedans as the vehicles slowly drove by the front of the station. The four burly occupants in each vehicle returned the glare from the Pinkerton men and decided to move on. The show of force had served its purpose.

Van Duzer nodded to his men and returned to his prior position. He was pleased by the progress they had made in light of the change in their original plans. The schedule was moved up a day because of the approaching hurricane.

The weather forecasters revised their prediction as to when the deadly hurricane would make landfall. They now expected the hurricane would hit West Palm Beach the next morning with winds up to 150 mph. They anticipated the hurricane would cause severe damage between Miami and Ft. Pierce. Later, it would be defined as a Category 4 hurricane and recognized as the second worst hurricane in Florida's history.

Van Duzer's eyes were drawn to the train in front of him. It consisted of a sleek black engine that was built in 1924 in upstate New York at the Schenectady Locomotive Works. It glistened in the rain. The numbers 444 were white-lettered below the cab window. The locomotive had a black coal tender and a mail express car that was armor-plated with 5/8-inch steel on the car's roof, floor and sides. It was fitted with two large, walk-in safes.

The primary activity was taking place at the armored mail car. Six rough-looking uniformed Pinkerton guards cradling shotguns oversaw several men loading a number of boxes from an armored truck to the car. The guards ever-vigilant eyes pierced the rainy darkness for any signs of trouble.

Within thirty minutes, the mail car was loaded and its secret cargo stored securely in the two safes. The six Pinkerton guards stepped aboard as the conductor looked at his watch, and then glanced toward the corner of the building where Van Duzer had been standing.

"We're ready," the conductor yelled through the rain as he peered out from the armored car. He started to slide the armored door closed after the six guards had boarded and the armored van drove away.

Van Duzer nodded and approached the conductor. "You have a safe trip."

"I'm counting on it. This weather should give us nice cover."

"You just never know. Can't be too careful," Van Duzer cautioned as the conductor secured the door shut from inside the car. Van Duzer then affixed a large padlock to the outside of the door and locked it. There were two keys to the padlock—his key and a key in New York City. He walked up to the engine where another armed Pinkerton guard looked down from the protection offered by the engine cab.

"Are we ready to go?" the guard asked as the engineer and fireman peered over his shoulder at Van Duzer.

"All clear. Have a safe trip," Van Duzer replied as he looked at the three men, then returned to stand under the station's overhang.

The guard nodded his head as the engineer moved the throttle forward and the special train began moving northward through the driving rain toward its New York City destination.

Watching the train safely leave the station, Van Duzer glanced down to the depot floor where he saw six cigarette butts crushed on the ground. He smiled to himself as he reached inside his coat pocket for another one. His hand came away empty. He forgot that he recently had smoked his last cigarette.

Shrugging his shoulders, he walked around to the front of the station to talk with his other guards. "We're done, boys," he shouted to his men. "Good job."

The five guards walked over to two parked vehicles and left the area.

Van Duzer stepped into the rain and walked to his vehicle. It was like walking through a waterfall. He couldn't get any wetter. When he reached his car, he started it and drove to the airport where a Ford trimotor airplane was waiting to fly him out of St. Augustine before the weather worsened.

If Van Duzer had left at the same time as the train pulled out of the depot, he would have seen the two Ford sedans, which earlier had driven by, give chase after the departed train. The evening would have some interesting developments.

An hour later at the airport, the Pinkerton had finished a coffee and was listening as the wind picked up, causing the terminal building to pop and crack from its force. He was waiting to board the trimotor when the airport manager approached him.

"Mr. Van Duzer?" he asked. The man had a concerned look on his face.

"Yes."

"I'm sorry to bother you, but I just had an urgent message called in for you."

"Yes?"

"Engine number 444 and its cars made it to Bowden Yard in Jacksonville."

"Good. I would expect that," Van Duzer replied.

"There were armed men aboard the engine and they made the rail workers turn the train around," the airport manager stated with alarm.

Van Duzer stood in silence. As he did, he reached for a cigarette that was tucked behind his ear. He had bummed it from an airport worker earlier.

"Someone shot the engineer and fireman. They found their bodies in the rail yard next to the tracks," the man added.

"Did the caller have any idea where it's headed?" he asked calmly as he thought about the situation. Remaining calm in the face of adversity had been one of the personal strengths that enabled Van Duzer to advance in the Pinkerton organization.

"Not north," the man answered as he watched Van Duzer light the cigarette and inhale deeply before speaking again.

"How far is it from here to Bowden Yard?" Van Duzer asked as his mind worked furiously.

"About thirty miles."

"I want you to call Bowden Yard and every station within thirty miles of Bowden to watch for the train."

"I hope I can." The station manager appeared agitated.

"What do you mean?"

"The phone went dead. We probably have phone lines down because of the storm," he explained. "Probably have telegraph lines down, too."

Van Duzer took another deep draw on his cigarette. "See what you can do now and I'll be in touch." Van Duzer looked at the trimotor pilot. "Let's head out."

"Are you going to try to find the train?" asked the stunned airport manager.

"That's our plan," Van Duzer said confidently.

Taking a notepad from his inside pocket, Van Duzer scribbled a phone number on a blank page as he clenched his cigarette tightly between his lips. He ripped the page from the notebook and handed it to the station manager.

"This is the number for the Pinkerton office in New York. When the phone lines are back in service, call them and tell them what's happened. And tell them that I'm going after the train," he instructed as he buttoned up his raincoat. Van Duzer pulled his fedora down tightly upon his head before following the pilot out the door to the waiting plane.

As they walked through the driving rain, the wind threatened to tear Van Duzer's coat away. He clenched his hat tightly and climbed aboard the plane. He took the co-pilot's seat as the rain peppered the plane's corrugated metal skin with hail. When he peered out the window, he could barely see the lights from the airport lobby. Van Duzer had a smile on his face and was pleased with the evening's events.

The pilot started the three 7-cylinder, 235-horsepower Wright Whirlwind engines and then slowly taxied to the runway. There, the pilot pushed the throttle forward and the plane moved quickly down the rain-slicked runway. The trimotor became airborne and disappeared into the inky canopy of relentless rain.

CHAPTER 2

Present Day
Booger Blake's Bar
Key West, Florida

Tempers were running high throughout the crowded bar. Bartenders were stressed, servers were unhappy and a tempest was brewing among the patrons. Something was soon to erupt in the hot, humid night. It didn't help that the air conditioning system in the bar had succumbed to an operational heart attack earlier in the day.

A repairman had provided an initial systems assessment and would return the next day with the needed parts to make repairs. Until then, large fans, which were brought in to dilute the thick humid air and provide some degree of comfort, achieved little by mid-evening to suppress a gathering of low-paid, overworked employees and raucous customers.

Using a bar towel, a bearded bartender paused and wiped the beads of sweat from his brow. His long hair was pulled back in a ponytail. He also had a large red birthmark on his cheek below his right eye.

"How long did you say that you've been bartending?" the balding, t-shirted owner asked his recent hire.

"Not very long, Blake," the bartender answered.

"Yeah. I figured. I saw you looking up drink recipes several times, Manny."

"It's this PTSD I'm dealing with, man. Sometimes, I just forget stuff," the barkeep replied.

"Yeah. Sure, you do," Blake said in disbelief. Looking toward the end of the bar, the owner instructed, "You take care of those two guys down there. They're regulars and spend good money here."

Manny Elias looked to where Blake was pointing.

Blake continued. "The one with the red hair is separated from his wife for almost a year. He hasn't filed for divorce yet and he's miserable. Caught her having an affair. The skinny guy next to him. That's Carl. He's got two kids and can't do anything right, according to his wife. She treats him like garbage, always wants to spend his money and complains all the time. He works two jobs and tries to save his money, but she spends it faster than he can earn it. Think Home Shopping Network and Amazon."

"Why doesn't he leave her?"

"In one word, co-dependent. They can't exist without each other. They swim in their misery and can't break out of it." Blake lowered his voice as he added, "Remember. We are their psychologists. We listen and try to give them advice and all for the cost of a drink."

"And a tip," Elias grinned at his boss.

"Right. I feel bad for some of the people who come in here. Real nice folks and just in some plain bad situations. Just don't get pulled down by their depression. Cheer them up, Manny."

"I can do that."

"You hear a lot of stories. Stuff that they can't do, places they can't go, how they have to act or think or how they're surrounded by a sea of ungratefulness."

"Come on now, Blake. It can't all be bad," Elias said.

Blake looked at his apprentice bartender. "It isn't. You've got the fun ones coming in here, too. They're living the life. Living it high. Being successful. Having fun. Catching fish. Great sailing stories."

"Just send them down to this end of the bar. I like to be around positive people," Elias said half-jokingly. "Especially if it's a good-looking female," he added with a wink.

"Yeah," Blake agreed. "Them beauties can certainly make your day, but you get whatever sits across from you. Be good to them."

Blake walked down to the other end of the bar as Elias greeted and served two women who sat down at his end of the bar before moving down to talk to the two men that Blake had mentioned.

Later that night, Elias walked out of the bar as Blake closed it. He unlocked his bike from the rack and rode it down Whitehead Street to United Street where he turned left. A short distance later, he turned left into the trailer park and rode up to the trailer. He parked the bike under the porch and unlocked the door.

Elias stepped into the cool confines of his refuge from the heat and headed to the fridge where he grabbed a cold bottle of water. Rolling the bottle slowly across his forehead, he walked to the sofa and dropped his overheated body on it as he took off his wig. It indeed had been a tough night for Manny Elias, the alias that Emerson Moore resurrected as he went undercover to research a story on the drug trafficking between Key West and Cuba.

Unscrewing the bottle cap, Moore took a long drink of the frigid water and relaxed. He was disappointed in failing to uncover anything linking the bar owner to drug trafficking in the week he had worked. It might take time. He wasn't sure how long it would take, but he knew that he'd have to rise early and study the drink recipes for the next evening. At the rate he was going, the owner would fire him for being incompetent. Moore couldn't afford such a setback.

After he finished his drink, Moore headed for the bedroom. One thing he did appreciate was his former Navy SEAL friend, Sam Duncan, allowing him to use his mobile home while he was in town. It worked well. Duncan again was off on one of his own covert adventures.

Moore dropped his shorts and t-shirt on the floor and escaped to a cooling shower before crashing for the night. The next morning, he awoke, slipped into his running gear and enjoyed his run along Smathers Beach. When he returned to the trailer, he again jumped in the shower and shaved before making coffee and sitting at the kitchen table to study the drink recipes.

Upon arriving at the bar that afternoon, he was pleased that it was dramatically cooler inside since the air conditioner had been fixed. Moore was working his end of the bar and looked toward the owner as a patron entered the doorway. The patron stared at the owner whose eyes widened in disbelief. The patron then quickly turned on his heels and walked briskly out of the bar.

Blake grabbed the bar top. He was visibly shaken and looked like he had seen a ghost.

Moore approached him.

"Are you okay?"

"Fine. I'm just fine," Blake grumbled as he tried to compose himself.

"Did you know that guy?"

"Yeah. It's been a long time since I've seen him."

"A friend?"

A scowl filled Blake's face. "No. We used to do business together until it went sour."

"What kind of business?" Moore probed, hoping that this might be an opening to a discussion about drug trafficking.

"None of yours," Blake retorted angrily.

"What?" Moore asked, not comprehending.

"It's none of your business!" Blake repeated himself. Looking down the bar where two patrons seated themselves, he snapped at Moore. "You've got customers! Go and take care of them."

Blake turned and walked out to the cooler at the rear of the bar as Moore hurried to serve his new arrivals. The rest of the evening passed incident free.

Late the next afternoon, Moore arrived at the bar and began serving patrons. Five minutes later two police officers walked in, interrupting a conversation that Blake was having with Moore.

"We're looking for Blake," said an officer wearing a name badge showing his last name was Pieffer.

"I'm Blake," the owner spoke up.

The officer thrust out his hand. In it he held a photo. "I'm Greg Pieffer. Do you know this man?"

A shiver ran up Blake's spine. "Why?"

"Just a simple yes or no will do, Blake."

"No."

"Can you explain why he had your name, address and phone number written on a scrap of paper on the nightstand in his motel room?" Pieffer asked.

"I don't know," Blake replied.

It was the other officer's turn to ask a question. His name badge showed his last name was Fletcher. "Blake, do you own a handgun?"

"Yes."

"Could I see it?" Fletcher asked.

"Sure. It's right here," Blake said as he opened a drawer beneath the cash register and his face contorted into a look of surprise. He stood paralyzed.

"What's wrong?" Fletcher asked.

"It's gone. My gun is missing."

"Does it look like this?" Fletcher held up a Smith and Wesson .38 revolver. It was in a plastic evidence bag.

"Yes."

"Would you be surprised if I told you the serial numbers on this gun are the same that were registered for your .38?"

"What are you getting at?" Blake asked.

"We'd like you to come in for questioning, Blake," Pieffer directed.

"What for? It looks like someone stole my gun. You want me to file a police report?" Blake asked with a sense of confusion.

"This gun was found next to the body of a man murdered last night," Pieffer explained. "It was the man in the photo that I showed you," he added.

"Where were you last night?" Fletcher asked.

"I was here working and then…"

Moore saw an opportunity and interjected, "… and then he spent the night at my place. We talked business almost all night." Moore was taking a risk by lying about Blake's whereabouts, but he saw it as a way to get closer to Blake.

Fletcher looked closely at Moore and then Blake. "Is that true?" he asked suspiciously.

Surprised by Moore's alibi, Blake didn't respond right away.

"Is that true?" Fletcher asked again.

"Yes. That's right. I was with him," Blake answered as he gave Moore a look of appreciation.

"And who are you?" Fletcher asked.

"I'm Manny Elias. I just work here. That's all," Moore replied.

Unconvinced, the two officers eyed the men behind the bar.

"Blake, we still want you to come in for questioning. And you too, Elias," Pieffer spoke sternly.

"Can we stop in tomorrow morning at nine o'clock?" Blake asked. "We've got a bar to run."

"That will be fine," Pieffer responded before the two officers left.

Blake turned to Moore and asked, "Why did you cover for me, Manny? We weren't together." Blake was dumfounded by Moore's action.

"You were in a tight spot. I knew you couldn't have done it," Moore replied.

"I didn't," Blake offered.

"Don't worry about anything, Blake. I've got your back," Moore said.

"Thanks, Manny." Seeing a number of customers awaiting drinks, Blake said, "Let's take care of these folks. We'll talk after we close up tonight."

The rest of the evening passed without any other incidents. Moore was anxious to learn more from Blake. When they finished closing down for the evening, Blake approached Moore and poured himself a beer from the tap.

"Want one?"

"No, not really a beer drinker, Blake."

"Make yourself whatever you want, then," Blake said as he carried his beer around the end of the bar and sat at a nearby table.

Moore fixed himself a rum and Seven-Up and took a seat at the table.

"Thanks again, Manny, for standing up for me."

"No problem, Blake."

"I came in today and saw the gun was missing. You remember, right? I asked you if you saw it," Blake said anxiously.

"I do."

"I don't know who took it. I checked with the rest of the staff. No one took it."

"Any signs of a break in?" Moore asked.

"None. But some of the good ones don't leave a trail when they break in. Kind of quietly do it and slither away," Blake said knowingly as he took a long drink of his beer.

"I figured you didn't kill the guy."

"I would have if I had the chance," Blake remarked in a deadly tone.

"Why is that?"

Even though Blake knew that the rest of the staff had left, he looked around the bar. He sighed before he began his explanation. "The guy and I used to be business partners."

"You owned a bar together?"

"No, it was a different business." He took a long drink from his glass.

"What kind?"

Blake's eyes scanned the empty room again. "It was five years ago. I was short of cash and he gave me an opportunity. It was drugs."

"You sold drugs?" Moore feigned surprise as he fought to control his enthusiasm to learn more.

"Yeah. It was up in Miami."

"What happened?"

"Manny, you've got to understand that the dudes who we worked with were some tough hombres. They'd stop at nothing to get even with you if they thought you were stealing from them. They'd go after your family. They'd kill your parents. They didn't care."

"So, what happened?"

"He was skimming money off the top. I kept telling him to stop, but he wouldn't. So, I did the only thing I could do for my family. I ratted him out."

"You told the guys that he was skimming?" Moore asked incredulously as he sipped his drink.

"I did. It was the only way I could keep my family safe."

"And they didn't get him?"

"No, the lucky son of a gun. He told his brother to start his car because he forgot his cigarettes. He was in the house when the car exploded. Killed his brother. He knew that they were on to him and he disappeared."

"And he shows up here last night, in your bar," Moore reiterated.

"Yeah."

"And dead later that night."

"Yeah."

"And you really didn't kill him?" Moore asked.

"No."

"Any ideas who did?"

"No. I really don't know. I've been here for a few years. I keep a low profile. Mind my own business."

"You selling drugs again?" Moore probed, hoping for a break. He took another sip of his rum.

Blake didn't answer right away. He wrestled with how he was going to answer the question. He raised his glass to his lips and drank the remaining beer. He then stared at Moore, wondering what to admit.

"Manny, I'm going to let you in on a little secret." He furrowed his brow for a moment before continuing. "I am. There was this Cuban who started hanging out here. Nice guy. We seemed to hit it off. He invited me on his boat to go fishing a couple of times. Nice boat. Fifty-footer.

"One day, I was talking and I had too much to drink. I let slip that I was running behind on my payroll taxes and lease payments. He offered to help me out with a short-term loan. Then he pitched the idea of me pushing drugs for him. He thought I had a good location. I needed the cash and I knew how well I did before, so I agreed. Been doing it since," Blake explained.

"It's been good for you?"

"Yeah. Real good."

"How do I get in?"

Blake furrowed his brow as he studied the bartender. "You ever do anything like this before, Manny?"

"No, but I like the idea of getting some extra cash."

Blake slowly shook his head from side to side. "I don't know, Manny. I'm not sure that he wants anyone but me involved. You let me think about it for a few days and I'll let you know what I decide."

"I'd really like to get the extra cash, Blake."

"Yeah. Yeah. We all do. You just be patient, my friend."

Moore stopped pushing so hard. He realized that he could sour the relationship he built with Blake. "Has he been in this week? I didn't notice you hanging out with any Cuban-looking guy," Moore asked.

"No. He's back in Cuba. Picking up a load."

"Do you think there's any way he could have killed your ex-partner?"

"No. Like I said, he's in Cuba."

"Wonder who could have killed him and why they set you up?" Moore inquired.

"Yeah. It makes you wonder," Blake agreed. "Might be some of the boys from Miami and they figured they should eliminate both of us."

"Then, why didn't they just kill you rather than trying to set you up?"

"Who knows? These guys don't always think things through like us smart guys," Blake chuckled softly. He looked at his watch. "Okay. It's late and I need to get home to my family."

The two stood and finished cleaning up, then left the bar. Moore walked over to his bike and unlocked it from the tree where he had chained it. As he mounted his bike, he saw Blake walking down Fleming Street toward his apartment.

Moore pedaled his bike down Whitehead Street and enjoyed the late evening air. He turned onto United Street and rode to the mobile home park to Sam's trailer. Moore was pleased. He had succeeded in opening up a dialog about Blake's drug trafficking.

CHAPTER 3

A Few Weeks Earlier
Put-in-Bay
South Bass Island, Ohio

"Got to run. I'm late," the six-foot-two, tanned, dark-haired man in his early forties said as he rounded the corner into the kitchen, almost knocking over his aunt. "Sorry," he said hurriedly.

"You don't have time for breakfast, Emerson?" Aunt Anne asked as she walked to the stove.

"No. I've got to make the ferry. I've got a meeting in Bellevue," he replied as he grabbed his car keys.

"Here. Take this," she said as she handed him a cup of coffee that she quickly poured.

"Thanks Aunt Anne. You're the best," he said as he bent over and gave her a quick kiss on the cheek.

"Sure. Sure. Go on with you," she smiled as he took the to-go-cup and raced out the kitchen door. She poured herself a cup of coffee and wandered out to the front porch of her home on East Point. She sat silently in one of the wicker chairs and enjoyed her view of the water traffic entering and exiting the bay.

She was content and glad that her nephew, Emerson Moore, had moved in with her a few years ago after her husband had died. She wondered what exciting story he was working on this time. He was an investigative reporter for *The Washington Post* and Aunt Anne was his biggest fan.

On this beautiful Put-in-Bay morning though, Aunt Anne had a disconcerting premonition concerning her nephew as he commonly found himself in various sorts of trouble in pursuit of his blockbuster stories. While she did not know every detail of Emerson's past adventures, this day she sensed something terribly disturbing about his future, or perhaps the future of their relationship as aunt and nephew. She returned herself to the present moment, simply enjoying the boats passing nearby and remaining thoughtful of her daily blessings that included living on an island in Lake Erie and not living on the mainland.

Meanwhile, Moore drove his red Ford Mustang convertible past Perry's Monument on his left and Put-in-Bay's harbor on his right. He saw the high-speed Jet Express ferry glistening in the morning sun as it headed for its dock with a boatload of island visitors ready to explore the picturesque resort village located on South Bass Island in western Lake Erie.

Put-in-Bay, popularly known as the "Key West of the Midwest," and the surrounding islands served as a summer season tourist "hot spot" and a great getaway weekend destination. Visitors from a diversity of locales, domestic and foreign, each year flocked to the islands in droves to swim, sail, boat, fish, jet ski, dine and party at the various local attractions and venues. Most were from Ohio, its surrounding states and its closest international neighbor—the province of Ontario, Canada.

Moore turned left on Toledo Avenue and drove up to the

stop sign where he heard someone shout his name. He looked to his right and saw Peter Huston, his tall and lean, bearded friend with a large mop of white hair, wave at him from outside the nearby Chamber of Commerce office. Huston was the Chamber's ambassador.

Moore pulled through the stop sign and parked on the side of the road.

"Where you heading, Emerson?" Huston asked.

"Off island. Going to Bellevue to the train museum."

"I love that museum," Huston responded with modest enthusiasm as he adjusted his glasses. Then he added, "Did you know that Bellevue is where Henry Flagler got his start?"

"That's why I'm going. I'm doing a piece on him and his railroad to Key West for the newspaper," Moore replied.

"Sounds to me like someone is working on getting another trip to Key West for research," Huston teased.

Moore smiled. "You know it. Got to run to catch the Miller Ferry."

Huston glanced at his watch. "You're cutting it close," he warned.

"I'll make it," Moore said with confidence as he eased the car away and sped to Langram Road. He turned right and headed for the Lime Kiln dock. As his car picked up speed, he was relieved that there wasn't much traffic that morning.

When he turned left and drove up to the ticket window, he flashed his ticket at the attendant, who waved him through. He headed down the hill and saw that the ferry was halfway filled with vehicles, and passengers had started to walk aboard.

Moore drove around the first building and followed the first lane to where Billy Market, the co-owner of the Miller

Ferry, motioned for him to stop. They were longtime friends and Moore was a loyal Miller Ferry customer.

"Think I can get on, Billy?"

"You'll have to ask the man in charge," Market said as he turned to look at his four-wheeler. "Now, where did he go?"

"You mean him?" Moore asked as he pointed to Market's three-year-old son who was throwing rocks into the calm water.

"Liam, what are you doing?"

"I'm fishing, Daddy."

"With rocks?" Market asked with a smile.

"I don't have my fishing pole with me," the boy answered innocently.

"Guess he's got you there," Moore chuckled.

Market laughed. "What are you going to do with them?" as he looked back at Liam. "Should we let Emerson drive onboard?"

Liam looked toward the ferry and saw that the passengers had finished boarding. He nodded his head. "Yes. It's clear now, Daddy."

"Starting him at a young age," Moore observed.

"It's in our blood," Market winked as he took Moore's ticket and waved him toward the ferry.

Moore drove aboard and parked his vehicle. He could hear the noise of the ramp being raised behind him and locked in place. He settled back to enjoy the brief twenty-minute ride across the South Passage to the Catawba dock on the Ohio mainland.

An hour later, Moore turned his Mustang left onto Southwest Avenue in Bellevue and drove the short distance to the Mad River and NKP Railroad Museum, which was built on the site of Henry Flagler's home. The museum's name was derived from one of the first railroads in Bellevue, the Mad River and Lake Erie Railroad.

It was also named after the Nickel Plate Railroad (New York, Chicago and St. Louis Railroad Company) as Bellevue was the hub for its operations. It housed the principal classification yards, the largest roundhouse in the system, railway equipment maintenance, an icing station, diesel and steam engine terminals and the general superintendent's headquarters as well as the offices for four of the Nickel Plate's divisions.

Turning into the museum parking lot, Moore's attention was drawn toward an area across the street where a number of locomotives, passenger cars, cabooses, box cars, tank cars and a mail car were displayed as part of the museum collection. He saw several families climbing aboard and exploring the various cars. They made him recollect the first time he had visited a rail yard with his own father as a young lad. Emerson smiled to himself.

As Moore walked into the museum, he was greeted by a low voice. "Hello, Emerson."

Moore again smiled as he saw Ron Smith, a local attorney and fellow diver in the Bay Area Divers (BAD) scuba club in Port Clinton. The sixtyish, graying Smith volunteered at the museum and was going to give his visitor a customized tour. It was during a previous lunch at the Sandusky Yacht Club with Moore's attractive friend Lorraine Robinson that Moore learned about the museum. Robinson had been the mayor's assistant when she lived in Bellevue and suggested that Moore meet with Smith.

"Hi Ron," Moore said as he returned the greeting. "I appreciate you taking time to give me a tour."

"Hey, can anyone say 'no' to you?" Smith teased.

"I know some women who do," Moore teased back.

"I noticed that the operative word was 'some'," Smith kidded good-naturedly. "Come on. I'll show you around."

Escorted by Smith, the two men began their tour of the museum. They started with memorabilia from the railroading days and walked to the north end where two cabooses were housed in the structure.

"Ever since early childhood, the caboose has been my favorite rail car of all," Moore remarked, looking at them with a boyish envy.

"Well, now you have two, Emerson. Climb aboard," Smith suggested.

Moore went through the two cabooses, marveling at the simplicity of their contents. The men next toured several passenger cars that were on the other side of the cabooses. Moore was having a grand time.

When they finished touring the rest of the museum, they walked across the street and spent the next two hours climbing in and out of the various railroad cars and engines in the outdoor exhibition. Their last stop was the engineer's seat inside a massive diesel locomotive.

"This just made my day, Ron," Moore commented with a boyish grin.

"Thought you'd enjoy it. Hungry?" Smith inquired.

"I am."

"Then you're in for another treat."

"How's that?" Moore asked.

"It's a short drive over to Fremont. That's where Tackle Box II is located. They have the best yellow perch dinners in the state."

"You don't have to ask me twice," Moore grinned as he followed Smith to his car. The two men chatted during the relatively short drive on Route 20.

"I didn't realize that Henry Flagler started his career in Bellevue," Moore commented.

"He did. Flagler's originally from the little town of Hopewell, New York, in the Finger Lakes region. He went to work for his stepbrother's grain company here in Bellevue. After a while, he left to start up a salt business in Saginaw, Michigan. When that business collapsed, Flagler returned to Bellevue to work in the grain business again. Shortly after, he met another guy in the grain business. His name was John D. Rockefeller."

"I didn't realize he knew Rockefeller or that Rockefeller once worked in the grain business."

Smith nodded. "It was more than that." Smith continued. "When Rockefeller left the grain business in 1867 to go into oil refining, he asked Flagler to become his partner. And that was the beginning of The Standard Oil Company in Cleveland. Rockefeller attributed the company's success to Flagler's brains."

"How did Flagler get involved with railroading in Florida?" Moore asked.

"In the early 1880s, Flagler began stepping away from an active role with Standard Oil. His first wife was ill and he took her to St. Augustine for the winter. Liking the area, he built the 540-room Ponce de Leon resort hotel. When he realized he needed a better way to transport visitors to the hotel, he began buying up short line railroads. That was the basis for the Florida East Coast Railway.

"He built bridges and more hotels as he was trying to make Florida's coast into America's version of the French

Riviera. By the turn of the century, Flagler's railroad reached Miami and he began developing the Miami area. Flagler was a good guy. He encouraged fruit farming and settlement along his railway and also made cash contributions for building schools, hospitals and churches in Florida."

"Sounds like quite a guy," Moore agreed. "What about the railroad to Key West?"

"I was just coming to that," Smith said. "Flagler knew that Key West was Florida's biggest city. It was the closest deep-water port to the soon-to-be-built Panama Canal and would be a great location for additional trade to Cuba and Latin America. He decided to build a railroad to Key West. It was a monumental task that he completed in 1912. It was 128 miles from the end of the Florida peninsula to Key West."

"And a hurricane destroyed it, right?" Moore asked.

"Correct. The Labor Day Hurricane of 1935 destroyed major sections of the railroad. The remaining infrastructure was sold to the State of Florida, which then went on to build the Overseas Highway."

"A route that I'm very familiar with and enjoy driving. Especially Seven Mile Bridge," Moore smiled.

"There were forty-two bridges built down through the Keys," Smith added.

"I bet Flagler enjoyed Key West."

"Not really. He just made one trip on the train. It was the first train to Key West and they had a huge celebration when it arrived. All kinds of governors, senators and foreign dignitaries. Even the Cuban army showed up to greet them. Flagler was in his early eighties then and quite frail. He died sixteen months later in Palm Beach."

"Heart attack?"

"No. He fell down the marble steps at his home and never recovered from his injuries. He's buried in St. Augustine."

"Quite a guy," Moore surmised.

"In some ways, he reminds me of you, Emerson."

"How's that?"

"He had relentless energy and unlimited optimism," Smith said as he turned onto Sandusky Street and drove to the Tackle Box II. It was set on a bluff overlooking the Sandusky River and Brady's Island.

"How do you know so much about Flagler?" Moore asked.

"I'm a Flagler buff," Smith smiled.

Parking the car, the two men exited and Smith pointed to the island in the river. "That's Brady's Island. You ever hear of it?"

"No. This is my first trip to Fremont," Moore admitted.

"You picked the right guy to travel with. I'm such a history nut. Back in 1780, George Washington wanted to learn more about the strength of the Wyandot Indians here and sent his scout, Samuel Brady, out of Fort Pitt."

"That's where Pittsburgh is today, right?" Moore asked.

"Correct. Brady had been a scout for Washington during the Revolutionary War. He crossed the Delaware River with him to capture Trenton on that cold Christmas evening of 1776, but back to my story. Brady, with a few soldiers and Chickasaw guides, made his way through the wilderness to this island where together they observed the Indians and returned with their report. But things didn't go so well on Brady's second trip here."

"What happened?"

"The Indians captured Brady and were going to torture

him. He was able to escape and was pursued 100 miles to the east. When he reached the Cuyahoga River in Kent, he jumped across the river gorge. It was a twenty-two-foot wide jump and the Indians couldn't jump it. That spot is known as Brady's Leap."

"And he got away?" Moore asked.

"He hid in a nearby lake until the Indians gave up searching for him. It's known as Brady's Lake now. Let's go inside."

The two men walked into the tropical oasis.

"I don't know which way to look," Moore said as he tried to take in all of the oddities that the owner had collected. There were signs, lights, a statute of a female pirate just inside the door plus other memorabilia throughout.

"And that doesn't even compare to the perch," Smith said as the two men were escorted to a table on the Tackle Box's outside deck.

"Two perch dinners please," Smith offered to the waitress, who also took their drink orders.

While they waited, Smith leaned forward to Moore. "You're doing a story on Flagler's railroad, right?"

"Correct."

"There's something else that you should look into," Smith suggested.

"What's that?"

"I heard this story from my uncle who worked on Flagler's railroad. It goes back to 1928. There was a special train with armed Pinkerton guards. It was supposed to run from St. Augustine with a secret cargo to New York, but the train never made it."

"What happened?" Moore asked.

"The Okeechobee Hurricane was coming ashore that

night. It stirred things up, but it wasn't responsible for turning a train around in its tracks."

"What do you mean?"

"Somehow that train ended up on its way south to Key West. It got almost all the way across the Seven Mile Bridge when the bridge exploded. The engine, tender and express car were found submerged in the water next to the bridge."

"Did anyone survive?"

The men paused as the waitress placed their drinks and dinners in front of them. Moore hurriedly bit into a piece of yellow perch and exclaimed, "This is really good. Amazingly so."

"I knew you'd like it," Smith smiled.

"So, tell me about the folks that were killed on the train," Moore urged him.

"No bodies were found. And you know what was most interesting?"

"What?"

"Six Pinkerton guards and the conductor had been locked inside the express car before the train departed St. Augustine. They had no way out, yet their bodies were missing when the train wreck was first discovered."

Moore stopped chewing and wrinkled his brow. "That's weird. What about the secret cargo?"

"The safe doors were unlocked and the divers found the two safes empty."

"But you said the express car doors were locked when the train left St. Augustine!" Moore remarked.

"They were. That's what makes it so mysterious."

"Any idea what the cargo was?"

"My uncle wasn't sure. There have been all kinds of

rumors over the years, but no one knows for sure or wants to talk about it."

"This happened after Flagler's death, right?"

"Yes. Fifteen years later." Smith took a sip of his beer. "There's one more thing, Emerson."

"What's that?"

"The head of the Pinkerton detail, who oversaw the loading of the train, had boarded a plane that night following the train's departure."

"During a hurricane?" Moore asked in disbelief.

"Yep. The fool went up in the air during a hurricane to go after the train," Smith confirmed.

"Is that how they knew the train was off the bridge?" Moore asked.

"No. Railroad workers were checking the tracks after the storm and saw the damaged bridge. Then they saw the train submerged in the water below."

"What about the plane?"

"The plane just disappeared. No one has seen hide nor hair of it since. Nor its occupants for that matter."

"No crash debris?" Moore asked as he pushed his empty plate away.

"None. She probably went down in the water somewhere and sank. You wouldn't know where to look."

"You've piqued my curiosity," Moore said as he looked at Smith.

"Figured that story would," Smith smiled.

The two men finished their drinks, paid their bill and drove back to Bellevue. Moore thanked Smith for the tour and meal, then sat alone in his car pondering the story he had heard. He reached for his phone and called his boss, editor

John Sedler, at *The Washington Post*. As he drove back to the Miller Ferry dock in Port Clinton, en route back home to Put-in-Bay, Moore updated Sedler on what he had learned and his plans to visit St. Augustine and the Florida Keys.

"That's interesting, but it sounds a bit like a wild goose chase to me," Sedler groused.

Moore protested. "I think there's something there."

"I'm sure there have been a lot of people trying to find that train's missing contents. I'm just not going to sign off on another treasure hunting trip for you, Emerson."

Sedler paused as he thought how he could accommodate his fervent reporter.

"There might be a way where you could do some work on this while working a major story for us," Sedler suggested.

"I'm all ears."

"I heard that there's a Congressional subcommittee beginning to do an investigation on drug running from Cuba to Key West. You interested in doing some undercover work in Key West and see what you can ferret out?"

"Like you had to ask?"

Sedler smiled. "I'll email what I have and you can review it. Let me know your thoughts and you might soon be on your way."

"I'll get right on it," Moore said as he pressed the accelerator harder. He was anxious to get back home and start reviewing the material. They ended their call and Moore's mind raced.

His hand reached up and absent-mindedly stroked his chin. When he realized what he was doing, he decided that he needed to grow a beard and let his hair grow longer than it was, or maybe resort to wearing a wig. He looked in the rearview mirror and decided that he should add a fake birthmark to his face.

Maybe it was time to resurrect his old alias from a previous adventure and become Manny Elias again. Moore grinned at the thought.

When he arrived home on South Bass Island, he spent the rest of the evening reviewing the emailed material from Sedler and researching background information on the internet. He was stunned by what he discovered.

Colombian smugglers were shipping millions of tons of marijuana and cocaine to the United States aboard motherships, which rendezvoused with smaller feeder boats. The smaller boats would shuttle the drugs to the Florida coast, mostly to Key West. One of the biggest risks was when the motherships sailed through the Windward Passage, a fifty-mile wide strait in the Caribbean Sea between the eastern tip of Cuba and Haiti.

Cuban gunboats would lie there in wait for unsuspecting ships and seize them, confiscate their drugs and kill the crew. That all changed when a Cuban criminal boss saw an opportunity although his country's gunboats were causing the Colombians all of their problems. His name was Henri Baudin, also known as El Patrón. He was involved in a number of nefarious criminal activities from his lair in the Sierra Maestra Mountains on the southeast coast of Cuba, just east of Santiago.

Moore further learned that for a payment of $2 million per vessel, El Patrón would guarantee the safety of the motherships and provide his own fleet of feeder boats to carry the offloaded cargo to the Florida Keys. The Colombians agreed and entered into a partnership with El Patrón. It was better to pay him than risk losing a drug shipment that averaged $12 million.

Additionally, El Patrón had connections throughout the

Cuban government and military. He knew who to bribe to have them look the other way. The Cuban drug lord took it one more step as he contracted with the Colombian motherships on their return trips to transport illicit arms to Colombia to be delivered to insurgents throughout South America.

Over the next couple of weeks, Moore did additional research. He had several conversations with Sedler in Washington, D.C. and contacted his friend former Navy SEAL Sam Duncan in Key West to see if he could stay at his trailer while going undercover. Duncan readily agreed and wanted to connect Moore with the Joint Interagency Task Force South at the Truman Annex in Key West, but Moore begged off. The intrepid reporter instead wanted to go in with no connections. He didn't want any leaks developing in Key West that could hamper his undercover investigation and any opportunity to get to El Patrón.

The night before he caught an early morning flight to Miami, Moore took the Miller Ferry from Put-in-Bay over to Catawba and drove through Port Clinton to the Overboard Bar and Grill on West Lakeshore Drive. It was just past his friend's business, New Wave Scuba. He was going to have dinner with legendary Put-in-Bay entertainer Mike "Mad Dog" Adams.

Pulling into the parking lot, Moore parked his Mustang convertible at the side of the gray-painted building and smiled as he looked at the huge plastic shark that overlooked the outdoor patio. When he walked in, he always felt that he was entering a bar in the Keys.

The interior of the bar was painted in a variety of vibrant tropical greens, blues, oranges, yellows and pinks. The tiki-bar décor was definitely island-style. A "Don't Give Up the

Ship" sign hung on one wall. The rope winding around the two pillars at the bar was painted a bright blue. A surfboard hung over the bar and below it was a guitar signed by entertainer and musician Jimmy Buffet. Next to Buffet's guitar hung another that was personally autographed by the equally popular, local island entertainer and musician, Mike "Mad Dog" Adams.

"Hey Emerson," owners Cory and Lindsay Sipert greeted Moore. They had purchased the old Wharf Lounge and completely remodeled the interior. He got to know the couple during his frequent stops to have their delicious burgers.

"Hi guys," Moore returned the greeting as he walked over to Adams, who was seated at the bar playing Keno.

"The usual, Emerson?" dark-haired Lindsay asked, knowing that Moore liked rum and Seven-Up.

"You know it," Moore smiled as she turned to get his drink.

"You winning anything?" Moore asked as he sat on a bar stool next to Adams. The burly entertainer was wearing a beige Put-in-Bay ball cap and a blue t-shirt that read "I Work Harder Than an Ugly Stripper" in white letters.

"Not doing bad at all," Adams grinned as he turned to look at Moore who was completing his meal order form. The gray and white cards had boxes for patrons to check for their meal selections.

Moore placed the form on the counter as Adams asked, "How are you doing, Emerson?"

"Getting ready for an undercover project."

"I think I told you that I do my best work under the covers," Adams chortled.

"Yes, you did tell me that," Moore laughed. "Did you

order yet?" he asked as he saw a partially consumed mixed drink on the bar in front of Adams.

"Yep. I gave it to Lindsay and told her to put it in when you arrived." Adams took a sip of his drink as Lindsay placed a rum and Seven-Up in front of Moore.

"You confuse me, Emerson," Adams quizzically said as he looked at Moore's drink.

"What do you mean?"

"I know you're pretty consistent in ordering a rum, but what's behind the switching from Coke to Seven-Up thing you do? I just don't get it."

"It's easy Mike. If I don't mind the caffeine keeping me up late, I take the Coke. But if I want to make sure I get to sleep early, then I have it mixed with Seven-Up. And I've got to drive to a Cleveland hotel tonight to catch an early flight to Miami tomorrow morning."

"That's where you're going undercover?" Adams asked in a serious tone.

"I'll get in character there."

"Is that beard a part of going undercover or are you just trying to look cool?" Adams asked.

"Part of my disguise," Moore smiled.

"The beard looks good on you."

"Thanks, Mike." Moore continued. "I'll catch the shuttle at the Miami airport and head to Key West."

"Ah, Key West, one of my favorite stomping grounds. You need any help down there? I can hook you up with some of my buddies. You remember meeting C.W. Colt, don't you?"

"Oh yeah. Quite an entertainer and I loved that sound studio he has. Thanks for connecting us, but I'm really doing this low-profile."

"Well, I was just saying."

"I know Mike. You're always trying to help me and it's appreciated."

"That's what friends are for," Adams said as he reached for his drink, took a sip and placed it back on the counter. He leaned in toward Moore and asked in a low voice, "So, can you tell me what you're up to down there?"

Speaking in a low tone, Moore answered, "Drug trafficking. You remember John Sedler?"

"Your boss at the paper?"

"Yes."

"I met him when he came out to Put-in-Bay a while back when we all thought you were missing and dead, and they had a memorial service for you," Adams recounted.

"Yeah, that's right," Moore agreed. "John gave me information on drugs coming into Key West through a chain that traces back to a guy in Cuba."

"You going to Cuba, too?"

"If things work out and I can get connected, I am."

Adams shook his head with concern. "And you'll go there by yourself or with the DEA folks?"

"Probably not DEA, because the Cuban government wouldn't think kindly to them being there. It sounds like the government there is on the take from this guy."

"How about your buddy Sam Duncan? Is he going to help you on this caper of yours?" Adams knew Duncan. They had both been Navy SEALs.

"No. Sam volunteered to connect me with some folks, but I'm doing this one on my own."

Lindsay returned with their burgers and set them on the counter in front of the two men.

"Can I get you two anything else?"

Both men shook their heads as they reached for the salt and pepper for their food.

Moore bit into his cheeseburger. "Oh my. This is absolutely the best," he said as he reached for a napkin to wipe his mouth.

"I like them, too," Adams said as he chewed. "Hey, you've got to help me understand something, Emerson."

"Sure. What's that?"

"I thought you were allergic to onions. They do weird things to your stomach."

"They do," Moore agreed as he took a bite of his onion ring. "This is really good."

"Come on. Are you playing with me?"

"Why?"

"You're allergic to onions, but you're sitting there chomping on an onion ring."

"I know what you mean," Emerson remarked. "It's strange. I can eat a few onion rings with no problems, but you put onions or scallions in my food and I get sick within thirty minutes. Intense stomach cramps."

Adams stared at Moore. He wasn't sure that he was buying into the explanation. Adams shook his head and leaned toward Moore as he changed the subject.

"Emerson, like I always tell you, you need to be careful. I don't want to go to another memorial service for you in the near future and I have an uneasy feeling in my gut about this one, my friend."

Moore chuckled quietly. "Come on Mike. I'll be fine."

"I don't know. Sometimes you remind me of that Asian pilot who died in the plane crash the other day," Adams said with a mischievous look.

"What pilot?"

"Sum Ting Wong," Adams snickered, then a serious look crossed his face. "You need to be careful because neither Sam nor I will be there to rescue you if something goes wrong," Adams warned.

"I get it," Moore chuckled and agreed.

The two friends continued to banter as they finished their meals and paid their bills. As they each headed for the exit door, Cory walked out of the kitchen.

"Where have you been Cory?" Moore asked. "You let Lindsey do all of the work?"

"No. I was on a break. I'm reading a really good book. It was written by a friend of mine who writes award-winning mystery adventure novels set in Put-in-Bay."

Moore smiled and looked at Adams who also was grinning.

"I think we both know who you're talking about. I hope you're enjoying it," Moore said with a suggestive wink. "Watch out too, because that guy really is a big fan of good burgers—sort of our local Burgermeister."

"I am and he loves our burgers," Cory responded as he watched the two men walk out the door.

Before he got in his truck, Adams turned to Moore. "Hey Emerson, did you know that Perry's Monument is starting to lean?"

"No, I didn't," Moore responded in self-disappointment for not noticing it since he lived just past it. "Which direction is it leaning?"

"Toward the east end of Delaware Ave where the topless beach is. They've got too many guys on that side of the monument with binoculars."

"I didn't know there was a topless beach there," Moore said as he wrinkled his brow.

"There are two on the island. The other is at the state park. Why do you think Bob Gatewood located his boat business there?" Adams joked.

Moore chuckled in response.

"You be safe, my brother," Adams said as he entered his truck.

"That I will do, amigo," Moore said as he got in his Mustang. As he started to pull out, Moore recognized another of his lake friends, Clay Cozart. Moore waved at Cozart, who was stepping out of a black limousine that had parked in front of the building.

"You're styling!" Moore chuckled as he lowered his window.

"It helps when you know the right people," Cozart countered.

"And Clay knows all of the right people," a voice yelled.

Moore swung his head around and smiled when he recognized the handsome limo driver. It was another friend, Carl Thompson, who was known as Carl the Limo Man.

"I'm sure he does," Moore grinned as he responded to the driver. "Enjoy the food," he added as he started to drive out of the parking lot.

"It's burger time," Cozart called.

Moore waved and headed east for Cleveland to check into the hotel.

Along the way, he stopped at a costume shop to get the wig and the ink he needed to make a birthmark on his face. The next morning, Moore checked out of the hotel and drove to the nearby Hopkins International Airport where he parked, entered the terminal and checked in for his nonstop flight to Miami.

When he landed in Miami several hours later, Moore headed for the restroom where he worked on changing his appearance. He inked a birthmark on his face and stepped back to look at his artwork. It was passable. Reaching into his duffel bag, he pulled out the dark long-haired wig and fussed with it for a bit before becoming satisfied with how it looked.

"It is good-bye Emerson Moore and a new hello to Manny Elias," he thought to himself as he looked in the mirror.

Leaving the restroom, he realized that he still had his Emerson Moore Ohio driver's license in his wallet. He would take it to Duncan's trailer and hide it. He still had his cell phone and laptop, but wasn't concerned about them. He'd stash those personal items at Duncan's place. His laptop required a strong password to access and he felt relatively comfortable that it was well protected, at least while it was at Duncan's place.

Moore walked through baggage claim and out to the Keys Shuttle pick up. It was almost noon when he boarded the twelve-passenger van to Key West.

After a drive of several hours, the van crossed Seven Mile Bridge and Moore peered out the window, trying to imagine where the train wreck was located. He vowed to visit the wreck site when he had a chance on this trip.

Shortly thereafter, the shuttle crossed the bridge from Stock Island to Key West, the anchor for the long emerald chain of fossilized coral and limestone islands. Surrounded by clear, blue-green water, Key West was Florida's crown jewel.

The shuttle followed North Roosevelt Boulevard which changed into Truman Avenue. The vehicle drove past a variety of pastel-painted tropical houses trimmed out with white gingerbread and surrounded by lush vegetation.

Many of the alluring tin-roofed homes featured white picket fences on small lots that were filled with white, pink and lavender oleander and laurel trees. The dark-stained front doors and dark green shutters on many of the one-and-two story houses provided an aesthetic balance to the brightest of whites, which many of the houses were painted.

Catching the shuttle driver's attention, Moore was allowed to be dropped off at the intersection of Truman Avenue and Grinnell Street. He walked about three blocks to his new home in a small mobile home park off United Street. It was hot and he was perspiring.

Ambling down a narrow lane, he spotted in the near distance Sam Duncan's faded yellow mobile home with its covered patio. The patio was screened from the lane by white latticework desperately in need of a fresh coat of paint. The patio area itself was littered with three chairs in disrepair that surrounded a worn and stained rattan table. A few potted plants dotted the patio and were in dire need of water. A number of colored lights and two wooden parrots hung from the ceiling.

He remembered that Duncan told him that a key would be hidden over the door sill. Without looking, Moore reached up and felt a sharp pain on his fingers. He jumped back and noticed that there were several bees flying out of the hidden key area. He shook his head and smiled. It would just be like Duncan to have hidden the key by a bee's nest. He'd be sure to tease Duncan about his bee stings.

Moore looked around and spotted a rusted coat hanger under the porch roof. He used it to carefully extract the key from its hiding place. No sense in stirring up a bee's nest, Moore thought. Pulling out the key, it dropped to the ground.

Moore picked it up, unlocked the door and walked into the cool air of the cozy trailer, throwing down his small duffel bag.

To the right was a small living room complete with an easy chair and small sofa. A beat-up coffee table was covered with magazines and files. Moore's eyes were drawn to one side of the room that housed the latest in Duncan's entertainment technology. There was a big screen TV with surround-sound for the TV and CD player.

The next day, he would go to Booger Blake's Bar on Whitehead where Duncan thought drugs were being sold. Moore was pleased with his progress as his plan was coming together.

Tossing his duffel bag into the guest bedroom, he returned to the kitchen table and set up his laptop. He chuckled as he entered the password to Duncan's Wi-Fi. It was WHAM_BAM_ THANK_YOU_LAN. Only Duncan would have a password like that, Moore mused.

Moore savored any visit to idyllic Key West, the party island famous for its casual and relaxed approach to life as well as a lot of piña coladas and Jimmy Buffet. There was nothing like finishing off a hot day with the nightly sunset festival on Mallory Pier or the mile-long block party along historic Duval Street.

There was a huge Cuban influence in Key West's history. It was heightened by a large wave of Cuban immigrants arriving in 1868 who were escaping the brutality of Cuba's ten-year war for independence. In 1869, a Spaniard, who supported the Cuban rebels, established the first cigar-making factory in Key West. He realized, like Cuba, Key West had the perfect temperature and humidity that allowed tobacco to remain pliable throughout the cigar manufacturing process. At its peak, Key West's cigar industry included more than 200 factories that produced more than 100 million cigars each year.

The Cuban immigrants of the time also brought their love for cock fighting to the island. That's why hundreds of roosters still run wild on the narrow streets and lanes near the Naval Station. Their crowing can be heard throughout the island as they strut their lustrous orange-red plumes.

In 1871, Cuban immigrants and revolutionaries also founded the San Carlos Institute at 516 Duval Street. The two-story, white building, trimmed in gold, hosts concerts, art exhibits and plays. It has a library and museum on Key West history that is primarily focused on 19th-century and 20th-century Cuban exiles.

The biggest connections that culturally linked Cuban-Americans to their homeland was their music and food. Moore enjoyed their food, although his stomach was challenged by the inclusion of onions in their cooking. Cuban food is a Creole cuisine, influenced by Spanish and African cooking with meats, legumes, onions, garlic, pepper, starchy fruits, vegetables and citrus.

Moore spent some time on his laptop at Duncan's trailer as he researched Key West and its reputed drug trafficking. He wished he could get into some of the black ops programs that Duncan had access to, but that wasn't going to happen.

Shutting down the laptop, Moore headed out to dinner. He unlocked the bike under the patio cover. Moore was hungry for Cuban food. It would be a short bike ride a block over to El Siboney Restaurant on Catherine Street.

He was a big fan of Put-in-Bay's Topsy Turvy Restaurant and their Cuban sandwiches. He planned on getting one for dinner at El Siboney. The Cuban sandwiches were made of roast pork, ham, Swiss cheese, pickles and mustard on Cuban bread, and a flaky-crisp baguette with a buttery white middle.

When making the sandwich, it was usually placed briefly in a press to melt the cheese and meld the juices. Many of the Key West Cuban restaurants used Serrano ham, a dry cured meat that added extra flavor.

After a tasty dinner, Moore hopped on his bike and headed for Duval Street. He never tired of taking in the famed street, which ran a little over a mile between the Atlantic Ocean and the Gulf of Mexico. It was lined with art galleries, seafood restaurants and quaint hotels with wicker chair-filled balconies. The northern half of Duval was populated by a number of t-shirt and souvenir shops. Festive partiers crowded Duval Street and overflowed on the adjacent streets.

Moore slowed as he neared his favorite Key West restaurant, Jack Flats, which was across from Margaritaville and near the intersection of Duval and Fleming Streets. He'd have to make sure to eat there one night, he thought as he rode to the end of Duval Street and then biked over to Whitehead Street. As he neared the intersection with Caroline, he spotted the First Flight Island Restaurant and Brewery which had been owned by movie star Kelly McGillis.

The white-clapboard building was the original headquarters of Pan Am Airways when it first started its business in 1927 by delivering mail to Cuba from Key West. Using a Fökker trimotor airplane, Pan Am expanded its service by transporting passengers in 1928.

Moore continued his ride along Whitehead Street, slowing as he rode by Booger Blake's Bar where he was hoping to get a job the next day. Sedler had passed along a tip from one of his local sources to Moore that the owner was dealing drugs. He pedaled on down the street and returned to the mobile home park. He planned on relaxing for the rest of the evening.

CHAPTER 4

Present Day
Key West Police Department

The two-story, coral-colored building with white trim on North Roosevelt Boulevard was a far cry from Key West's first police operation in 1828. It started with a town marshal and a ship's brig at the harbor's edge serving as the jail.

Earlier this morning the police had grilled Blake about the murder and Blake's missing gun. There was however, nothing more that Blake could offer in explanation since he hadn't been involved in the man's apparent homicide.

Moore's turn at the interview desk as Manny Elias was also quite bland. Other than the alibi which he had provided Blake, he didn't have anything useful to offer.

The two men were talking under the portico in front of the police station while the police turned to running down other possible leads on the man's death and to ascertain his identity.

"Thanks again, Manny, for giving me that alibi," Blake said appreciatively.

"Glad to help out," Moore replied.

"Those guys can go figure out who murdered him. I didn't," Blake underscored. Turning to Moore, he asked, "Can I drop you anywhere?"

Blake had picked up Moore at his trailer that morning and gave him a ride out to the police department.

"It's almost lunch time," Moore said as he glanced at his watch. "Are you hungry?"

"No," Blake said. "I'm still a bit tense from that interview, but I can drop you somewhere."

"Sure. How about Jack Flats on Duval?"

"I know right where that is."

The two men walked over to Blake's truck and Blake drove Moore to Jack Flats near the intersection with Fleming Street.

"Thanks again, Manny," Blake said as he stopped in front of Jack Flats.

"Any time. See you tonight," Moore replied.

After Moore exited the vehicle, Blake headed for his bar. He had work to catch up on.

Moore entered Jack Flats, a popular sports bar featuring banks of TVs and several pool tables at the rear. He grabbed one of his favorite tables right next to the open floor-to-ceiling window that fronted the sidewalk. It was a great place to people watch.

Moore thought back to the last time he had been at Jack Flats. It was with that rascal Willie Wilbanks, the famed shipwreck hunter. He allowed his mind to wander with the memories of that adventure in finding a sunken Nazi U-boat. Nostalgically, he recalled the woman named Asha and what might have developed romantically with her prior to her sudden and unexpected death. Moore was somber about the remembrance, but then was interrupted by the arrival of his server.

"Can I get you something to drink, hon?" she asked as she eyed the handsome reporter.

"Just a sweet tea," Moore responded.

"Did you get a chance to look at the menu?"

"Don't need to. I'm a creature of habit and I love your grilled grouper sandwiches," Moore answered.

"Got it," she smiled as she reached for the menu and scurried off. A few minutes later, she returned with his tea.

Sipping it, Moore gazed out to the sidewalk, which was filled with tourists going in and out of the souvenir shops. Although it wasn't quite noon, Moore noticed a couple of sunburnt tourists had already had too much to drink. He could tell by the way they stumbled down the sidewalk.

After he finished his meal and paid, he exited the building and started walking down Duval Street toward Truman Avenue. The sound of a car backfiring drew Moore's attention. He turned his head and looked down Duval. He chuckled as he watched the strange-looking vehicle approaching him.

It was a faded yellow, 1975 American Motors Gremlin. It had sunflower pin wheels affixed upright on its two fenders. There were two red bicycle horns attached to the two outside mirrors. An agitator from a washing machine also was attached to the car's roof. It rotated in the wind as the car moved forward.

As the rattle trap neared, Moore saw that a black arrow was painted on the roof. It was pointed forward. He also saw that someone had lettered a message on the roof. It read "This side up!"

The passenger door was held shut by a sliding bolt.

Bumper stickers weren't doing a good job in covering the rust holes on the lower quarter panels. A twisted clothes hanger acted as the vehicle's antenna. A faux fox tail was tied to the makeshift antenna. The car was missing its hubcaps and the tires appeared to be of different brands and sizes.

As the car passed, it smelled like something was burning. White steam was emanating from the grille. The windows were peeling from a do-it-yourself tint job. As the car slowed to turn left in front of Moore, he could see the driver. The bearded driver was wearing dark sunglasses and a hat pulled low over his brow. He was manually working the signal lever up and down. There was something familiar about the driver, but Moore couldn't place him.

The driver, in turn, stared momentarily at Moore before he turned his attention back to driving around the corner. The blast of an oncoming garbage truck's horn filled the air as the hooptie turned abruptly in front of it. The screeching of truck tires, curses from the truck driver, two more backfires from the Gremlin and a cloud of black smoke filled the air.

Moore laughed as he watched the vehicle, with a hanger struggling to hold a muffler off the ground, drive away. The muffler had definitely seen better days.

Moore resumed his walk back to the mobile home park on United Street, but his mind lingered on the driver of that odd-looking vehicle. Moore couldn't place him, but his sixth sense told him that their paths had crossed in the past.

Late that afternoon, Moore hopped on his bike and pedaled to the bar to work his shift. The rest of the evening passed calmly.

The next night, Moore saw a Hispanic-looking man enter and approach the bar. He had a backpack slung over one shoulder. Moore watched as the man greeted Blake and saw the two men disappear into Blake's office at the rear. Moore wondered if the man was Blake's Cuban drug source.

Within thirty minutes, the man reappeared and left the bar. He carried his backpack with him. Two minutes later, Blake emerged from his office. He had a contented look on his face as he busied himself with the bar's patrons.

The rest of the evening was uneventful other than the arrival of one short, chubby patron. He was wearing a straw hat and a dark beard. He took a seat in a far corner and ordered a beer from one of the servers. As he waited, his eyes carefully scanned the room. He was looking for somebody.

When the server returned with his beer, he spoke. "Thanks, Sherry," he said to the blonde server as he read her name badge. Before she could walk away, he asked her, "Who is that bartender over there?"

She looked to where he was pointing. "You mean Manny?"

"Is that his name?"

"Yeah. Manny Elias," she answered. "Do you know him?"

"Naw. He just looks like someone I knew some time ago," the man lied as he shrank back into the shadow. "Do me a favor."

"Yes?" she asked.

"Don't mention to him that I asked," he said as he slid a double sawbuck across the table. "And keep the change, sweetheart."

She took the twenty-dollar bill and grinned at the man. "I never saw you come in," she said as she turned and walked away. "It's none of my business," she added as she smiled.

Manny Elias, I wonder what you are up to, the man thought to himself as he hurriedly finished his beer and walked his chubby body out of the bar.

CHAPTER 5

The Next Afternoon
Booger Blake's Bar

Moore arrived early. Blake wanted to meet with him before the bar opened. He chained his bike to the tree and walked to the back entrance where he knocked twice.

Blake quickly appeared and cracked the door open. "Manny?"

"Yes, it's me, Blake."

"Thanks for coming in. Go on into my office," Blake said as he pushed the door wide open, allowing Moore to walk inside. Blake stuck his head out of the doorway and looked to the left and right to be sure no one had followed Moore. He closed and locked the door before walking into the small, cluttered back room that doubled as his office and a storage room.

Motioning toward a wooden chair that had seen better days, Blake instructed Moore, "Take a seat."

Blake dropped into a well worn and torn leather chair that had been a deep green at one time. Now it was just faded from being in the sun too much. Blake had bought it at a yard sale. He was known for being thrifty.

"Have you given some thought to my pitch the other day?" Moore asked eagerly.

"I have, Manny. I have."

"And?" Moore asked eagerly as he leaned forward.

"I want to move slowly on this. I'll look for some ways to work you in since you backed me the other day," Blake said as he eyed Moore carefully.

"I was hoping to jump right in," Moore responded impatiently.

"Not so quick, my friend. You and I are still getting to know each other. It will take some time, but it will eventually happen."

"I was hoping sooner than later," Moore urged.

"Slow down. You in a big rush for cash?" he asked as he tried to determine why Moore was so hopped up.

"No. It's nothing like that. It just sounds like this could be my big break," Moore said as he tried to hide his disappointment.

"Be patient." Blake encouraged Moore. "Refresh my memory. What did you say you did in Ohio?"

Moore let out a deep breath in frustration. He had explained his background when he interviewed for the job. But if Blake wanted to hear it again, Moore was willing. "I kicked around. Mostly odd jobs and various gigs when I could find work. Worked on a ferry boat for awhile as a deckhand. Did some landscaping work." Moore had prepared a cover story that he regurgitated when necessary.

"And you don't have a driver's license?"

"No. I lost it."

"Or did they take it away from you?" Blake pushed.

Moore paused before answering. "Yeah. I got caught for a hit and run."

BOB ADAMOV

"And you were drunk?" Blake guessed.

"Yeah," Moore continued with his cover story.

"Did you do time?"

"Yeah."

"You do drugs?"

"You asked me during my interview," Moore noted.

"Yeah and I'm asking again," Blake pushed.

"Just some weed. That's all," Moore answered in character.

"Nothing heavier?"

"No."

Blake nodded. He appeared to be satisfied with how his questions were answered. He pointed to a box of unopened liquor. "You can take those out front and stock the bar."

Moore stood and did as instructed.

An hour later, Moore saw the Cuban with the backpack enter the bar and walk into the back. Moore assumed that he was going to meet with Blake again and decided to take a risk. He called to Sherry.

"Can you cover the bar for a few minutes? I need to run out back."

"Sure, Manny. Got ya covered," she replied as Moore took one quick look around the interior and the sparse early afternoon crowd.

Cautiously, Moore walked into the back to the closed office door. He could hear Blake and someone, most likely the Cuban, talking. He placed his ear up against the gap between the jamb and door. He strained his ear to hear what they were saying.

"This is big. That's why I need your stuff, too. I'll replace it on my next trip and give you a better price," a voice with a Cuban accent said.

"But I haven't had a chance to move any of it," Blake protested.

"Blake, this is a big one. Stop stalling and fill the backpack," the Cuban ordered.

"When's this going down?"

"Tonight. Around six. You don't need to be there. It's some of the boys from Miami and this could open up a new buyer for me."

Just then the compressor for the air conditioner kicked on and Moore struggled to hear where the meeting was taking place. He managed to hear the name of the hotel and decided to go there to observe what he could. Quietly, he slipped back out front to return to his duties.

"Thanks, Sherry," he said as he walked past her to wait on a patron who had taken a seat on a bar stool.

"No problem, Manny," she smiled. She liked the nicely mannered bartender.

At the end of his shift at five, Moore rode his bike back to the trailer and cleaned up, changing into a white linen shirt and black trousers. He checked his fake birthmark to make sure that it still looked good and then headed the few blocks to the hotel near Smathers Beach.

Parking his bike, he walked over to the main entrance to the hotel and looked at his watch. He had about fifteen minutes before the Miami group was scheduled to arrive. He decided to scope out the property and walked inside. He saw a waiter pushing a cart of freshly cut fruit through the lobby and, on a hunch, stopped him.

"Is that for the six o'clock meeting?" Moore asked.

"Yes. Don't worry. I'll have it set up on time," the man said nervously.

"And you know where to take it?" Moore pushed.

"Yes. Meeting Room B."

"Are the drinks in there already?"

"Yes. Your associates sent me to get this fruit." The man was anxious to stop the chitchat and deliver the fruit.

"Go ahead, then. Be sure to have it ready," Moore advised, pleased to uncover the meeting location so easily. Things were falling into place better than he expected.

Moore returned to the main entrance and engaged the valet parking attendant, Jerry, in conversation.

Within two minutes, a black Cadillac pulled up. The valet ran up to the driver's side as four swarthy-looking men stepped out of the car. They were wearing tropical shirts and carried briefcases.

"Jerry, you can park them close by and I'll show them to our meeting room," Moore said, acting as if he worked there.

The valet had a perplexed look on his face, but did as he was directed.

The four men approached Moore who acted like he was there to show them to the meeting location. "Welcome to Key West. You're right on time gentlemen," Moore smiled.

"I'm always on time," the leader of the group snarled.

Ignoring the comment, Moore led the men through the lobby to Meeting Room B, passing the waiter who was making his way with his now empty fruit cart down the hallway.

"Thanks for the fruit," Moore called as he continued his sham in front of the visitors.

When they reached the door to Meeting Room B, Moore stopped and opened the door. As the men entered the room, they were greeted by the Cuban that Moore previously had seen at Blake's bar and two of his companions. It was obvious to Moore that everyone was armed. Moore followed the last one into the room and stood by the door as if he was assigned to guarding it.

"Welcome, Jaime," the Cuban greeted the man who had snarled at Moore.

"We need a drink," Jaime replied as he and the other three set their cash-filled briefcases on a table near four cocaine-filled briefcases which the Cuban had placed there earlier.

"There's liquor there and a few bottles of rum that I brought from my last trip to Cuba," the Cuban explained. The four men moved to the portable bar and began mixing drinks.

"Your man at the door can have a drink, too, if he'd like," the Cuban said as he looked at Moore.

"Our man? He's not our man. I thought he was your man," Jaime growled as a .45 handgun appeared magically in his hand.

"He's not my man!" the Cuban said as he and his two companions produced their semi-automatic handguns and pointed them at Jaime and Moore. All hell broke loose with each one thinking that the other had set up a bad deal.

Moore moved quickly when Jaime made his comment. He had opened and run through the doorway as the first shots rang out. The room was filled with the sound of gunshots as the two parties began firing at each other.

As several men dropped dead to the floor, a burst of automatic fire came through the windows, breaking the glass and killing the remaining occupants. The gunman opened the door from the outside patio and walked into the meeting room. He kicked at the bodies to make sure that everyone was dead. When one groaned, he put a few rounds into him. He looked at the briefcases for a moment and thought about taking the drugs and cash, but decided against it.

He walked around the front of the building where he saw Moore standing next to his bike. A Cuban had a gun pointed at him. He was a backup.

"Hey Emerson, you need a hand?" the gunman shouted as he accomplished his goal in distracting the Cuban. As the Cuban swung his handgun toward the gunman, he fired a round into the Cuban's torso, instantly dropping him to the ground.

Moore stood with his mouth open. He was stunned as he recognized the gunman. It was like looking at a ghost! It was Fat Freddy Fabrizio, the five-foot, five-inch-tall, generously overweight Italian-American from Moore's past. He sported a shaved head and a beard.

"Yeah, it's me," the gunman yelled as he dropped his weapon. "Now you and I need to get out of here before we have to do a lot of explaining to the police."

"My bike," Moore stammered in shock.

"Leave it. We'll come back for it." Fat Freddy grabbed him by the arm. "Come on. My car is parked over there," he said as he half-dragged a stunned Moore to the vehicle.

Still in a daze, Moore allowed himself to be taken through the parking lot to the strange-looking Gremlin he had first seen driving down Duval Street a few days ago. "This is yours?"

"Yeah. People focus on the car and not the driver. Helps protect me," Fat Freddy laughed as he slid open a locking bolt on the passenger door and opened it. He shoved Moore inside and closed the door, sliding the bolt shut. He walked around to the other side and tried starting the vehicle. The engine sputtered once, and twice, then caught on the third try. He eased the car out of the parking lot and drove along Smathers Beach.

"I thought you were dead," Moore finally managed a comment as he stared at Fat Freddy.

"Yeah. Everyone did," said Fat Freddy.

"But I heard the police officer yell that you were dead."

"Stupid rookie. The paramedics found a slight pulse and gave me some sort of shots and an IV. They rushed me to the hospital from the marina and I pulled through."

Fat Freddy slowed the car as they approached the main part of Smathers Beach where the food trucks lined the street. "I like to park over here. Lot of hot babes walk over in those skimpy swimsuits to get food," he chuckled as he parked across the street from the food trucks.

"Freddy Fabrizio, I never thought I'd see you again," Moore said as he took a deep breath.

"No one did. A lot of the guys are dead. Jimmy Diamonds is gone. Santoro is gone. I decided I'd better scoot or I'd be permanently gone, too," the cherubic gangster explained. "I'm in the Federal Witless Protection Program now."

Moore chuckled when he heard Fat Freddy substitute witless for witness. "How did you manage that?"

"I worked out a trade. I gave the feds some valuable inside info on some bad boys in Detroit. They gave me a new life and I picked Key West."

"That's great, Freddy," Moore said, happy that his friend was alive and well.

Fat Freddy held up a finger. "No, no. I'm not Freddy any more, Emerson. My new name is Bones Aiken."

"That's original," Moore muttered.

"Yeah, it's because my bones were aching up in those cold Michigan winters. I told the feds that I wanted to use the name Luke Skywalker and they didn't think that was a good idea."

Moore smiled.

"Then I suggested Luke Warmwater and they didn't like it either. So, I landed on Bones Aiken. It works for me."

"And you grew a beard and shaved your head, Freddy," Moore noted.

"Women loved the shaved head look and the beard adds an air of mystery to my face," he responded with a sensuous smile that made Moore chuckle quietly.

Then Aiken's face transformed into a serious look as he waved a finger at Moore. "You've got to remember to call me Bones. Got it, Emerson?"

"Yes, and you have to call me Manny Elias," Moore cautioned in return.

"The name Jimmy Diamonds gave you? That's just perfect. I was over at Booger Blake's and one of the gals, who I think was hot for me, told me your name was Manny Elias. And you've got this beard and long hair now, and that birthmark on your face. But I'd know you anywhere, my friend."

Moore laughed quietly as he saw that the rotund Aiken still saw himself as God's gift to females. "Yes. The birthmark is fake and I'm wearing a wig. I needed to rough myself up for this assignment."

"Okay, Manny. You're on an assignment which probably explains why I had to save your ass back at the hotel. Those were some bad dudes you were messing with. And lucky for you they were Cubans and not Colombians. Colombians would cut off your cojones with a dull knife when they got their hands on you."

"I was going to ask you about that. What made you show up?"

Aiken allowed a snide smile to cross his face. "I'm your guardian angel, Emerson."

"Manny," Moore corrected him.

"Yeah. That's what I meant. Manny," Aiken smiled.

"So how did you get wind of what was going down?" Moore asked.

"That day I thought I saw you on Duval Street ..."

"You recognized me even then?" Moore asked with surprise.

"Yeah. I saw right through that getup. I started nosing around to see if I could find you. I didn't turn up anything until I happened to walk into Booger Blake's. When I heard that you were using the Manny Elias name, I figured you were up to something or you lost your memory again. By the way, how is that memory working for you?"

"I'm completely recovered other than a few headaches every now and then."

"Well, we all get headaches from time to time. On the days you have a headache, just stick an out of order sign on your forehead and call it a day," Aiken offered.

Moore snickered. "You didn't answer my question. How did you connect the dots and show up at the hotel?"

"I know about Blake and his connection to Cuban drugs. It was pretty easy to guess that you were doing an undercover job on him. Am I right?"

"He was my starting point."

"Yeah and I know about that Cuban running drugs. He works for a real bad hombre in Cuba. You don't want to mess with these people. They make Jimmy Diamonds look like a Girl Scout."

Aiken continued as he allowed his eyes to take in one skimpily-attired blonde approaching one of the food trucks. "I kind of kept an eye on you from a distance. When a couple of friends told me that the Cuban was doing a big deal with some of the boys from Miami, I figured you'd be there and out of your league; it turns out that I was right."

"I thought I'd get a big break on the story."

"The only break you'd get from those boys is a broken neck. You can't mess with them, Manny."

"I actually got into the room," Moore said, quite proud of his subterfuge.

"And what were you thinking? Walking in there with them? How long did you think it would take before they realized you weren't with them? You dumb schmuck!"

"Probably not one of my brightest decisions," Moore agreed.

"Yeah, and I almost had a heart attack running my little legs around the building so I could watch through the window. When they drew their pieces and started firing, you gave me little choice. I had to open up," Aiken said as he popped a handful of gummy bears in his mouth.

Suddenly Aiken started choking on the sweet treats.

"You okay, Bones?" Moore asked with a panicked look.

Aiken pointed at a bottle of water at Moore's feet which Moore picked up and handed to Aiken. He quickly opened it and took a deep gulp. After coughing a few times to clear his throat, Aiken said, "I hope if I ever choke to death on gummy bears that people will just say that some bears killed me."

Moore smiled. He always liked Aiken's warped sense of humor. "Thanks for bailing me out back there, Bones," he said appreciatively.

"What if I hadn't been there? I'll tell you what I'd be doing. I'd be getting ready for your funeral. We'd be burying whatever pieces of you were still around, including that bad wig!"

"And now we'll probably end up getting questioned by the police," Moore suggested. "Especially if they spotted your car," he added.

"Probably. I'll call my guys at the Witless Protection Program and see if they can help in getting us off. You didn't kill anyone. You were an innocent bystander if I can stretch the truth. Me? Well, I did the feds a favor and took out some bad guys. I was tempted to take the cash and drugs, but it would be better to leave them. They can write it off as a drug deal gone bad. That might satisfy the boys up in Miami."

"You think the feds would do that for you?" Moore asked, surprised.

"Yeah. I gave them a boatload of information. They'll owe me for years. They can smooth it over with the local police here."

"That would help. I don't need to be in front of the Key West police," Moore said appreciatively as he thought about his previous visit with them.

Aiken glanced at his watch. "Hey, I've got to get going," he said as he started the car and began driving. "I've got to get to work."

"Work? You've got a job here?"

A huge smile crossed Aiken's face. "Oh yeah. I've got the perfect job. I'm the night cook at Candyland."

"Candyland?" Moore asked.

"Yep. It's a strip club near the end of Duval Street. Best place for me to hide. Who is going to come in there and look for me when they'd be distracted by all of that eye candy walking around?"

Chuckling, Moore said, "I guess you're right. Who would notice you?"

"That's the idea. Same thing with my wheels here. People stare at the car, not me." With a sly glint in his eye, Aiken continued. "And those babes at Candyland, they come back in the kitchen to pick up food for the customers. Sometimes, I'll whip up something special for them. And in return, I get all of the lap dances I can handle!"

"Sounds like the perfect job for you, Bones."

"I get my bones warmed all of the time. Them broads can't resist me," he grinned. "Now, where can I drop you?"

Moore gave him directions to the mobile home on United Street and Aiken drove him there. As Moore stepped out of the car, he added, "Don't forget to set the record straight with the police here. I don't need them messing up the rest of my plans—and don't tell them what I'm up to."

"No problem. Zippo. Nada. I don't tell anyone anything I don't need to tell them. I'll give the feds a call before I go to work. Hey, give me your cell number so I can have it."

Moore rattled off the number as Aiken punched it into his phone and called Moore. "There. You have my number, too."

"My phone's inside. I don't carry it with me," Moore said.

"That could be good or bad. I'll call you tomorrow and update you."

"I'll be at work tomorrow night and without the phone."

"I'll call you before you go. Hey, you need to stop by the club. I can get you a free lap dance," Aiken teased.

"Maybe. I'll see." Moore closed the car door and leaned toward the open window. "Thanks for saving my life, Freddy."

"Geesh! What a slow learner you are. It's Bones, you dumb ass!" Aiken spun his wheels as he accelerated the Gremlin. It sent small stones spinning in the air as Moore turned his back and entered the trailer.

Locking the door behind him, Moore enjoyed the cool comfort of his home away from home. He walked over to the refrigerator and grabbed a cold drink, then headed for the corner recliner. Dropping into it, he took a long swig of the icy drink. Before setting it on the nearby end table, he ran the cold beverage across his brow, enjoying the momentary distraction it offered from the evening's chaotic events.

As he sat, Moore thought about how foolish he had been to walk into that room to see the drug deal go down. What had he been thinking to walk in there, especially unarmed? It was just one of those stupid things we do as humans when we're not thinking clearly, he thought.

And what about Fat Freddy returning from the grave? He had to admit that he was happy to see the little Mafioso was still alive. His reappearance couldn't have been timelier. He had saved Moore's life by getting involved.

Moore looked forward to spending time with Freddy. "Oops," he spoke out loud as he remembered that he needed to call him Bones. Tired, Moore stood and walked down the hallway to the bedroom where he allowed his body to fall onto the bed.

Even though he was tired, he couldn't fall asleep right away. The gunfight at the hotel and his encounter with Fat Freddy, aka Bones Aiken, danced through his mind. Finally, he fell into a fitful sleep.

CHAPTER 6

The Next Morning
Smathers Beach

After an early morning run along Smathers Beach, Moore picked up his bike where he had left it at the hotel and rode it back to the trailer park. He fixed a ham and cheese omelet and some fresh fruit for breakfast. He was washing the dishes when his cell phone rang. He looked at the caller ID and saw that it was Bones Aiken.

"Hi Bones," Moore answered.

"Manny, I wanted you to know I talked to the feds last night and told them what happened. They called me back a little while ago and told me that they smoothed out everything with the Key West police, although I was surprised to hear that the police already know you. They really wanted to talk to you since they saw you on the surveillance footage at the hotel. Something about you being involved in a murder here?" Aiken asked.

"Not really. I just covered for my boss." Moore relayed what had transpired when the police stopped by Blake's bar to question him and the visit afterwards to the police station for further questioning.

"Manny, you just can't stay out of trouble," Aiken hissed. "Just don't go and do anything that's going to cause me to be in any pictures. I'm supposed to be low-key here, remember?"

"I get it, Bones. Being on anyone's radar screen is not what I want either."

"Then be smart and stay cool, Manny. Listen. I got to go. I'll be in touch."

They ended their call and Moore finished up his dishes. He saw on the wall clock that it was time to head to work and headed out the door to grab his bike. He made the ten-minute ride to Booger Blake's without incident and locked his bike in front of the bar.

As he entered the bar, Sherry walked over to him. "Hey, Manny."

"Yes?" Moore answered.

"Be careful around Blake today," she cautioned.

"Why?"

"He's really in a foul mood. He's been angry all morning."

"Any idea what's bothering him?" Moore asked, although he guessed privately that it might involve the death of the Cuban, Blake's primary drug source.

"No."

"Fight with his wife?" Moore asked.

"I don't know. I haven't seen him like this in the past."

"Thanks for the warning," Moore said as he walked behind the bar and started washing some dirty glasses in the sink.

A few minutes later, Blake walked behind Moore, bumping him as he carried two bottles of liquor. "Guess I've got to do everything myself around this dump," Blake snarled as he set the bottles on the shelf behind the bar.

"I can help, Blake."

"If you wanted to help, Manny, you'd have checked the inventory out here and restocked it," Blake snapped angrily.

"I'll get right on it," Moore replied quickly.

"Yeah. Yeah you will," Blake said sarcastically as he walked back to his office.

Manny looked over the bottles on display and took note of which ones needed replaced. Hurriedly, he went in the back and brought out new bottles. He focused on his work and his customers for the rest of his shift, interrupted only occasionally by Blake and his bad attitude.

After the bar closed for the evening, Moore found himself alone with Blake and decided to see if Blake would open up to him.

"Hey, Blake," Moore called from behind the bar.

"What?"

"I've got about three shots of Patrón left in this bottle. I'll buy you two and myself one. Interested?"

Blake cast a wary eye toward Moore as he thought for a moment. "Yeah, maybe I should." Blake walked over to a corner table and plopped on a chair. He swung his feet up on another chair as Moore approached with the bottle and two shot glasses.

Moore sat and placed the shot glasses on the table. He then filled them and set the nearly empty bottle on the table. Pushing one of the glasses to Blake, Moore said, "Here's to washing your troubles away."

Blake reached for the glass and spoke as he raised it to his lips. "It will take more than this to wash away my troubles." He threw down the shot as Moore set his empty glass on the table and picked up the bottle.

"Let me refill it," Moore offered as he poured Blake another round.

"You might want to go get another bottle," Blake said somewhat sarcastically as he reached for the glass and drank it down.

Moore ignored the comment. Instead he pushed. "What's been eating at you today?"

Blake's eyes narrowed. He looked like he was getting ready to confide in Moore—and he was. "I've got this kind of silent partner."

"The guy I've seen come in here from time to time?"

Blake jerked back in surprise. "You're pretty observant."

Moore smiled. "I try to be."

"Yeah. That's the guy."

"There's a problem with him?" Moore asked.

"Yeah. Big problem."

"What do you mean?"

"He isn't sucking air any more."

"He's dead?" Moore asked, playing dumb.

"Yeah. Bought it yesterday."

"What happened?"

Blake looked around the empty bar before he leaned toward Moore. "I'm going to let you in on something, Manny. I trust you for what you did with the police and for giving me an alibi the other night."

"Sure, Blake. I don't tell anybody anything."

"My partner and I run drugs out of the back. Coke."

"You do?" Moore asked in mock surprise.

"Yeah." It was Blake's turn to smile. "I guess you're not as observant as you thought you were."

Moore let it go. "I guess not."

"He was my main contact with our source."

"Somebody in Miami?"

"No, Cuba. We did some stuff for the Miami guys, but that all went bad last night."

"Deal gone bad?"

"Yeah. And to make matters worse, I'm into the Miami boys for some big bucks."

"What about your Cuban guy?"

"Him, too."

"What are you going to do?"

"I got to figure this all out." He looked toward the bar. "Bring me another bottle, would ya?"

"Sure, Blake."

Moore stood up from his chair and walked behind the bar where he grabbed an unopened bottle of Patrón. He quickly returned to the table, opened the bottle and poured Blake another shot.

"Pour yourself one while you're at it." Blake instructed.

"Sure."

The two men downed the shots.

"You ever been to Cuba, Manny?"

"No."

"Would you be interested in going?" Blake asked.

"Do you mean for you?"

"Yeah."

"Maybe." Moore didn't want to appear too eager. "Wouldn't it be dangerous since you owe this guy money?"

Blake didn't speak for a minute. "Probably. Pour me another."

Moore complied and then pushed the shot glass back to Blake who took it and downed it.

"Let me sleep on it, Manny. I'll figure something out." Blake wobbled as he stood from his chair. "Make sure that shotgun under the bar is loaded."

"I'll check right now."

"And be on alert for any unsavory visitors over the next few days. Who knows what our Cuban or Miami friends will be up to next?"

"I'll do that," Moore said as he watched Blake stumble to the back.

"I'm out of here. Lock up for me, Manny, and thanks."

"Okay," Moore responded as he heard the back door shut. He was elated that Blake was opening up to him. He hurriedly finished closing up and headed home. He would have a difficult time falling asleep as his mind raced about the evening's revelations.

CHAPTER 7

The Next Evening
Booger Blake's Bar

Blake seemed strangely aloof that evening. He was barely talking to the staff as his mind seemed to be elsewhere. Moore gave him space and didn't want to appear too pushy after the progress he had made with Blake the previous night.

Moore was focused on his customers and didn't see a man walk into the bar through the door. The man stopped and appeared to casually look around the room, but there was nothing casual about his sharp eagle eyes. He spotted Moore and slowly, but deliberately, walked over to the bar and took a seat. He waited for Moore to see him.

The man was in his late thirties—tall, lean and mean. His blonde hair was close-cropped and his slate blue eyes had a touch of cruelty in them. He had been dishonorably discharged from the U.S. Army Rangers and was involved with contract work, legal and illegal.

Moore stepped back from the bar as he saw out of the corner of his eye that someone was seated nearby. When he turned to face the man, he recognized him right away.

"Newt!" Manny acknowledged with surprise.

A couple of years ago, he had met Newton upstate in Cedar Key, about an hour west of Gainesville. It was during the time of his memory loss and when the Detroit mob had contracted with Newton to train Moore as a hit man under the alias of Manny Elias. It had been a tough and successful training regimen that Fat Freddy had overseen.

Newton's somber face cracked a small smile. "Hello, Manny."

Moore smiled to himself. He realized that Newton only knew him as Manny Elias. His real name had never been divulged to Newton.

Eyeing Moore's physique, Newton commented, "Looks like you've been keeping yourself in shape since Cedar Key."

"That I have. I learned a lot from you. Been working out almost every day."

"Good to hear."

"What's going on with the hair and birthmark?" Newton asked as he stared at Moore. "And you're looking scruffy with that hair on your face."

"I'm just chilling out. That's all," Moore responded, not wanting to talk about it in the bar with so many people around.

"Sure," Newton said with skepticism. He wasn't buying the explanation.

"What can I get you?"

"Bud Light."

Moore grabbed one and set it in front of Newton. "It's on me."

"Thank you, Manny," Newton said as he raised the beer to his mouth and took a large gulp.

"What brings you to town?"

"Just a little R&R," Newton drawled slowly.

"Fishing?"

"You might say that," Newton said with a glint in his eyes. "What are you doing down here? I thought you were up north."

Moore thought quickly. He knew that Newton tied him to the mob because of the training he had undergone. He also knew that Jimmy Diamonds, the Detroit crime boss, had been talking to Newton while Moore was training with him in Cedar Key.

"Letting things cool down. It was getting too hot up there, if you know what I mean," Moore explained quickly.

"I get it," Newton said as he nodded his head. "Whatever happened to your little fat buddy, Freddy?"

"He bought the farm," Moore answered, not wanting to let him know that Fat Freddy was still alive. Besides he could put Fat Freddy at risk.

"Sorry to hear that. He was a funny guy. I remember that fight with the bikers he got us into at Cedar Key."

Moore chuckled at the memory. "That was a great night." Moore wanted to talk more, but saw two customers take a seat at the other end of the bar. "I'll be back. Got to take care of those folks."

The bar became more crowded and Moore realized that he wasn't going to have time to chat with Newton. When he had a chance, he walked over to Newton and asked, "You want to grab lunch tomorrow?"

"How about a workout and a late breakfast?" Newton asked.

"Sure." Moore grabbed a piece of paper and scribbled

his cell phone number and address. "You want to stop over around 0800?"

"That works. I'll see you then." Newton stood and walked out of the bar while Moore busied himself with his customers.

As Newton left the bar, a figure scurried across the street and hid behind some bushes. He had recognized Newton and wondered what he was up to.

Later that night, Moore closed the bar and walked over to his bike. As he unlocked it, the figure stepped out of the shadows and spoke.

"What in the hell is Newton doing down here?"

"Bones!" Moore said startled. "I didn't see you."

"You're letting your guard down," Aiken said. "Answer my question. What was Newton doing here?"

"He's on a fishing trip."

"Fishing trip. Crap! Cedar Key is known for its fishing. Why would he leave there to come down here? Something's fishy, Manny," Aiken said as he chuckled at his own joke.

"I don't know. I'll find out more tomorrow."

"What do you mean?"

"He's coming over to my place and we're going to work out together," Moore said.

"You didn't say anything to him about me being alive, did ya?"

"No. Why would I do that?"

"Just be sure you don't."

Aiken heard a noise and turned in its direction. He watched two cats chase each other around the corner as he thought for a moment. "I don't like it. Him showing up like this. Out of nowhere. You don't know who he could be working for!"

"I'll be fine."

"Yeah. Well, you just watch your ass."

Moore could sense Aiken's angst. "I'll be careful, Bones."

"You do that," he said. "I got to go. I've got to give a couple of the girls a ride home tonight."

"I'm sure you'll enjoy that," Moore teased.

"I'm hoping I do," Aiken said as he turned and walked over to his car.

CHAPTER 8

The Next Morning
Sam Duncan's Trailer

Standing at the kitchen window, Moore saw a car pull up and park in front of Sam's trailer. He watched as Newton stepped out. Newton was wearing running shoes and shorts like Moore. He was shirtless and Moore could see his muscular chest. Moore finished his coffee and walked over to the door.

"Morning," Moore greeted Newton as he walked out of the mobile home and locked its door. He carefully reached above the door to avoid getting stung by the bees and put the key on the ledge. "Great day for a run."

"Every day is a great day for a run. It doesn't matter what the weather is," the tough ex-Special Forces ranger replied.

"Then, let's do it," Moore said as the two stretched out. A few minutes later, they were running. They initially ran to White Street and followed it to Atlantic Boulevard. After a quick jog to the right on Bertha Street, they were running on South Roosevelt Boulevard along the Atlantic Ocean.

"Over here, wimp!" Newton said as he ran off the

sidewalk and along the water's edge of Smathers Beach. "The sand is tougher to run in," Newton yelled.

"No problem," Moore smiled as he kept pace with Newton.

"No girls in bikinis?" Newton asked as his eyes scanned the beach.

"So, that's why you wanted to run here," Moore teased.

"No. That would be a side benefit."

Moore smiled. "Too early. Give them an hour and they'll be out."

They ran until the beach ended and then jogged along the sidewalk to the intersection with U.S. Route One to Stock Island. There, they turned around and retraced their route back to the trailer.

When they arrived back at the trailer, Moore reached into the small outdoor refrigerator and grabbed two bottles of cold water. They sat in two old rickety chairs under the awning. Moore took a slow drink of water and watched as Newton poured some of his water over his head before taking a sip.

"Good run," Moore said as he grabbed a nearby towel and wiped the sweat off his face.

"It was," Newton agreed. "You did well."

"You were testing me!" Moore exclaimed. "I wondered if you were."

Newton smiled. "I wanted to be sure that you didn't let my training lapse."

"I'll admit that I don't follow the vigorous workout you put me through, but I do my best to work out almost every day."

"Keep it up. You don't want to lose what you accomplished at Cedar Key, Manny."

"I'm with you," Moore agreed. "You want to shower before we go to breakfast?"

"Yeah. I've got a change of clothes in the rental car," Newton said as he stood.

As Newton walked over to his car, Moore carefully grabbed the key from its hiding place and opened the door. Both men cleaned up and changed.

Thirty minutes later, the two men were in Newton's rental car and driving over to Thomas Street to Blue Heaven.

"Been here before?" Moore asked as they walked the short distance from the parked car.

"No," Newton replied. "I've heard about it and wanted to try it."

They walked through the restaurant's gated entrance and down a brick sidewalk into an open courtyard dining area. It featured chairs and tables set on a sandy floor.

"Seriously, this place is one of the top ten best places to eat in Key West," Moore explained. "It's got a long history. They used to have cockfights here, and, according to local history, Ernest Hemingway once refereed some of the Friday night boxing matches. If I remember when we leave, I'll point out the rooster cemetery where they buried the dead roosters," Moore said as they walked onto the grounds.

They were seated inside and the waitress gave them menus and large cups of coffee. They each read their menu quickly and placed their orders.

Emerson opted for the Rooster Special, which consisted of two eggs, bacon and Betty's banana bread. Newton ordered Seafood Benedict, a fresh fish sautéed and served with poached eggs on English muffins with lime Hollandaise sauce.

"Cool place," Newton said as he looked around the interior.

"Did you see the shower stall in the courtyard?" Moore asked.

"Out of the corner of my eye."

"It had a sign on the side of it. It read that showers are one dollar and it's only two dollars to watch," Moore grinned mischievously.

Newton shook his head.

Moore pointed toward the stairs to the second floor. "The second floor of this building used to be a bordello years ago."

"Now that I'd like to see," Newton smiled.

"And they had spyholes on the doors so people could look in and watch," Moore added.

"Now that would have been interesting!" Newton grinned.

The waitress returned with their food and the men focused on their meals, chatting as they ate.

When they finished, Newton sat back in his chair. He took a last sip of his coffee and leaned toward Moore. "There's something I wanted to ask you, Manny."

"What's that?"

"You staying out of trouble down here?"

"Yes." Moore looked perplexed and was becoming suspicious. "Why do you ask?"

"After all, I was hired to train you as a hitman. You still doing that job?"

Moore's outward appearance remained calm, but inside, he was getting nervous at being asked the question. He wondered if Newton knew about the circumstances surrounding Jimmy Diamonds' death since Diamonds was the one who sent Moore to Newton for training. Or had Newton, Moore thought, in some strange way become aware of his connection to the Cuban's death the other night?

Moore took a slow breath before responding. "I'm just laying low now. That's why I took the job here."

"Not for the money, huh?"

Moore saw a smile break on Newton's face.

"Definitely not for the money. There isn't any here," Moore responded.

"Remember what I told you in Cedar Key. Don't …"

"… trust anyone. I remember," Moore finished the sentence for Newton.

Newton looked at his watch. "I should be going. I'm going deep sea fishing today. Want to come?"

"I'd like to, but I've got an early shift tonight. Maybe another time."

"Sure. That sounds good to me," Newton replied as he threw down cash to pay for their breakfast.

The two men returned to the rental car and Newton dropped off Moore at his trailer. Later that afternoon, Moore returned to the bar to work his shift.

CHAPTER 9

The Next Morning
Booger Blake's Bar

After getting a frantic call from Sherry at Booger Blake's Bar, Moore left the trailer and pedaled as fast as he could to the bar. When he arrived, he saw two police cars parked in front. A covered body was being wheeled out on a gurney to the ambulance. It appeared that whoever it was had died.

"Manny! There you are," a red-eyed Sherry shouted as she emerged from the bar.

Manny secured his bike and walked over to her as she crumpled in his arms. "What's wrong?"

"It's Blake. Someone murdered him."

Moore's brow wrinkled with concern. "Just now?"

"No, I found him on the floor when I walked in this morning. Someone shot him," she sobbed.

"Was it a robbery? Anything taken?"

"I don't think so. I just got here and saw him on the floor by the bar. I really didn't look around."

Moore looked inside the building and saw several officers going through the crime scene. He recognized one of the officers from the visit a few days ago. It was Pieffer.

"Manny!" Pieffer called.

"Yes?"

"I'd like to talk to you," Pieffer said as he approached. Sherry walked away to talk to another employee who had arrived.

"Sure. What can I do to help?"

"What do you know about this?"

"Nothing. I was here on the late shift yesterday. I left around 1:00 A.M. this morning. Nothing seemed out of place. I didn't sense any problems," Moore stated matter-of-factly.

Pieffer spent another ten minutes questioning Moore before letting him go and telling him that the bar would be closed for the next couple of days while everything was sorted out.

After Moore unlocked his bike, he began wheeling it to the sidewalk and wondering what his next move should be.

"Hey, Manny. Need a lift?" a voice called.

Moore looked up and saw Newton.

"We can throw your bike in the trunk and grab breakfast. You look like you're in shock. We can talk," Newton suggested with a look of concern.

"Yeah. Maybe that's what I need," Moore replied as he pushed the bike to the rear of the car where he was joined by Newton. They put the bike in the trunk and tied down the trunk lid.

As they sat in the car, Newton spoke. "How about going over to Schooner Wharf Bar?"

"That sounds good to me. I'm not really hungry, but I could use a drink," Moore said solemnly.

"You're certainly not yourself this morning," Newton said observantly.

"You're spot on," Moore murmured.

"So, what happened?" Newton asked as he turned left onto Duval Street.

"My boss was shot. He's dead," Moore answered somberly.

As Newton stopped the car for a red light, he watched as a pedicab pulled up next to them on Moore's side of the car. Suddenly, Newton shouted, "Duck!"

Reacting quickly, Moore dropped down in the passenger seat as a .38 caliber semi-automatic handgun appeared quickly in Newton's hand. He fired it twice, killing the nearby pedicab driver. Newton floored the accelerator as the car turned right and sped away.

"You okay, Manny?" Newton asked Moore as he glanced at him.

Moore's face was ashen gray. "What was that all about?" he asked.

"Hit job on you, man."

"What?" Moore asked in disbelief.

"Yeah. The guy pulled up next to us, looked at you and started to aim a gun to take you out. Good thing you had me at the wheel. I'm always armed," Newton spoke proudly.

"Why would anyone put a hit on me?" Moore asked.

"I don't know. You tell me. What are you really doing in Key West, Manny?" Newton asked as he pulled over and parked the car.

Moore didn't respond.

"Get out," Newton ordered.

"Why? What are we doing?"

"The police will be looking for a car with a bike sticking out of the trunk. We're going to take that bike out and walk it the rest of the way to breakfast."

"What about the car?" Moore asked as they lifted the bike out of the trunk.

"Who cares. It'll take them awhile to run down the plates and trace it back to me. Doesn't matter, I used a fake ID to rent it. Come on. Let's walk and talk."

Moore set the bike on the sidewalk and began pushing it. Things were happening so fast that he was bewildered.

"You didn't answer my question, Manny. What are you really doing down here?"

Remembering Newton's sage advice not to trust anyone, Moore decided he still wouldn't reveal his real purpose in being in Key West.

"I told you. I'm just taking a break and laying low."

"You got the boys in Detroit after you for some reason?" Newton pushed. "It looks to me like you're hiding from someone, wearing that stupid wig, fake birthmark and hairy face."

Moore looked around as they started to cross the street. He decided that he'd let Newton in on part of the real reason he was in Key West although he'd twist it a bit. "Listen, Newt. The guy who owned the bar was making a bundle by selling cocaine out of the bar. I thought that I'd have a chance to get a cut, but then someone kills him."

Moore's mind was in turmoil. He needed to be alert and respond to Newton's questions, but he wasn't sure how he was going to go forward with penetrating the Cuban connection to drug trafficking in Key West now that Blake and his Cuban business partner were dead. There also was Blake's dead friend and who killed him. Bodies were piling up too fast and Moore didn't want himself added to the pile.

"That's life," Newton observed. "You never know when your best laid plans are going to go down the toilet," he added nonchalantly. They entered the Schooner Wharf Bar at the foot of Williams Street and found a table overlooking the boat-filled harbor, better known as the Key West Bight.

The weathered-looking bar was located on the site of the old Singleton Shrimp factory and was a tropical oasis filled with an eclectic mix of customers and their pets. It was known for its strong drinks and good seafood, plus the annual Mel Fisher Days bikini contest.

A server appeared next to their table. She was carrying a decanter of coffee. "Would you like to start off with coffee?" she asked.

"Perfect," Moore responded. "That's all I'm having."

"Tough morning?" she asked her morose customer. She'd like to find a way to cheer him up.

"You have no idea," Moore replied.

"I'll take coffee and a ham and cheese omelet with home fries and rye toast," Newton said as she turned and filled his cup. Newton wasn't letting anything like a morning murder kill his appetite.

"My, but you do have an appetite," she smiled at Newton.

When she left their table, Moore looked at Newton. "You have to excuse me. I'm not thinking clearly."

"No excuse necessary, Manny."

"What a morning! Blake killed. Pedicab driver tries to take me out. You kill that guy." Moore paused and stared at Newton. "By the way, I never thanked you for saving my life."

"Not necessary. It's what I do," Newton said before taking a sip of his coffee. "You think the stash of drugs in the bar was found?"

"I'm sure that if Blake had anything, the police discovered

it. It seems like they were swarming the place."

"Too bad. That could have been your seed money if you found it and sold it."

"Yeah. I guess I lost out."

"What are you going to do now, Manny?"

Moore thought for a few seconds. "Guess I'll veg out and try to figure out what my next steps are. I have a buddy here who I can confide in."

Newton set his coffee cup on the table and looked at Moore. His last comment grabbed Newton's attention. "You do?"

"Yeah. I've known him for some time."

"Who is it?" Newton pushed.

"I'd rather not say. He likes to fly under the radar." Moore wasn't going to rat out Fat Freddy's identity to Newton. After all, Newton might eventually recall meeting Fat Freddy when Moore was training with Newton in Cedar Key. No sense in creating a problem for Fat Freddy, Moore thought.

"Sounds like a guy who's connected," Newton said. "Maybe somebody who could help me," Newton tried again to uncover the real identity of Moore's friend.

Moore wasn't buying. "Like I said. He's flying under the radar and doing his own thing," Moore replied.

Seeing the conversation going nowhere, Newton turned to his breakfast which the server had placed in front of him and began to wolf it down.

Moore became unusually withdrawn as the gravity of morning events continued to sink in. Someone had killed Blake and the pedicab driver had tried to take him out. Moore's mind was filled with confusion as he tried to sort out who was behind all of these disturbing events.

Newton ignored Moore's introversion and finished his breakfast. He glanced at the check the server had placed on the table and pulled out a wad of bills from his pocket. He peeled off a twenty and threw it on the table and placed the remaining wad in his pocket. Finishing the last of his coffee, he looked at Moore. "Ready to go, Mr. Quiet?"

"Sorry, Newt. I'm not good company."

"Like I would expect you to be after the crap that went down around you, Manny? Come on. Let's go."

The two men pushed back from the table and walked out to the parking lot where Moore's bike was secured to a bike rack.

"Heading home, Manny?" Newton asked as he spotted a Key West cab and waved it over. "Might not be the best place to be if somebody's looking to kill you," Newton warned.

"Yeah. I'll be careful. I just need to sort things out."

Newton handed Moore a card from his wallet. "There's my cell phone number. Call me if you need anything."

Moore took the card and slipped it in his shirt pocket. "I'll do that. Newt?"

Newton had opened the back door of the cab. "Yes?"

"Thanks."

"No problem," Newton flashed Moore a quick smile as he entered the cab and it drove away.

Moore looked at his watch and bent to unlock his bike. Within a minute he was riding his bike. He wasn't headed home. He had another destination in mind.

CHAPTER 10

Twenty Minutes Later
Candyland

Pulsating music echoed through the open doorway of the baby blue-painted building with hot pink highlights toward the end of Duval Street. A red neon sign flashed on and off to passing cars to let them know that Candyland was open.

Moore pedaled his bike up to the club's parking lot where three customers had parked their cars. He found a bike rack and secured his bike next to two other worn bikes. As he turned to enter the building, he was almost run over by an older, bearded man in a Jazzy-powered wheelchair. He was wearing a ballcap that showed he was a Vietnam War veteran.

"Sorry son," the man said as he hurried inside to catch the girls dancing on stage.

"Enjoy yourself," Moore smiled despite himself.

"Oh, I intend to. I certainly intend to," the man called over his shoulder.

Moore followed the man into the dimly lit club. To his left, he saw a raised stage with a stripper pole. A young, semi-nude woman was dancing seductively on the stage, flirting with three senior citizens who were seated in front of the stage.

In their eager hands, they held dollar bills saved from their monthly retirement checks. They couldn't wait for the chance to stuff a dollar into the sides of the dancer's barely-threaded bikini bottoms.

Moore's eyes scanned the room and saw another bikini-clad dancer sitting at a table with a man in his forties. They were talking and watching the seniors. Moore spotted one other person at the bar who was turned around in his seat, watching the activity.

Moore walked over to the bar and waved the server over.

"Can I help you?" the server asked as she thought that she'd like to give the good-looking Moore a private lap dance.

"Yes. I was trying to find Bones Aiken. Is he in yet?"

His question surprised her. Nobody looked for Aiken. "Yeah. He's out back taking a break. You a friend of his?"

"Yes."

"I didn't think he had any friends. Nice guy. Thinks he's funny. Cracking jokes all the time."

"Yes. That sounds like him."

"Just go down that hall." She pointed to the right of the stage. "Then go out the rear exit. You'll find him there."

"Thanks," Moore said as he turned to head in that direction.

"One more thing," she called.

"What?"

"No stopping in the dressing room in that hallway. It's off limits. Capisce?"

"Yes. I get it."

Moore walked through the hallway and its dangling

colored beads as a dancer on her way to the stage bumped into him.

"Where do you think you're going?" she demanded, as she suspiciously eyed Moore up and down.

"Out back to see Bones," Moore responded.

The dancer shook her ample chest. "When you're done with him, you come in and watch me dance. Okay, honey?"

Moore grinned at her flirtatiousness. "Maybe." He suddenly realized it was the first time he had smiled that morning.

"No maybes, baby. You come see me. I'll make it worth your while," she teased as she turned and walked through the dangling beads.

Moore continued his trek down the hallway and out the back door. As he walked outside, he spotted a perspiring Aiken.

"Bones, what's up?"

"What in the hell are you doing here, Manny?"

"It's a long story. You have a few minutes?"

"Yeah. I'm just recovering from an incident inside."

Moore became alarmed at the thought that someone identified Aiken. "Bad news?"

"Not for me, but it was for that stupid raccoon."

"What raccoon?"

"There was this raccoon that would do everything it could to get into the building."

"What?" Moore asked.

"Yeah. He learned the ladies had food in their dressing room. About fifteen minutes ago, one of the ladies came into the kitchen and told me that he was back. So, I grabbed my butcher's knife and I go into the dressing room.

"There's that raccoon sitting on top of the vanity table and munching on an open bag of Fritos like he owned the place. When I charged it, it skedaddled under my feet and knocked me down. The stupid raccoon carried the bag of Fritos with him. I chased him down the hallway and he pushed open this screen door and ran out. I'll get that crazy raccoon," Aiken said as he looked around.

"Sounds a bit like Elmer Fudd looking for that 'cwazy wabbit' to me," Moore chuckled.

"Not funny, Manny!" Aiken snapped before turning serious. "So, what brings you here? Wanted to check out the beautiful ladies?"

"No. It's been a rough morning." Moore went on to detail the morning's tragic events.

When he finished, Aiken asked, "Was that the pedicab driver who wore a flower power shirt all of the time?"

"I don't know about all of the time, but I do recall he had something like that on."

"That's good to hear if it was him. I didn't like him. Anytime I caught a ride with him, he'd charge me for two passengers because of my weight," Aiken groused.

Even though he thought the comment was funny, Moore didn't break a smile.

"And you say that Newton showed up? Just like that! Out of nowhere?" Aiken asked.

"Yes," Moore replied.

"It smells. I'm telling you it smells," Aiken said quietly.

"Why do you say that?"

"Out of the clear blue sky, Newton shows up in Key West. Then your boss is killed and the pedicab driver is killed."

Aiken turned to stare at Moore. "Did you see the pedicab driver aim a gun at you?"

"No. Newt had me ducking. I didn't see anything but the floor," Moore answered.

"And didn't you tell me that an old friend of Blake's was killed?"

"Yes."

"How long has Newton been in town?"

"I don't know. He didn't say."

"I don't like it. It all sounds too coincidental to me. I'd suggest you be very suspicious of Newton. You packing?"

"No, but I'm sure I can find a handgun at the trailer."

"Do that. Make sure you have one handy. I don't like the way this all is going down, Manny. I don't like it one bit," Aiken grumbled.

"I'll do that."

Aiken looked to make sure no one was around. "So, what are you going to do about your story now that you can't make the connection through the bar owner?"

"I don't know."

"I might be able to help you," Aiken offered.

"How's that?"

"There's a woman in town who could help you as long as you don't spook easily."

"What do you mean, Bones?" Moore didn't know where Aiken was taking the conversation.

"She's known locally as Madam Jean Seres," Aiken said as his beady little eyes looked up at Moore.

"Right, Bones. Listen, I don't plan on going to see a madam," Moore muttered, thinking of the kind that managed a whorehouse.

Aiken chuckled as he realized Moore was going down the wrong track. "No. Not that kind of madam. She's a fortune teller. Her sign says Haitian, but she's really Cuban."

"And why do I need my fortune told?"

"It's not that. She knows people in Cuba. She might be able to help you."

Moore was skeptical. "I don't know."

"I'm telling you she can help you," Aiken urged.

"Maybe tomorrow," he said hesitantly.

"You've got to go and see her." Aiken gave Moore the address and ushered him inside the building, talking as they walked.

"I know it's been a rough day for you. What you really need to do is get a lap dance. You'll forget everything that's bothering you," Aiken said as he escorted Moore into the main room.

"Connie, come over here," he yelled to a statuesque brunette with two of the biggest brown eyes. The bikini-clad dancer ended her conversation with another dancer and started toward Aiken.

"Hey, bring Donna with you," he shouted as he saw the dancer talking with Connie. "Manny, you're going to get something real special. I call it a 'twofer'," Aiken grinned as the ladies arrived.

"I don't know," Moore started as the two women realized what Aiken wanted and began to caress Moore's face and shoulders.

"You want to come with us?" Connie asked as she grabbed one of Moore's arms and tried to pull him toward a secluded area where the lap dances were given.

"Crap!" Aiken bellowed.

The three stopped and looked at Aiken, who was staring wide-eyed at the doorway. A man was entering the club. His attention was riveted on the topless dancer on the stage. It was Newton.

"I can't let Newt see me," Aiken said as he turned to head to the kitchen. "He can do me serious damage with all of the people he knows," Aiken called over his shoulder to Moore.

"I'll take care of him," Moore assured Aiken as he disengaged himself from the two women. "Hey, Newt," he called as the two dancers walked away with frowns.

Seeing Moore, Newton headed toward him as he kept one eye on the stage, watching the dancer spin on the stripper pole. "Trying to forget this morning's woes?" he asked sardonically.

"Yes," Moore responded, hoping that Newton hadn't seen Aiken scurrying away. "Thought I'd give it a try."

"Is it working?"

"Not really."

Newton turned to the server. "Honey, he needs a stiff one. Give him a shot of Captain Morgan and one for me. No, make that a double for both of us," Newton added.

"What brings you here? You stalking me?" Moore asked. He was suspicious about Newton's impromptu arrival.

"No. The cab was driving by and I asked him to pull over so I could check out this joint," Newton responded nonchalantly.

Moore wasn't convinced. It was too coincidental.

"You come here often?" Newton asked.

"No. This is actually my first time," Moore replied.

"I think if I lived down here, I'd be spending a lot of time here. Nothing like this in Cedar Key," Newton said as he looked around. "We're so small that we don't have a Subway."

"Or McDonald's," Moore added as he recalled his previous visit to Cedar Key where he first met Newton.

The two men downed their shots and conversed for a few more minutes before they stood and left the club. They didn't know that Aiken had been furtively and nervously watching them.

Once outside, Moore unlocked his bike.

"Heading home now?" Newton asked as he looked down the street for a cab.

"Yeah. I'm just going to veg out and go into recovery mode," Moore said as he hopped onto his bike. "I'll give you a call in the next day or two and we can get together."

"Sounds good as long as I'm not out on a fishing boat. I'm going to land a big one this trip," Newton called as Moore pedaled away.

An hour later, Moore's cell phone rang. It was Aiken.

"You home, Manny?"

"Yes. I was just sitting here and relaxing. What's up?"

"You got to tell me. Did Newton see me? Did he say anything about me?" Aiken asked in an agitated tone.

"No. I don't think so. You're in the clear."

Aiken sighed with relief. "Good. I hope that's true. I don't need my cover busted. That Newton knows all kinds of wiseguys. If he tipped off my whereabouts, he'd be into some big money. And I mean big."

"I think you're okay," Moore assured Aiken.

"Don't forget what I told you about visiting Madam Seres. She could be a good connector for you," Aiken urged.

"I plan to see her late tomorrow morning and then head

over to Blake's to see what's happening with the bar."

"And don't forget to stop by the club again some time. You never did get that lap dance from Connie and Donna. They were disappointed they didn't get to give you one."

"We'll see," Moore replied hesitantly. It wasn't like he wouldn't enjoy it, but he wanted to show them respect as women. It was just something with the way he had been raised. They ended their call and Moore spent the rest of the day replaying the morning's events and researching on his laptop.

CHAPTER 11

The Next Morning
Madam Seres' Parlor

Parking his bicycle on Whitehead Street, Moore walked to
the weather-beaten building housing Madam Seres' business.
It was a low, one-story building with a red-tiled roof. An
open wooden door beckoned potential customers.

He entered the darkened interior and became immersed
in its mysterious ambiance, filled with the aroma of burning
incense and collection of herbs. Moore's eyes eagerly took in
the shelves displaying traditional African, Cuban and Haitian
artifacts and masks.

The purple-painted walls were lined with flimsy shelves
holding voodoo dolls, blessed chicken feet, mojo beans,
evil-eye charms and necklaces, tarot cards, incense, Madam
Seres' lettered coffee mugs, beer glasses, ball caps and t-shirts,
tribal masks and statues, hand-carved candles, oils, powders,
potions and assorted books. There were a number of spell kits
displayed for sale like "Hex Your Ex" and "Other Attorney
Be Stupid."

A sign over the doorway to the rear listed the cost for
a palm reading, psychic medium reading, card reading or

evil spell casting. The doorway had strings of colorful beads hanging from the door sill.

Moore chuckled when he spotted a voodoo doll wearing a top hat and smoking a cigar. It had three pins sticking from it and it had a special sale price. As he walked past the rear doorway, a short, gray-haired woman collided with him. The collision caused her to drop a vase she was carrying, and the dusty contents spread across the floor.

"I am so sorry," Moore apologized as the woman stopped dead in her tracks. She had a look of agony on her face.

"I'll help you sweep up that mess. Do you have a broom and dust pan?" Moore asked, eager to make amends.

"That won't help," she sobbed as her gold-studded nose ring glimmered in the dimly lit room. "Those are my husband's ashes."

Moore's face had a panicked look on it as he realized the emotional gravity of the situation. "I am really sorry."

"His spirit is disturbed. It will now wander aimlessly. His soul will be restless," she moaned.

"Is there anything I can do?" Moore was visibly distressed by his action.

The woman seemed to be in a trance.

"Is there anything I can do?" Moore asked again.

The woman held up her finger to quiet Moore. "Shhh. I'm trying to communicate with his soul," she whispered softly. Thirty seconds passed before the woman answered in the singsong cadence of a Haitian. "I've been able to contact him."

Moore wasn't sure what he should say. He took a chance. "Good. Is he peaceful now?"

The woman held up her finger again. "I will ask him," she

said in a low voice. Her eyes were still trance-like. She then spoke some gibberish for a few seconds as if carrying on a brief conversation with her husband in a heavenly language.

When she halted her murmurs, she seemed to relax and her eyes returned to a normal state. She looked at Moore and spoke. "He'd be peaceful if you gave me a thousand dollars to restore his soul."

Moore wised up quickly. He knew a scam when he saw one. "I don't think so," he commented as his composure returned.

The woman eyed Moore carefully, then closed her eyes and extended her hands over the scattered remains. After a minute, she spoke, "My husband says that he'd be content if you paid me five hundred dollars. That's a real special deal, believe me."

"Listen," Moore warned. "I'm not buying into this at all."

"Okay then. For a hundred dollars, I'll take the curse off of you," she offered firmly.

"What curse?"

"The one I'm going to put on you for distressing my husband," she replied expectantly. "It's a Madam Seres special curse. Very bad mojo!" she cautioned.

"That's not working for me at all," Moore concluded. "Let's just do a palm reading."

"That will be twenty-five dollars up front. And you can tip me when we're done," Seres said as she held out her hand.

Moore pulled twenty-five dollars out of his pocket and paid her.

"Follow me," Seres said as she walked through the beads.

"What about your husband?" Moore said as he carefully stepped over the remains.

"I'll get to him later," she said as they approached a small table covered by a dark red cloth and a desk lamp that she turned on. "Sit there," she instructed as she reached for a bottle of rum.

"Thanks, but I don't need a drink," Moore said as she raised the bottle.

"This is not for drinking. Hold out your hands," she ordered brusquely. "We must cleanse our hands."

She sprinkled the liquor, which Moore could tell by the smell was not fine rum, over both of their hands. They each washed their hands in the clear liquid as she doused them again.

"Now, wipe the back of your neck."

Moore complied and wiped the back of his neck with his rum-coated hands.

"We are spirit cleansing now," she explained.

Next, she poured a small amount in a shallow bowl and picked up a chicken's foot which she dipped into the rum. She walked around the room shaking the rum off the chicken's foot as she chased away evil spirits. When she finished her performance, she sat and pushed a piece of paper and pencil toward Moore. "Write your name and birthday, but not year."

"Sure," Moore said as he complied by writing down his alias name. Moore guessed that she was going to use handwriting analysis and astrology. He slid the paper across the table to her.

"Let me see your palm, Manny," she directed as Moore extended his open palm to her.

"Good lifeline," she said as she closely examined it.

"Is it a long life?"

"Yes, but you do seem to have some brushes with death," she observed as she looked closely at the marks on the life line which ran from the area between the thumb and the first finger to the base of the thumb.

If only you knew, Moore thought.

"I see you have a double life line."

"Where? Can you point it out?"

"Yes. It's this line which runs parallel to your life line," she said as she pointed to it. "It tells me you are very confident and successful. Are you a risk taker, Manny?"

Moore chuckled before answering. "I am."

"Is your primary purpose in life your career?" she asked.

"I'm not sure that I'd agree with that," Moore responded uneasily. He knew he had a tendency for not relaxing enough.

"Your lines are telling me that you devote most of your time and energy to your job," she added as she studied his palm.

"I'm known for being a hard worker," Moore agreed.

"That doesn't surprise me. What do you do?"

"I'm a bartender," Moore replied.

Seres let go of Moore's hand and stared at him. "You're a what?" she asked with a hint of skepticism.

"I'm a bartender."

Seres closed her eyes and wrinkled her forehead as she concentrated. Moore became a bit nervous, hoping that she wouldn't discover that he was on an undercover reporting assignment. He thought about immediately ending the session. It was getting spooky and he didn't like this mumbo jumbo stuff.

"No. I see more."

Moore's heart skipped a beat when he thought she was

saying his real name, but relaxed a little when he realized he had misinterpreted what she had said.

She continued. "No. I see you doing more than bartending." She opened her eyes and stared directly into Moore's eyes.

Moore realized what she was going to do. It was something that he watched for when he interviewed people for stories. You could tell if they were being untruthful if they looked away when asked a direct question. He prepared himself.

"Are you a writer?" she asked as her eyes pierced his and looked deeply into his soul.

Moore didn't show any reaction. Not flinching as he returned her look and answered confidently. "Yes. I'm an author." He didn't want to say reporter and thought that being an author was close enough. It worked.

"I knew you were more than a bartender. What you doing? Researching your next story?" she asked proudly.

"I'm taking a break. Like you said a minute ago, I could relax more," Moore admitted, not wanting to reveal what he was really doing.

"I see," she said as she picked up his palm and examined it again. "Good heart line and head line."

"Which one is the heart line?" he asked as he peered at his palm.

"It's this top line. Yours runs up to the mount of Jupiter," she said as she pointed to the mound below the forefinger.

"And what does that tell you?"

"You have love to give, great dreams and high expectations."

Moore nodded in agreement.

"See these two forks at the end?" she asked.

"Yes."

"That's a good sign. It means you are responsible, friendship means a lot to you and you are popular with your friends," she explained

"And what's this second line?" Moore asked with his curiosity geared up.

"That is your head line. You have a long and straight head line. That tells me that you have a strong analytical ability and you're a good thinker. You're practical, dedicated and very considerate of others. But there's a downside."

"What's that?" Moore asked with intrigue.

"You have a tendency to get yourself into blind alleys."

More than you know, Moore thought. "That's interesting," he commented.

"Are you married?"

"I was."

"Did it end abruptly?" she asked.

Thinking about the death of his wife and child in the car accident some years ago, he responded, "It did." He then asked, "Do you see marriage in my future?"

She turned his hand and examined it. "I'm not sure, but women seem to be attracted to you."

"They are," he agreed. "I just haven't found the right one."

"I sense that you are a communicator," she said.

Yep, there's the handwriting analysis, Moore thought.

"You're the type of person who is always willing to help others without expecting anything in return. You empathize easily with others and are very intuitive."

"I thought I'd find you back here," a familiar voice boomed, interrupting the reading.

Moore looked up and saw Aiken's chubby face beaming

with a huge smile.

"You guys hitting things off okay?" he asked.

Before Moore could respond, Seres looked at Aiken and spoke, "This is a friend of yours, Bones?"

"Yes. Manny and I go way back."

"I didn't know," she said.

"Jean, I see you pulled the broken vase schtick on him." Aiken began to chuckle before turning to Moore. "Did you pay to quiet her husband's spirit?"

"No," Moore replied.

"She does that to everyone who comes in. I always see Jean at Kmart buying more vases," Aiken laughed.

Moore shook his head. He had been right. It was a scam.

Seres acted perturbed by Aiken's revelation. "Bones, how could you say such a thing? You hurt my feelings."

"Jean, let's get down to business," Aiken said as he grabbed a nearby chair and placed it next to the table before sitting on it.

"But I'm in the middle of a reading," she protested.

"No. That's okay. I'll pass on the rest of it. You were very good," Moore said.

"Thank you, Manny." Sitting back in her chair, Seres looked at the two men. "And what kind of business do you want to get down to?" she asked.

"My friend Manny here needs to make a connection in Cuba and I know that you know everyone over there."

"Maybe yes, maybe no. Who is it you want to connect with?" she asked.

"El Patrón," Aiken replied as he watched her reaction.

Seres shuddered involuntarily. "He's bad mojo."

"Yeah, we know. Can you connect my friend?" Aiken asked.

"No."

"Come on, Jean. You know everybody there."

"He's bad. Evil. Death surrounds him and people who get too close to him." She shook her head from side to side. "No. This is not a good thing for your friend. He should stay away."

"Maybe Manny could buy one of your protective spells and he wouldn't get hurt. He could then go to Cuba and meet El Patrón," Aiken suggested.

"No. His spirit world is too strong. I can't do this." She pushed her chair away from the table and stood. "We are done."

Aiken and Moore stood.

"Is there anyone that you can connect me with who could help me get to El Patrón?" Moore asked with a pleading look on his face.

Seres looked from Moore to Aiken and back. "I have a cousin who lives outside of Santiago, in the mountains."

"That's where I want to go," Moore said excitedly.

"I know. El Patrón lives in the mountains," she responded slowly as she thought about the danger she'd help put Moore in.

"How do I contact your cousin?"

Seres took a slip of paper and wrote her cousin's name, address and cell phone number on it. "Here," she said reluctantly. "He owns a small store in Santa Lucha. El Patrón lives above the town."

Moore glanced down at the information and looked up at her. "Thank you. Thank you."

"Okay, Manny, we need to get out of here," Aiken said as he pushed Moore to the front of the establishment.

Seres followed and asked, "Do you need a love potion or black magic spell, Manny?"

"I don't," Moore said as he turned and gave her a hundred dollar bill. "Thank you for your help though. I appreciate it."

Aiken chimed in. "Here's another hundred, Jean. Put a love spell on me and the women I meet and put one of your black magic spells on El Patrón. I know you said his evil mojo is strong, but just do it for me."

"I'll do the love spell, but El Patrón's mojo is too strong for me. I can't overcome it. But I'll put a spell of protection on your friend here," Seres said with concern. "Maybe it will help," she added.

"Thanks—and a little prayer would be good, too," Moore said.

The two men walked out of the building and to Moore's bike.

"Why did you show up and interrupt us?" Moore asked.

"I remembered you saying that you'd stop by late this morning. So, I drove over and saw your bike parked out here. I thought things might go better if Jean knew we were friends."

"Not sure how much better, but thanks, Bones."

"I just wish I could have been there when she dropped the vase with the fake ashes. I can picture your reaction," Aiken chuckled.

"Yeah. It was a moment. She had me at first, but I knew it was a scam when she asked for money."

"Tell me, Manny. Did she give you the stink eye?"

"Huh?"

"Yeah. She arches her right eyebrow and she has this little trick where she can make that eye bulge out. It's weird-looking and scary."

It was Moore's turn to chuckle. "Nope. She was probably saving it for later and didn't get to do it because you showed up," Moore guessed as he unlocked his bike from the stand.

"Where you heading now?"

"Blake's bar. I'm going to see what's going on there."

"What about Cuba?"

"I need to work out a plan for going to Santiago."

"Let me tell you one thing. From what I hear about El Patrón, you don't take a dump in Cuba without him knowing about it. He's got eyes and ears all over the place. He's got the police, military and the airport customs people in his back pocket. You enter the country and he'll know it. And my friend, you'll end up in the Caribbean Sea with cement shoes if not worse. Mark my words," Aiken warned.

"I get it," Moore acknowledged.

"You think about it today and stop by the club tonight. I'll see if I can come up with someone to help you over there," Aiken said as he headed to his car. "There's a guy in Cudjoe Key that I know. Chuck Meier. He might be your ticket into Cuba."

Moore settled on his bike and began to pedal down Whitehead Street. "Sounds good. I'll see you tonight," he called after Aiken.

Moore pedaled over to Booger Blake's and saw that it was still closed. He didn't see any of his co-workers and decided to head home. With the hot sun beating down on his head, Moore worked up a sweat as he rode into the trailer park and pedaled to Duncan's mobile home. He dismounted and parked the bike under the patio cover.

That's when a man stepped out of the shadows of the covered patio. The swarthy man held a .45 caliber semi-automatic handgun in his hand and it was pointed at Moore.

"Don't do anything stupid," the man said as Moore looked at him.

"What do you want?" Moore asked.

"We'll talk about that inside," the man said. He motioned with his weapon for Moore to open the door.

Moore began to reach over the door frame.

"Hold it!" the man said. "What are you doing?"

"I hide the key up there," Moore replied. "I was just going to get it."

"What do you think? I'm some kind of schmuck?" the man growled as he motioned for Moore to step away. "You probably have a hideaway gun up there," he said as he walked over and stuck his hand into the gap over the doorway.

He quickly withdrew his hand and shrieked in pain from the stings of several bees. While the man's attention was distracted, Moore saw a chance to escape. He suddenly raced through the patio and ran through the neighbor's lot to the adjoining lane.

Meanwhile the man was swearing at losing Moore and swatting at the angry bees. He stepped into the lane and waved at a car parked a short distance away. Still swatting at the bees that were attacking him, he jumped into the car when it arrived and the two men fled.

Moore waited a few minutes after hearing the car screech around the corner, guessing it was the getaway car. Carefully, he walked down the lane and around to the trailer. He looked up and down the street and toward the patio, but didn't see anything that concerned him.

Approaching the trailer cautiously, he pulled the key out of his pocket. He unlocked the door and entered, relocking the door behind him. He then found one of Duncan's hidden .22s and placed it on the kitchen counter.

He wondered who was after him. That was the second attempt on his life in two days. He picked up his cell phone and began to call Newton, but hesitated. He decided he'd better calm down and carefully think things through.

Grabbing a pitcher of sweet tea from the fridge, he poured himself a glass and carried it to the desk. Sitting back, he replayed the events of the last few days, trying to determine who might be after him and why.

Moore was very frustrated and perplexed. He tried to distract himself by turning on his laptop and researching what he could find on El Patrón and making his plan to infiltrate the drug lord's lair in the Sierra Maestra Mountains. He couldn't focus, so he closed his eyes and bowed his head forward in momentary relaxation.

His mind was spinning as he stood and ambled over to the cabinet where he found a half-empty bottle of aspirin. He poured out two and downed them with a glass of water. Moore then returned to his laptop. It was futile. He still couldn't get his mind off the man accosting him outside of the trailer.

CHAPTER 12

Two Hours Later
Candyland

Moore rode his bike over to talk to Aiken at Candyland. Between talking with Aiken and the atmosphere at the club, Moore thought he might have a good shot at relaxing his mind.

The parking lot was full and the music throbbed through the open doors onto the sidewalk where Moore was securing his bike to the bike rack. He paid the burly bouncer at the door five dollars to enter and stepped inside.

The club was packed with men and couples drinking and watching the dancers move provocatively on the stage. Money and whiskey were freely exchanged.

Moore made his way around to the back of the club and started to go down the back hallway when another bouncer seemed to step out of nowhere.

"Where do you think you're going, buddy?" he growled.

"I'm going to see Bones," Moore explained.

The bouncer eyed Moore skeptically. He had heard all of the excuses for men trying to go backstage to the dancers' dressing room. Using Bones as an excuse was a new one to him.

"Sure, you are," he said unconvinced.

"No, really. Bones is a friend of mine," Moore protested when suddenly he felt a warm arm go around his side and rub against his right arm.

"Hi honey. Did you come back for that lap dance?"

Moore turned and saw Connie, the dancer he had met on his previous visit.

"Hi Connie. I'd love to, but I need to see Bones," Moore explained.

"Wouldn't you prefer to go over on the other side and let me climb all over your bones?" she asked provocatively.

Before Moore could respond to the invitation, the bouncer asked, "You know this guy?"

"Not as good as I'd like," she said as she allowed her hand to run up Moore's arm to feel his bicep. "Nice," she cooed.

"Is he a friend of Bones?" the bouncer asked as he ignored her comment.

"Yes. He's Bones' friend, but I'd like to have him be a closer friend to me," she teased.

Smiling as he separated himself from Connie, Moore commented sincerely, "Another time. Another place. Who knows what could have developed, Connie?"

He turned back to the bouncer as a look of disappointment replaced the smile on Connie's face. "Can I go in the back now?" Moore asked as Connie huffed away.

The bouncer stepped aside, allowing Moore to walk down the corridor where he stuck his head in the kitchen.

"Hey Bones," Moore called.

Finishing up two sandwiches, Aiken placed them on plates

and slid them across the counter to be picked up by one of the scantily-clad servers.

"What?" he shouted without looking in the direction of the person who had called his name.

"Can you take a break?" Moore asked.

"What?" Aiken asked as he turned his head to see who was trying to interrupt him. "Manny, what are you doing here?"

"Come on out back and I'll tell you," Moore urged.

Aiken turned to the grill cook and said, "Cover for me. I'll be back in a few."

The grill cook nodded as Aiken left the kitchen and led Moore out the back door.

"Can't relax so you decide to come down here and bother me?" Aiken groused as he sat on an upturned wooden crate.

"Somebody tried to kill me," Moore said as he eased his frame into a faded beach chair.

"Now you're having memory problems again, Manny. You already told me about the pedicab driver," Aiken groused.

"I remember telling you, but I had another attempt," Moore explained.

"That's your life, Manny. Somebody is always out to get you." Aiken looked around before speaking in a hushed tone. "You should come and join me in the Witless Protection Program," he teased.

"That might not be a bad idea," Moore agreed.

"Okay, so what happened now?" Aiken asked in a serious tone.

Moore related the assault by the gunman at the trailer and his subsequent escape.

When Moore finished, Aiken commented slowly, "Boy, oh

boy. Someone's got it in for you. It sounds like there's a hit put out on you. Maybe our buddy in Cuba is behind it."

"I don't know."

Aiken thought for a moment. "You think Newton has anything to do with this?"

"Why would you ask that?" Moore questioned.

"Think about it. When did people start dropping like flies around you?"

"I can't believe it. Besides he saved my life when that pedicab driver tried to kill me," Moore argued.

"The pedicab driver was disposable. There are people in my world who are disposable and he'd be one."

"So that Newton could gain my trust," Moore thought aloud.

"Come on, Manny. Cut to the chase. That Newton works both sides of the street. He could be setting you up to bag you and I'm talking a body bag, my friend."

Aiken glanced at his watch. "I need to get back to work. Why don't you go back inside and let the girls take your mind off everything? A couple of nice lap dances will ease your mind."

Moore shook his head from side to side. "Not sure that it would help. Maybe I'll just hang out back here."

"Suit yourself. I've got a half hour to go. I'll check back with you when I'm ready to leave," he said as he stood and headed toward the kitchen.

"Sounds good," Moore said as he sat back.

Moore soon lost himself in thought with no concept of how much time was passing.

"Hey Manny, they're about ready to close up," Aiken's voice brought Moore back to reality and he looked at his watch. It was late. It was two in the morning.

"I guess I better be going," Moore agreed as he stood. He followed Aiken through the club and out the front door which the bouncer unlocked for them.

"Can I drive you home?" Aiken asked.

"No. I have my bike, plus I need to make a stop at the all-night convenience store over there." Moore pointed a half a block away.

"Okay. Don't say I didn't offer," Aiken said as he walked over to his car and entered it. After starting it, he eased his head out of the window and cautioned Moore. "You be careful tonight."

Moore grinned. "Yeah. I know, and don't let the bed bugs bite."

"Unless their name is Connie," Aiken cracked as he put his car in gear and started to drive away. He suddenly stopped and leaned over to shout at Moore.

"You really missed it tonight."

"How's that?" Moore asked.

"When Connie came in, she was telling everyone how she got out of a speeding ticket this afternoon."

"How did she do that?" Moore asked, figuring that Aiken had a funny spin to the incident.

"Lucky for her that she was wearing her low cut GET-OUT-OF-JAIL-FREE t-shirt," Aiken guffawed as he accelerated his car and drove away.

Moore chuckled at his friend's comment and rode to the store. He picked up bread at the all-night corner grocery, then headed home.

When he rode up to the trailer, he saw a motorcycle parked in the dim street light by the spot where he parked the bike. He wondered if Sam Duncan had returned home early. If he had, he could update Duncan on the incidents from the last few days. Moore was mildly excited about seeing his friend, although he noted that there were no lights on in the mobile home. Then again, it was late and Duncan might be in bed.

Moore parked the bike and retrieved the key from his pocket. Before he could insert the key, he sensed someone approaching him from around the corner of the trailer. His body tensed and he whirled into a defensive stance to confront the intruder.

"Easy there, tiger. It's me," Aiken said softly as he walked over.

Relaxing, Moore asked, "What are you doing here? I thought you went home."

"Yeah. That's what I told you. But it turns out that I had something more important to do."

"What's that?"

"It's called saving your ass, Manny."

"What do you mean?" Moore asked, not comprehending.

"Got a flashlight?"

"Yeah. On my cell phone." Moore switched on the flashlight app.

"After I heard about your altercation today, I decided to scout out your place before you got home to be sure it was safe. I had a suspicion."

"And what was that?" Moore asked.

"Here. I'll show you. Shine your light in here." Aiken opened up one of the saddlebags on the rear of the motorcycle. "Know what that is?"

"IED?"

"Good guess! You're right," Aiken's chubby faced beamed.

"What for?"

"I'm getting to that. This is a remotely detonated device,"

he said as he reached in and gently withdrew it.

"Aren't you worried that they'll detonate it now?" Moore asked with serious skepticism.

"Not now, I'm not," Aiken grinned confidently.

"They were waiting for you tonight. When you arrived, they were going to detonate it and poof. No more Manny Elias. No more Emerson Moore, either," he said quietly.

"Who is they?"

"Come on. I'll show you."

The two men walked to a car parked in the shadows one hundred feet away.

As they approached, Moore looked nervously at the IED in Aiken's hands. "Aren't you concerned that they will trigger it?"

"No."

"Why not?"

"They're dead," Aiken said as if it was a daily occurrence. "Look inside."

Moore looked in the passenger window and saw two figures slumped over. "That's the guy who came after me earlier today."

"Yeah. That's Billy No Balls. He came back to finish the job. He's with the mob in Miami. I got here early enough to see him ride up on the motorcycle and park it by your trailer. He then walked back to this car which was parked back here. I knew they weren't up to any good, especially when I recognized Billy. I used a .22 with a silencer. Took them both out. You recognize the driver?"

Moore leaned in and looked closely. He was absolutely stunned when he saw that the driver was Newton. "Oh crap!" Moore muttered in shock.

"Yeah. That's our buddy from Cedar Key. The guy you thought was going to help you here. It was all a set up. Sort of like a cat playing with a mouse before it kills it."

"Oh, no!" Moore was beside himself.

"Look in your buddy's hand. He has the detonator. He was going to blow you into cat litter."

"Freddy ...," Moore started, forgetting himself.

"No, stupid. It's Bones!" Aiken warned Moore quickly.

"Bones, I mean. How did you figure this all out?" Moore asked suspiciously.

"Don't get your underwear all bunched up. I wouldn't have lasted this long in the mob if I didn't learn to go by my instincts. I've been watching and I've caught Newton stalking you. I had to be careful because I don't know if he saw me and recognized me. He could blow my cover in the Witless Protection Program. Plus, I didn't know if I was next on his target list and I can't chance it. I wouldn't be surprised if Newton was behind all of the murders here, including your boss and his buddy from the past."

Aiken looked around before speaking again. "I'm out of here when we're done tonight."

"And leave that dream job of yours at the strip club?" Moore teased for the first time that night.

"I'll disappear and reappear somewhere. As for the ladies at the club, you know how it is with me. I'm just a natural chick magnet." Aikens' chubby frame shook as he chuckled quietly.

Looking at the two dead bodies, Moore asked, "And what are we going to do now?"

Aiken opened the door behind the passenger and carefully placed the IED on the floor. Closing the door, he motioned for

Moore to follow him to the driver's door.

"Help me pull Newton out. We'll put him in the back seat," Aiken said as he reached over Newton and withdrew the detonator, placing it on the car's roof.

The two men dragged Newton out and placed him in the back seat. Grabbing the detonator, Aiken instructed Moore. "I'm going to drive back to your place and you trot down there to meet me. We'll then lift that motorcycle into the trunk."

"Sure," Moore was content to let Aiken take the lead.

A minute later, they were lifting the motorcycle into the trunk and tying the lid shut. Moore was thankful that it was a small-sized motorcycle.

"Now what?" Moore asked.

"I'm going to take the detonator over to my car."

"Wait! You're not going to explode this car here in front of the trailer, are you?" Moore interrupted.

"Easy. Easy there, Pancho. No. You're going to get in this car and follow me over to Higgs Beach. You park this car there and walk over to where I'll park. I won't be far away. Just make sure no one is watching, then we're gone."

"I'm going to drive this car when there's an explosive in it?" Moore asked skeptically.

"Yeah. You'll be fine. Remember I have the detonator with me," Aiken smiled, teasing.

"Oh, that should give me a great deal of comfort," Moore said sarcastically as Aiken walked away to retrieve his car where it was parked a short distance away.

While he waited for Aiken's return, Moore sat in the driver's seat. He cast a wary eye at the two dead occupants and the IED on the floor in back. While he waited, he felt sorry for Newton. He seemed like a good guy, but then again, one never knew. One of Newton's earlier comments haunted Moore. Newton had said to never trust anyone. He was right. It applied to Newton and Moore also wondered if it should apply to Aiken, too.

But Moore was still confused. Who was behind the series of attacks on him? Who wanted him dead? Was it the mob in Miami, or did El Patrón know that Moore was after him? Moore sighed as the sound of the engine from an approaching car caught his attention. He squinted through the darkness in the rearview mirror and recognized Aiken's car. The headlights were off as he drove up.

"You ready, Manny?" Aiken hissed through the open passenger window.

"I guess so," Moore replied nervously.

Aiken couldn't help himself. He held up the detonator and waved it at Moore. "No speeding. I don't want to attract any attention. Otherwise, I'll have to make you go boom," he snickered.

"Not funny," Moore retorted. He didn't see any humor in driving a car with two dead bodies and the IED anywhere.

Aiken accelerated slowly and Moore followed him.

Within ten minutes, Moore saw Aiken pull his car over and park. His hand stuck out the window and he waved for Moore to drive on to Higgs Beach, which was about a block further.

Moore understood. Aiken didn't want anyone to see his car park next to the one they were going to blow up. His car was too easy to identify. Moore drove by and parked in one of the parking spaces under a burned-out street light. Moore turned off the ignition and exited the car. Locking the doors with the key fob as he walked away, he spotted a nearby trash can and tossed the fob inside.

When he arrived at Aiken's car, he saw that Aiken had turned it around and it was pointed in the opposite direction.

"Ready for our getaway?" Moore quipped as he entered the vehicle.

"More like get out of my way," Aiken retorted as he eased his foot on the gas pedal and slowly drove away. Moore looked over his shoulder and through the rear window.

"You going to detonate it?"

Aiken didn't respond. Instead he depressed the detonator and the parked car exploded in a ball of flames. Lights in the neighborhood flicked on as residents began looking out to see what exploded.

Aiken was already two blocks away and drove back to the entrance to the mobile home park. Aiken leaned toward Moore.

"I'm dropping you off here, Manny. I don't need to have my car seen in there because you don't know who's awake now."

"You heading out now?"

"Yep, after I pick up a few things at my place. I travel light these days."

"Thanks for saving my life tonight," Moore said appreciatively.

Aiken couldn't help himself. "That's me all right. A lifeguard. Picture me in my speedos, Manny. I drive the girls nuts!"

Moore smiled as he exited the car. "Or do you mean away?"

"Well, I'm on my way, my friend."

"I hope our paths cross again, Freddy," Moore said as he used Aikens' real name.

"I do too, Emerson," Aiken said as he reciprocated by using Moore's real name. "You're a good man."

"And deep down inside that little mischievous heart of yours, you are, too," Moore countered sincerely.

Aiken smiled and accelerated slowly away as he spoke, "Call Meier in Cudjoe Key. I told him to expect a call from you. He'll help you. He owes me one. Don't forget."

"Will do. Good luck."

Moore watched as the car drove down United Street and disappeared. He was going to miss that chubby mafioso and hoped he would be safe. Moore turned and began walking back to the trailer park. He was lost in thought as he ran the events from the last twenty-four hours through his mind. Moore was also concerned if El Patrón had gotten wind of what he was up to.

As he cautiously approached Duncan's trailer, his senses were steeled for a confrontation. His eyes scanned the shadows as he tried to see any signs of pending danger. There was no reason for him to be alert at this moment, though. The danger had passed.

Moore unlocked the trailer and entered. He walked to the counter and took a small glass from the shelf. He then filled it with ice cubes and poured himself a double shot of rum. He needed it to relax. Leaning against the counter, he shook the glass, listening to the ice cubes clink against the sides. He took a sip, then held the cold glass against his forehead. He had a headache and the cold glass provided temporary relief.

Over the next two hours, Moore's mind wrestled with the events of the last few days. Finally, he decided to call it a night and headed for bed as he carried a .22 handgun with him. He was looking forward to meeting Meier the next day and seeing what he could do to help him.

CHAPTER 13

Late The Next Morning
Cudjoe Key

It had been a twenty-mile drive east of Key West to Cudjoe Key and Moore enjoyed the drive in the rental car that he had secured with his driver's license that morning. He had temporarily discarded the Manny Elias disguise including the wig. What made it more enjoyable was that he had rented a Mustang convertible which reminded him of his own. It was parked at the Cleveland Hopkins Airport.

As he drove, he thought about his upcoming meeting with Meier. He was looking forward to meeting this ex-Special Forces veteran. Moore was intrigued about meeting him after he researched Meier on his laptop.

The guy seemed like a master of all trades. If you thought it could be done, he did it. Meier was a successful entrepreneur with a skill set that no one would believe. He'd been a boat captain, sky diver, scuba diver, sheriff's deputy, gun instructor, fireman, pilot, pirate, mercenary, minister, motivational speaker, strip club messiah and self-proclaimed purveyor of the fine feminine form. He'd been around the world twice and talked to everyone once. The guy had also authored three books, *Letters From The Sandbox, Corset Chronicles* and *Key West Iguana Killers Club Cook Book.*

During one of his tours of Iraq as a defense contractor, Meier was near six explosions when he worked on a team that confiscated and destroyed enemy ammunition and weapons in Tikrit. One day two IEDs exploded, nearly injuring him. Later that day, a truck explosion took his leg below the knee. After he recovered, he began wearing a prosthetic and was back up to full speed.

Moore sensed from his research on Meier that this was a guy who lived life to its fullest and beyond. He wouldn't be disappointed. Meier could be a very interesting guy to interview, Moore thought.

Moore slowed his car as he turned off the Overseas Highway and down a lane. He carefully watched the house numbers until he spotted Meier's house. He pulled into the driveway and parked next to a black Jeep Laredo.

Moore eyed the pastel blue home on stilts. He could see a canal on the other side and several boats tied alongside the dock that spanned the width of the property. Exiting his vehicle, Moore walked under the house and to the canal to look at the boats. Suddenly a loud, gravelly voice boomed overhead.

"Are you Moore?"

Moore turned and looked up at the wooden deck attached to the second level of the house. He saw a red-haired, bearded six-foot-four-inch giant of a man. He was nearly 300 pounds of natural force.

"You must be Chuck Meier," Moore replied as he looked at the titan who was wearing a black t-shirt and khaki shorts. The t-shirt was lettered on the front. It read: "Be Nice To Me, You're In Range."

"I'm that one-legged ass-kicker people talk about. Come on up to the crow's nest and join me and a couple of my knuckle-dragging friends," Meier offered as he erupted in loud laughter.

Moore walked upstairs to the deck that overlooked the bay toward the Navy base. He realized this guy had a wicked sense of humor. He also reminded Moore as being a cross between Put-in-Bay's Mad Dog Adams and Westside Steve Simmons. Like Simmons, Meier had long red hair. It hung below a horned Viking hat he was wearing.

"Grab a beer from the cooler and join my coconut commando team powwow," Meier invited as he pointed at a nearby cooler.

Moore did as he was instructed and grabbed a beer. He twisted off the cap and sat in an empty chair.

"I hear you move like a ghost in the night," Moore said to open the conversation with this battle-hardened veteran.

"I don't know who told you that crap. I'm the opposite. I'm more like a bull in a china closet or a deadly storm in the middle of the night. You'll hear me coming like the thunder and I leave a path of destruction in my wake," Meier roared.

Then Meier introduced his two friends who were wearing shorts and sleeveless t-shirts.

"Meet Kerby," Meier said as he nodded to a powerfully-built, dark-haired man sitting to his right. "We call him the Kerbinator."

Without cracking a smile, Kerby commented in a slow drawl, "Yeah. That's because I'm like a Kirby sweeper. I clean up the messes Big Daddy gets us in."

"And you wouldn't have it any other way." Meier turned to Moore and added, "Kerby was a bad kid growing up. He peed on Santa. And he did it on purpose!" Meier guffawed at his revelation.

Moore grinned. He was going to enjoy being with these rascals.

"Now, this other one here is a real pistol. This is Bobby Banger," Meier said with a wink.

"Oh?" Moore asked.

"Now, I know what you're thinking there, Emerson. And it's not that kind of banging. He got that moniker from his shooting ability. Like bang, bang," Meier snickered as he explained.

"I much prefer the other type of banging, Emerson," the tough-looking man with a shaved head said.

"I know what you mean," Moore said agreeably.

Banger added, "You're in with a tough crew here, Moore."

"I gathered that," Moore agreed.

"Take Big Daddy there," Banger said as he pointed at Meier. "He prefers to use the stone age approach on operations."

"How's that?" Moore asked. "He uses a club?"

Meier jumped in with the answer before Banger could respond. "You need to understand that there are two philosophies in warfare. The first is the surgical. It's like using the ball-peen hammer approach. The second one is the sledge hammer approach. When it absolutely, positively has to be destroyed overnight, I'd go in swinging the sledge. Seems to get the point across," Meier explained with a devilish grin.

Moore could tell that he enjoyed combat and living on the edge. Based on what he had seen in a few short minutes, he really liked Meier and his team.

"Okay, you've met my battle buddies and I've checked you out," Meier said. "I know you're a pretty good investigative reporter. I also know that we have a mutual friend."

Before Moore could guess that it was Bones Aiken, Meier continued, "Roe Terry up on Chincoteague Island. He and I go alligator hunting together in Louisiana."

Moore's face lit up. "I didn't know you knew Roe. The Duc-Man is quite a guy. Master duck carver. Just a good guy," Moore said as he remembered how Terry had helped him out with his investigation into the NASA rocket explosions on Wallops Island, Virginia near Chincoteague Island.

"We've done some black ops stuff together. You know he was a Navy SEAL, don't you?"

"I had no idea. He never told me," Moore replied, stunned.

"Roe's kind of a humble guy. I'm not surprised that he didn't say anything to you about that."

"He never mentioned it. I do know that he loves to ride his bike all over Chincoteague."

"Yep. And he's won a few bike races. I bet he didn't tell you that either," Meier smiled.

"He didn't."

"Back to business. Now what can we do for you?" Meier asked.

Moore explained his undercover work from the last few days and his goal of infiltrating El Patrón's Cuban headquarters.

When Moore finished, Meier stared at him. "You must have a King Kong sized pair of brass cojones or you're just a plain stupid jackass. Do you have any idea who you are going up against? This guy is big time. He makes Tony Montana look like Prince Charming. You don't want to run into this badass. There's no comparison."

"I've dealt with tough guys before," Moore countered

confidently.

Meier shook his head negatively. "This guy lives in a fecal position," Meier remarked loudly.

"You mean fetal position," Moore corrected Meier.

"No. You just aren't listening. I said fecal and I meant what I said. He's a Godzilla-sized pile of shit," Meier roared.

"I've done some research on him," Moore started weakly.

"Yeah, that's what your little buddy said when he asked me to meet with you." Meier eyed Moore with skepticism. He wasn't sure that he wanted to help him.

"Oh, I'm glad you brought that up. How do you know Bones?" Moore asked.

"Well, let's just think a moment there, Sherlock. Where does Bones work?"

"Candyland," Moore replied.

"Think about it, Emerson. What does Candyland offer tired-eyed bros like us?"

"Eye candy."

"Bingo. Give the man a cigar," Meier chortled.

"I thought Big Daddy said we were going out for fish and chips and he really said fish and chicks," Kerby muttered with a slight grin.

"You just don't listen well, Kerbinator," Meier quipped.

"So, you bumped into Bones there?" Moore asked as he took the discussion back on course.

"Saved his ass is more like it. He was trying to help out one of the girls when a couple of drunks got a little too frisky with her. They turned on your little chubby friend when he tried to rescue her. Bobby, Kerby and I sort of interrupted their party and booted the two drunks out of the place. We sent them urban surfing down the sidewalk. Bones made sure that we had free drinks for the rest of the night. I gave him one of my cards after he and I chatted for a bit."

"He's a piece of work," Moore offered.

"Lovable little guy, isn't he?" Meier asked. "So, he called me and gave me a brief rundown of your predicament, but I wanted to hear your version in person."

"Can you help me?"

"Commit suicide?"

"I'll be careful," Moore replied.

The three men chuckled at Moore's comment.

"Listen here, Shirley Temple. The DEA has sent guys in there and they've disappeared. Why do you think you could survive?"

"I've been in and out of jams before and I've survived," Moore countered.

Meier eyed Moore skeptically. "Dealing with El Patrón is like dueling with hand grenades. The results are not pretty."

"I'll take the chance," Moore retorted stubbornly.

"Bobby, why don't you give Emerson a little background on El Patrón?"

"I've researched him," Moore offered again.

"Not like our Bobby who has been involved with helping U.S. agents land there. He's sort of like a walking history book on Cuba. And first-hand experience trumps online research any day, dontcha think?" Meier turned to Banger and said, "Go ahead, Bobby. Show him what you got."

"Sure," Banger said with a smile. "Let me take you back to Cuba's war of independence from Spain. That was in 1898. The youngest general in the war was a Cuban by the name of Gerardo Machado. The United States occupied Cuba at the end of the war and Machado went on to serve as the Mayor of Santa Clara, about 160 miles southeast of Havana. Funny thing happened while he was mayor."

"What was that?" Moore asked.

"A fire swept through the city hall and destroyed the files that showed that Machado and his father had a criminal past."

"How convenient," Moore observed.

Banger nodded, then continued. "Machado ended up serving in a number of ministry posts for the government and became Cuba's fifth president in 1924. He became so powerful with his iron-fisted governing style that it led to public unrest and assassination attempts. Then, the 1929 stock market crash in the United States crushed the Cuban economy."

"Wait. Go back to 1928 and the U.S. president's visit," Meier interrupted.

Banger nodded. "Coolidge, his retinue and a bunch of reporters took Flagler's train to Key West in January, 1928."

Moore held up his hand at the mention of Flagler's train as he thought about the sunken treasure train and missing trimotor airplane. "I want to come back to the train."

"We can do that," Meier said. "Go on, Bobby."

"You need to remember that Prohibition was in effect in the United States, but this was Key West. You didn't even need a password to get into the bars for a real drink. So, the Coolidge retinue partied that night and left the next day for Havana on eight naval vessels. Coolidge was on the *USS Texas*, which anchored right over the spot where the *USS Maine* blew up in Havana Harbor. When Coolidge landed, Machado greeted him and so did a bunch of other people. Like 200,000 people."

"Why did President Coolidge go to Cuba?" Moore asked.

"I was just coming to that. Cuba was in an uproar because of the high tariffs the U.S. placed on their sugar. The other reason was that the Pan-American Union countries were having a conference and Coolidge wanted to address them. He needed to defuse a lot of the criticism the U.S. was getting for military interventions in Nicaragua, Haiti and the Dominican Republic."

Moore was stunned by Banger's knowledge base. "So, what does all of this have to do with El Patrón?"

"I was just coming to that. In late 1928 and early 1929, Machado gets a benefactor. A rich one. It's a Frenchman from Santiago, on the southeastern side of Cuba. The guy starts throwing cash at Machado and his cronies. They all look the other way as this guy grows his criminal syndicate in Santiago and the mountains overlooking the city. His name is Vadim Baudin."

Moore's eyes lit up. "And his grandson is Henri who is El Patrón, right?"

"Give Poindexter another cigar. I knew you were smart," Meier said sarcastically.

"That's right," Banger agreed. "But let me finish my story. Every government leader from then on had the financial support from the Baudins, including Batista and Castro. In return, they turned a blind eye to their criminal activities and drug running. In fact, some people will tell you that Castro worked drug deals, too."

"Where did the grandfather get all of his money?" Moore asked.

"It goes back to around 1800. The Baudins had sugar cane plantations in Haiti. Then the slaves revolted against the French. It was the biggest slave revolt since the days of

Spartacus, and it was bloody and successful. Most of the French sugar plantation owners moved to Cuba, including the Baudins. The family still owns several sugar plantations in eastern Cuba. Opportunity to increase their wealth soon came knocking from the United States," Banger said.

"Opportunity? What do you mean?" Moore asked perplexed.

"Prohibition. Baudin's friend Bacardi began taking molasses, a byproduct from the sugar refining process, and fermenting it into rum. And Baudin joined in, starting his own rum manufacturing business. That's where he got most of his money. Baudin acquired more plantations and eventually moved from Santiago up into the mountains."

"So, the Baudin family's power base in the Santiago area grew," Moore murmured.

"It did. They were always on the lookout for ways to make money. El Patrón connected with Colombian drug runners. They'd meet Colombian ships off the coast of Cuba, then offload cocaine, heroin and bales of marijuana onto El Patrón's go-fast boats. Then the boats would be run up to Florida. Nice money for El Patrón," Banger said.

"And El Patrón or Baudin, whatever you want to call him, is a snake in the grass. He tortures people when they disobey him. He poured gasoline on one guy's eyeballs then flicked a match at them. This guy, I'm telling you, is bad business," Meier explained. "He manipulates people like they're chess pieces."

"I get it," Moore said without hesitation.

"He and his cronies are ruthless and rich beyond belief. They can buy anything—and anyone. If they woke up and were hungry, they would fly a private jet to Cancun for lunch," Meier added. "Then they'd roll to Venezuela to check out a new casino. They'd go Maserati shopping by helicopter so they could look at the cars from the air. They had hookers waiting for them in every hot spot and all the drugs they wanted. They are the ultimate party animals!"

Moore was not going to be dissuaded. He turned to Banger. "So, you help agents get to the island?"

Banger looked at Meier and grinned. "Yes. And sometimes we do a little more."

Meier stepped in. "When you were researching Baudin, did you see anything about him buying an old Russian submarine for $5.5 million to transport cocaine?"

"Yes, I did. But it exploded in Santiago Harbor and he couldn't use it," Moore replied as he looked at the three smirking men sitting in front of him.

"You did that!" he exclaimed as he realized why they were smirking.

Meier answered for the three. "Let's just say that we won't be invited anytime soon to his house for dinner."

The three men guffawed at the remark.

Moore shook his head from side to side. "Listen, you guys need to help me get to this El Patrón."

"What are you going to do? Knock on his door and ask if you can interview him?" Meier asked incredulously.

"In a perfect world, yes. I'd like to penetrate his organization and see what I can learn, then do a story about it."

"The only story coming out of your adventure is your obituary," Meier warned. "Besides, the only kind of El Patrón I like is the tequila kind!" he added.

Moore nodded. "I've been in and out of scrapes in the past. I'm a survivor," he replied confidently.

"You don't know what you are getting into," Meier said

as he shook his head. "Like we said, El Patrón owns Santiago. He has paid so much money to people there that no one will cross him. If you make it through the city and get to the town near his compound, your odds of surviving are even less. People in Santa Lucha are his first line of defense. If they spot a foreigner, El Patrón will know immediately," he warned. "He wouldn't trust an outsider. No way."

Banger nodded in agreement. "The townspeople wouldn't cross him for anything. He's upgraded their electric service. He put in a new water system and sewers. He's brought in prefab housing for the town. That town has done very well by him," Banger explained.

"And many of them work for him," Meier added. "They're his guards and compound workers, and some transport drugs for him. I wouldn't be surprised if he had a cocaine processing lab nearby where they work and earn a living."

"There's basically one road into that town and to his compound on the other side. It's surrounded by thick forest. His compound is virtually impenetrable," Meier said ominously.

"As is the forest," Banger added.

"I don't see this working for you, Emerson," Meier voiced his concern.

Moore thought for a moment as he watched the three men finish off their beers.

"I'll just go in as a reporter doing a story on the mountains. That's where Fidel Castro started the revolution, so it's plausible that I'm doing a travel story. The highest summit in Cuba is in that mountain range, so I could include a hike to the top to throw them all off."

"And how do you get an interview with El Patrón?" Meier asked.

"I don't know. I'll try to work some of the locals to introduce me," Moore suggested.

Kerby, who had been relatively quiet during the exchange, spoke. "Guys, he may have something there. Let him go in under the pretense that he's writing a travel story. If he can get in to interview Baudin, then he can take it from there. Otherwise, he leaves."

"Thanks, Kerby," Moore said gratefully.

"I think that's plain dumbass stupid. What if El Patrón knows that the Manny Elias character who they tried to kill is really Moore? You'd walk into a trap and you're no roadrunner playing with Wile E. Coyote. It's the real deal there," Meier objected. "El Patrón isn't stupid. He's heard it all. Seen it all."

"I don't think he knows who Manny Elias was," Moore interjected. "I'm willing to take the risk," he added.

"Think about it, Emerson. That Newton buddy of yours shows up out of nowhere and our little buddy Bones offs him when he finds him planning to take you out. Somebody was behind that hit contract on you and I'd wager my wife that it was Baudin," Meier stormed.

Moore wasn't going to back off. "I'm going. One way or the other, with or without your help, I'm going."

"I can fix a lot of things, but I can't fix stupid. This is stupid, Emerson," Meier said firmly. "We're going to end up laying out body bags like we're going on a shopping trip to fill them."

"Listen, if you guys don't want to help, I'll just fly into Havana and catch an island hopper over to Santiago. Then make my way up to Santa Lucha. I can do this on my own. I'll just use my cover story about writing a travel piece."

"Yeah and they'll be on you as soon as you land. I don't like it," Meier said.

"Then I guess I'm wasting my time and your time," Moore said as he stood. "Thanks for the beer."

Meier stood and spoke. "Hang on a second. You're getting squirrely here. Why don't you go below and walk out to my boat? Let me and the crew talk a bit."

"Sounds good," Moore said as he turned and walked down the steps to the boat. He wasn't going to let them talk him out of going, no matter how dangerous they made it sound. He was determined. He'd always been successful on his past reporting assignments. This would be no exception as far as he was concerned.

Five minutes later, he was looking over the boat and the canal which led to the Gulf of Mexico when he heard approaching footsteps. He turned and saw Meier.

"What's the verdict?" Moore asked.

"You certainly have a death wish," Meier started. "If you're hell-bent on destruction, we're here to help you out. No promises that you'll live to tell about it, understand?"

"I do, and I appreciate your help and insight," Moore replied.

"You heading back to Key West tonight?"

"No. I can't take a chance of another hit squad coming after me there. I'll find a room close by."

"You can stay here. I've got extra rooms. Grab your gear and I'll show you where you can stow it."

"Thanks, Chuck," Moore said as he walked over to the car and grabbed his gear and laptop from the trunk.

He followed Meier into the house and to the bedroom which contained a single bed, a small worn dresser and a desk with a chair. Meier suggested he make himself comfortable and gave him the password to his Wi-Fi.

After Meier left, Moore unpacked and set up his laptop. He spent the rest of the afternoon researching El Patrón, Santa Lucha, the Sierra Maestra mountains and the hike to the summit of Pico Turquino.

Three hours later, a knock on the bedroom door interrupted Moore's research.

"You still alive?" Meier's voice boomed. "Or did you change your mind, open the back window and run away?" Meier listened for a response. He didn't have to wait long.

"Come on in," Moore said as he stood from the desk.

"The boys and I cooked up a special surprise. You hungry?" Meier asked as he opened the door and allowed his huge frame to fill the doorway.

"Sure am."

"Come on down then," Meier said as he turned.

Moore followed Meier down the small hallway and the stairs to ground level where Kerby and Banger were sitting at a table with several bowls of fresh fruit.

"Come on over here, son," Meier said as Moore followed him to an outdoor grill.

"What are you cooking?" Moore asked as Meier lifted the grill top.

"What do you think?"

"I have no idea," Moore replied.

"That, my friend, is nothing but the best Key West iguana you'll ever taste. That's marinated, barbecued iguana brought to you compliments of the Key West Iguana Killers Club," Meier beamed.

Moore raised his eyebrows as he looked at the iguanas cooking on the grill. "I heard some of the folks in Key West talk about the iguana infestation. Somebody said they're living under the gravestones at the cemetery."

"These used to live there," Meier chortled as he took the lid off a pot. "And over here, we've got iguana stew. Some carrots, potatoes and big chunks of iguana."

"I'm willing to give it a try," Moore said, not really excited about eating a lizard that may have feasted on cadavers.

"You'll like it. I call it chicken of the tree," Meier laughed again as he dished some on a plate and handed it to Moore, who then took it over to the table where the other men were already downing their plates full of iguana.

The men spent two hours telling tales, eating and drinking.

After Kerby and Banger left, Meier invited Moore for an evening boat ride. The two men walked down to the dock where a 20-foot long Carolina skiff awaited them. She had a 90-horsepower outboard engine on the stern and the bow had shark's teeth painted on it.

"That's *The Goat*," Meier explained as they boarded his boat. "She can run through the mangroves and fly through the flats. She ain't much to look at and she drives like a dish plate, but she'll get you where you need to go and back again."

Within a minute, Meier started his boat and they were moving down the channel.

"This here is real pretty country," Moore said as they neared the end of the channel to the Gulf.

"I enjoy it anytime I can. I like the freedom of being on the water, if you know what I mean," Meier commented.

"I do," Moore confirmed.

When they cleared the channel, Meier rapidly accelerated and they headed eastward through the back country.

"With you living so close to the Seven Mile Bridge, do you know anything about a train that derailed into the Gulf in 1928?"

"Know about it? Yeah, I've dived it," Meier reacted.

"It's still there?"

"Oh yeah and it's a great place for the locals to dive," Meier confirmed.

"It's the engine, tender and express car. Right?"

"Yes. I'll head over that way and point her out to you. You can see her in her watery grave."

"I heard that no one survived. Is that true?"

"Not that I know of. They said she was going full throttle across the arched bridge."

"How did they know that?"

"When they first dove on her, they could see that the throttle was wide open," Meier explained.

"What about the explosion?"

"I heard tell that the bridge exploded just before she hit dry land."

"And no one saw how that happened?"

"No, and if they did, no one is admitting it. It's been one of the biggest unsolved mysteries in the Keys ever since," Meier commented. "No bodies were found down here."

"That's strange," Moore said, puzzled.

"They disappeared into thin air. I heard there were only two keys to the padlocks on the express car door. There was one in New York and that Pinkerton agent in St. Augustine had the other. He personally locked the armored express car doors before the train departed St. Augustine. It's like Houdini was on board and made the agents and treasure disappear," Meier said quietly.

"There was a treasure?"

"That's the rumor. No one knows. The safe doors were wide open when she was first discovered. The big boxes they carried in are still down there. They're all empty. I saw them when I did a dive there."

Moore wrinkled his brow. "Hey, wait a minute. How did the express car door get unlocked?"

"The guy who did the recovery dive back in 1928 took bolt cutters with him."

"Did he take the treasure?"

"No. There were too many people around when he dove it. There were several others who went down with him."

Meier eased back on the throttle and the boat slowed as they neared the end of Seven Mile Bridge.

"Maybe the Pinkertons pulled off the heist. I heard there was one aboard the engine itself. He could have killed the engineer and fireman," Moore proposed.

"And how would he have gotten inside the locked express car?"

"What if he had bolt cutters? He could have stopped the train, cut the locks and unloaded the treasure. Then put new padlocks on the door," Moore suggested.

"I don't know. The Pinkertons inside the express car would have had to be in on it," Meier mused. "The odds of getting them all to buy in on the heist are slim."

"But remember, they found the bodies of the engineer and fireman near Jacksonville that night. They'd been murdered," Moore commented.

"None of the bodies of the other Pinkertons were ever found. Who knows, they could have decided that it would be a great payday and hijacked the treasure themselves. Then off to South America, amigo!"

"I heard that the Pinkerton in charge of the shipment, Van Duzer, went after the train. He tried to chase it from the air in a Ford trimotor during the Okeechobee hurricane."

"I heard the same. That's another example of stupid is what stupid is. Probably lost at sea is my guess. What kind of fool would go flying in a hurricane? It's not like they had hurricane hunter planes back then."

"Do you know what kind of treasure the train carried?" Moore asked.

"Nope. There were all kind of rumors. Some said Confederate gold that had been hidden away for years. Others say it was cash that Flagler hadn't paid taxes on. Who knows? We probably won't ever know."

"There's the locomotive," he said as he brought the boat to idle over the wreckage.

Moore peered over the side and could see the train engine below. It was on its side and partially covered by sand. As Meier eased the boat forward, Moore could see the coal tender and the armored car. They were also partially covered in sand.

"That wreck has been dived on by so many people over the years and no one has found a clue worth solving the mystery." Meier glanced at the horizon where the setting sun was being covered by dark storm clouds. "We better head back. There's a storm brewing," Meier added as he turned the boat and accelerated toward home.

They beat the storm back. When it reached the house, it unleashed its fury with a downpour pounding on the metal roof of the house for an hour.

The next morning Moore went on his daily run. When he walked into the house, Meier was drinking a cup of coffee. In front of him on the table was a map of Cuba that he had been studying.

"Here I went and thought you were sleeping in."

"Trying to stay in shape," Moore grinned as he enjoyed the air-conditioned comfort of the room and looked toward the Mr. Coffee coffeemaker. "Any left?"

"Help yourself," Meier responded as Moore walked over and poured a cup. "Serving people coffee is not in my job description."

"Chuck, I saw a bunch of old shoes hanging from that tree behind your house."

"Yeah. What about them?"

"I just wondered why they're hanging there?"

Meier had a somber tone when he answered. "If you took the time to read what's written on each shoe, you might have an understanding of why they're out there."

"Humor me. Just tell me what it's about," Moore countered.

"Each shoe has a name written on it. The names belong to my bros that have been lost on ops that we've run. Each shoe has a sole. They remind me of the souls that have been lost. I will never forget them," he explained.

"I see," Moore responded somewhat surprised by Meier's explanation. It showed that Meier did indeed have a soft side hidden within that hardened exterior of his.

Walking to the table, he joined Meier in looking at a map. "So, are you going to help me?" Moore asked with a smile as he took a sip of the chicory-flavored coffee.

"Don't get your hopes up. I'm just taking a look. Besides, it's more fun than contemplating my navel lint," Meier cracked.

Moore heard the toilet flush and the water running in the bathroom sink. Shortly afterwards, the door opened and Bobby Banger stepped out.

"I don't know what I ate last night, but I've got the runs," Banger lamented.

"I've got a solution for you, bro. Just line your boxers with mini pads!" Meier chortled.

"Thanks for being so concerned," Banger said sarcastically.

Turning to Moore, Meier ragged on Banger, "That boy spits thunder and pisses lightning." Pausing for a moment, he added, "Well at least he farts thunder!"

"TMI!" Banger roared.

"That's what battle buddies are for!" Meier retorted before turning to the map.

"What do you have there?" Moore asked, eager to change the topic to his needs.

"Before Bobby's last run to the crapper, we were studying ways to get you to Cuba without alerting any of the bad guys."

"So, you're going to help me?" Moore asked again earnestly.

"Slow down, amigo. We're just thinking about it," Meier said as he tried to put the brakes on Moore.

"If you go in through any of the normal points of entry, El Patrón will be on you," Banger cautioned. "Like you said, you don't know if he knows that you were behind that alias, Manny Elias."

"And it wouldn't take long for information about an investigative reporter landing in Cuba to get to Baudin," Meier added.

"But I'd use my cover that I told you about last night," Moore protested.

"I mean to tell you that you should rethink this whole thing. You're after a story. Let the real dudes go after him and bring him to trial."

"It sounds to me that he's untouchable. Especially since

he has the Cuban authorities in his back pocket," Moore responded. "You can't just drop in and kidnap him."

"That wouldn't work. That's been looked at in the past. He does have a heliport in his compound, but he has so many armed guards, it wouldn't stand a chance at succeeding. The odds against us are too strong. And hell's bells and buckets of blood, it'd cause an international incident for the U.S. to do a snatch and grab in Cuba."

"Why don't you just send in a sniper team and take him out?" Moore asked.

Banger looked at Meier who gave him a wink. "That was tried from what we've heard. Both the sniper and spotter were outed and killed. It wasn't pretty. They were disemboweled and hung from a tree in the town as a warning. They mailed pictures to the DEA here."

Moore clenched his teeth. He couldn't help it as his stomach did a flip flop at hearing how brutal Baudin was. "I still want to go."

For the next few hours, the three men reviewed the map and possible points of entry into Cuba, discarding most of their preliminary ideas. They paused for a late lunch of cold cuts and fresh fruit, which they ate in the crow's nest.

Late that afternoon, Meier made a decision. "Any non-Cuban watercraft have to enter Cuba through one of their international marinas. That means showing your passport, clearing customs and announcing to everyone on the island that you've arrived. That's not good for you, Emerson. Like I said, Baudin will know you're on the island. That coconut telegraph line works too good."

"You're going to use Captain Congo, right?" Banger asked.

"You read my mind, Bobby. That's where I was heading," Meier said in confirmation.

"Captain Congo?" Moore asked.

"Cool dude, Emerson. He has ice running through his veins. Runs a fishing boat out of Marathon Key," Meier answered.

"Former Navy SEAL. Helps us on some black ops," Banger added.

"Captain Congo moves like a ghost on water," Meier threw in.

"I don't get it. If he's going to take me to Cuba, we'll still have to go through customs—or do you have something else in mind?" Moore asked as he looked from Banger to Meier.

"Bobby, I knew we had a smart one here," Meier sneered.

Banger nodded his head in agreement and smiled.

"Let me explain what we're going to do." Meier took him through the plan that had been cooking in his mind that afternoon.

"I like it," Moore said.

"Good. I'm going to call Captain Congo and see if he's available and you can figure out how you're going to pay him," Meier said as he reached for his cell phone and walked out to the deck.

Meanwhile, Moore went to his bedroom and grabbed his own cell phone. He placed a call to his *Washington Post* boss, John Sedler, and told him the plans for the next step.

"Not sure that I like the risk you're taking Emerson," Sedler's voice was filled with concern.

"When have you ever been comfortable with any of the risks I've taken?" Moore asked.

"I haven't. It's going to catch up to you one day," Sedler cautioned. "You'll be the story instead of your byline crediting the story. That's not we want."

Moore smiled. He knew that the crusty editor had a soft heart somewhere under that rough persona he displayed, and that he truly cared. "I'll be fine, John."

They talked a few minutes more and ended the call after Sedler agreed to pay Captain Congo for the trip to Cuba. Moore walked out of the room and rejoined the two men at the table.

"Are we a go?" Moore asked as he looked at Meier.

"Can you pay Congo?" Meier asked in response.

"Yes. It's all set up. My boss will call him and send his bank a wire transfer."

"Then we are a go," Meier replied. "Congo is checking his charts and the weather. If it looks good, you're on your way tomorrow night."

"Good," Moore commented. "Hey, who's the brunette on that poster in the hallway?"

"You noticed the poster, huh?"

"Couldn't miss it," Moore answered. "It's a naked woman wrestling a shark!"

Meier grinned.

"Ahhh! That deep-diving, buck-naked, bubble-blowing, fin-slapping shark tickler! That's my old lady, Dallis. She's the only woman on this planet that has the ability to put up with me and my bullshit shenanigans. She has been with me through it all. Back room bordello bar fights, Bangkok, Baghdad, Waffle House and back again.

"Hell, after I got my ass handed to me with those IED's, she got me home when those government boys conveniently wanted to leave me for dead, rotting in that hospital in Germany. Dallis was by my side the whole time. Nursed me back to health, fattened me up, wouldn't let me give up. She grabbed me by the back and sack. Took no shit from nobody and drug my ass back to the side of light and the side of right, back to life and the land of the living.

"She cooks, cleans, keeps the bills paid, A/C running, fridge filled, beer chilled, shoots, loots, boots, scoots, can build a house from the ground up, digs ditches, terrifies bitches, drives big trucks, can back trailers and can run any boat like a mad banshee. She keeps my sweet ass in line. How's that for a description? I love that woman!"

"I guess that sums her up pretty good. I've got to admit I've never heard anyone describe his wife like that," Moore said stunned.

But Meier wasn't finished.

"If you cross her, you'll only do it once, and you will know about it. She will work your ass to the water line. So, mind your p's and q's around her. She takes no shit from no one. If you're dishing it out be prepared to get it back in spades. And don't get mad if you get your fragile little feelings hurt. It's just business, son."

"Is she here?" Moore was eagerly looking forward to meeting this one-of-a-kind wife.

"Nah. She's up in Ft. Myers visiting our daughter." Meier turned back to the table. "Now that I got your attention, come on over here and take a look at this."

"I'm disappointed I won't meet her," Moore said as he walked over to the table.

"She's the wife of a lifetime! Now, look what we figured out for you," Meier said as he turned back to the map.

The men went over their plans until Banger had to leave. The two men continued their conversation over a grouper dinner that Meier prepared.

Later that night, both men were seated in the crow's nest overlooking the canal where they were drinking rum as they chatted.

"Chuck?"

"What?"

"I wasn't snooping, but I noticed a stack of letters tied with a red bow on the dresser in my room. Are those love letters?" Moore asked.

Meier's face transformed into a somber expression.

"They're love letters from one of my bros," Meier replied.

Moore noted a touch of sadness in the response. "Nice."

"Not really."

"What do you mean?"

"My battle buddy was dying. It took a couple of days. He couldn't write, but he dictated what he wanted to say to his wife, and I wrote it down for him. He wanted me to mail his final letters to his wife."

"And you didn't mail them to her?" Moore asked in shock.

"No."

"Why?"

"His wife died in a car accident on the way to see him at the hospital."

"And you didn't tell him?"

"He was in so much pain. I didn't need to add to his burden."

"Oh my," Moore muttered. "That is so sad!"

"I figured that they ended up seeing each other when he passed. I just keep those letters as a reminder of my bro and how delicate our lives are. We're all just one heartbeat away from death," Meier explained.

"Isn't that the truth?" Moore agreed, pleasantly surprised by another look into the inner Meier's soft psyche.

"Those two days I did something right. There are too many days that the things I do make the devil happy," Meier lamented sadly.

CHAPTER 14

The Next Evening
Marathon Key

The next evening, the three men drove to Marathon Key and parked Meier's Ford F-150 Crew Cab truck next to the dock where Captain Congo's 46-foot Viking Convertible Sportfish was secured.

The vessel was powered by twin 890-horsepower Detroit Diesel inboard engines with Johnson & Towers Twin Turbos. She had a tuna tower with controls and could seat eight on the flybridge. She also had two staterooms and a mid-level galley and dinette below deck. The aft deck featured a high-grade steel fighting chair and various assortment of sportfishing rods well secured in their rack.

Moore grabbed his gear from the pickup truck and began following the other two men to the boat. Suddenly, Moore stopped and stared at the boat's name on the stern. He hoped it didn't foretell his future. The name read *Mis Fortune*.

A deep voice spoke behind Moore. "Not bad for being built in 1987, is she?"

Moore turned and saw a crusty African-American with dark leather skin dotted with age spots. His beard and close-cropped hair were graying. A pair of oversized sunglasses covered his bloodshot eyes, unwanted evidence of another night of heavy drinking.

"Captain Congo?" Moore guessed.

"Congo is all that you need to call me, son," the captain replied.

"I'm Emerson Moore," the reporter said as he extended his hand to the ship's captain. Congo was dressed in a ragged t-shirt and well-worn shorts that were covered with a variety of oil, fish and blood stains.

"Thank you," Congo said as he deftly avoided a handshake and handed Moore a tote bag to carry. "Nice of you to help an old codger like me." Congo walked past Moore and joined the other two men on board. Moore hurried to catch up as the men exchanged greetings.

"What's popping, Big Daddy?" Moore heard Congo ask Meier as he boarded.

"Like I told you on the phone, I've got this pilgrim," he nodded toward Moore, "who needs your *Mayflower* to transport him to the New World."

Congo chuckled as he eyed Moore up and down. "Think this one will live? None of the others did," he commented stoically.

"Nah. I already ordered his headstone," Meier responded sarcastically.

Moore ignored their chatter. He knew that they were playing with him. At least half-playing, he hoped.

"You're coming with us, right?" Congo asked Meier.

"I'd love to, Congo. But the Cuban Coast Guard has a bounty on me and the Cuban intel service isn't too fond of me, either. There's little chance with my red hair and prosthetic leg that I could go unrecognized if they'd board you," Meier retorted. "But Bobby will be going with you."

Congo looked at Banger. "I guess I can put up with Toots!" he teased. He knew Banger well and his flatulence problem.

"I'm a good one to have in case you run out of gas," Banger shot back without hesitation.

In a more serious tone, Meier asked, "You clear on the plan, Congo?"

"I got it. Thanks for giving me a call this morning. I don't figure we'll have too hard of a time with getting your friend ashore. We might run into a few squalls, but that could help keep the Cubans away."

"I wouldn't count on it. You never know what's going to happen when you get inside their territorial waters."

"It's always a risk, you know," Congo replied.

"And that's our life. Risk taking," Meier echoed. "Live fast, die young and leave a good-looking corpse," Meier smiled. "Did you get paid?"

"Yes. I saw the money wired to my account this afternoon."

Meier looked at Moore. "He has a good policy about being paid up front. Pay now because you may not be around to pay him later."

Moore nodded somberly.

They spent the next thirty minutes going over the equipment and gear, then Meier prepared to leave. As he did, he placed his hand on Moore's right shoulder.

"It's not too late to back out."

Moore grinned confidently back at him. "I wouldn't miss this for anything."

"It's your life. You'll be mostly on your own once you land."

"Not my first rodeo, Chuck. I'll do fine," Moore said assuredly.

"Emerson, I have a parting gift for you," Meier said as he handed Moore a small box.

Moore's eyes widened as he took the box and looked at it. "What! What are these for?" he asked surprised.

"No one should go into Cuba without a bunch of condoms," Meier grinned.

"Listen, I'm not going to need these. I'll be very focused on my mission," Moore said as he started to hand the box of condoms back to Meier. "You don't understand."

"No, you're the one who doesn't understand," Meier said as he pushed Moore's hand and the condom box away. "The Cubans, men and women, are going to love you for having these."

"I'm not buying what you're saying," Moore said not knowing where the conversation was heading—especially with the comment about men.

"Listen to me. The Cuban economy is poor. Store shelves just don't have a lot of merchandise, so the Cubans improvise. They use condoms as hairbands and they blow them up and use them for balloons at kids' birthday parties."

Moore chuckled. "Nice try, Chuck. You're playing with me."

"I'm serious. There's a real shortage of basic goods there. Even fishermen use them."

Moore looked at Meier with skepticism.

"Very few of the fishermen have boats because the government is worried about them fleeing the island. So, the fishermen will inflate the condoms, tie them together and use them as floats with hooks dangling below them. That way they send them out to deeper water with the tide to catch bigger fish, then haul the lines back in."

"That sounds more plausible."

"Some of the folks make wine in their garages and they'll take a condom and place it over a bottle of grape juice. When fermentation starts, it releases gases that inflate the condom. When the condom collapses, then you know the fermentation process is complete and the wine is ready to sell," Meier explained proudly.

Moore hefted the box in his hand. "All right. I'll throw these in my duffel bag," he agreed reluctantly.

"I wish you well, then," Meier said as he stepped off the boat as Congo started the engines.

"You left your cell phone and laptop in my truck, right?" Meier asked.

"Yes, and my driver's license."

"Like I said. They can be used to identify who you really are."

"Right," Moore agreed. "I'm not carrying any type of identification."

"And you remember where to head if you get in trouble, right?"

"Yes. That's a great backup if I need to be extracted."

Nodding, Meier cast the lines to Banger and the *Mis Fortune* eased away from her dock and motored quietly through the channel at no-wake speed.

"When you get back, you owe me a beer. Make that several," Meier shouted.

"You can count on it," Moore yelled back.

With the setting sun behind them, Congo opened up the engines once they cleared the channel, and instantly, they were flying across the water. In their wake, the setting sun's rays fell like glitter and danced like sparkling diamonds upon the disturbed water.

As the twilight slowly turned into darkness, Moore walked over to Congo, who was manning the helm.

"How far is it?"

"It's not terribly far," Congo replied. "We should get you there before dawn breaks. We want to make sure you land while it's still dark."

"Sounds good to me."

"We should have no problem until we pass the main fishing grounds. They're about halfway between Marathon and Cuba. The real problem starts when we're twelve miles off the Cuban coast and in their territorial waters."

"How's that?" Moore asked.

"That's when you're supposed to contact the Port Authority on channel 16 or 72 and identify yourself. They'll want to know your intentions and direct you to one of their marinas for customs inspection. That's when we go on high alert. They could send out a patrol boat to check us out when we don't call in."

"I see."

"And if they come out before we execute Big Daddy's plan, you could be in an awkward situation. We all would be," Congo confirmed.

Moore nodded, understanding the gravity of the operation. "How long have you known Chuck?" Moore asked to start a conversation with Congo.

"The human monster truck? I've known him for a long time. We ran ops together years ago when he and I lived in the dark world," Congo smiled coyly.

"You should have seen Big Daddy when he played football," Banger added as he joined them.

"I didn't know he played."

"Yeah. He was the blocking sled back in high school in Texas," Banger chuckled.

"No way!" Moore retorted.

"I was just kidding. He played linebacker and he destroyed quarterbacks. He was third team All-American," Banger explained.

"Quite a guy!" Moore agreed.

"Tell your buddy about the time Meier against his better judgement took a reporter with him on an op," Congo snickered. "You'll love this story."

Banger laughed before starting. "We're in the jungle somewhere that I can't reveal. And we get stuck with a know-it-all, green-ass reporter. I thought Big Daddy was going to shoot the guy. Anyways, the guy can't stand bugs and they're biting us left and right. We had hordes of bugs attacking us that night and the team just ignored him and his whining about his bug bites."

"What did he do?" Moore asked eager to learn the outcome.

"The guy pulls out a can of strong bug repellant and proceeds to strip naked and apply the repellant all over his body. While he was doing it, he spilt some repellant on his ball bag."

"Bet he didn't get any bug bites there," Moore chortled.

"Oh, no. But he ended up with a more serious problem than bug bites." Banger's face had a huge all-knowing smile.

"How's that?" Moore asked.

"He had one hell of a painful chemical burn. I think you

could have heard his shrieks for ten miles. We almost had to abort the mission because of this wet noodle."

"How did you get him to quiet down?" Moore pushed.

"Big Daddy solved it. I think he wanted to shoot him and put him out of his misery, but he reached in his pack and pulled out a tube of cream. He threw it at the guy and said that he shouldn't expect Meier to apply it."

The three men roared at the tale.

"Meier's the real deal. He'd give you the shirt off his back," Congo said.

"If you don't mind it being wet with sweat," Banger joked.

Moore smiled. "He's a pretty creative guy."

Congo nodded his head in agreement. "That's how he came up with this plan for tonight." Looking at Banger, Congo asked, "What did he call it again?"

"Operation Immaculate Deception. Guaranteed to get you on the island safely," Banger replied eagerly. "You might have one thing going for you at Baudin's compound."

"What's that?"

"Complacency."

"Huh?"

"Baudin has that town and area so wrapped up that his security may be a bit lax. He knows that the government will protect him from outside intrusion so he and his men may have let their guard down a bit."

"Overconfident," Moore suggested.

"Exactly. That could play very well for you."

"I hope so."

"It's going to be a few hours before we get there. You better go below and get some shut-eye," Congo suggested to Moore. "You're going to need to be well-rested for what you have in front of you."

Moore took one last look around before heading down. "Guess you're right," he said as he disappeared below deck. He made his way into one of the staterooms and dropped on the berth. He was asleep in a few moments.

The sound of raindrops hitting the windows like sharp arrows awoke Moore as a small squall passed. Moore rolled over and looked at his watch. He'd been asleep for three hours. He hopped off the berth and returned to the helm where he saw Congo and Banger staring at the radar scan.

"Trouble?"

"Not for us," Congo answered as the rain ceased. The ship rose up and down on the swells from the waves.

"See that blip there?" he asked as he pointed.

Moore looked and nodded. "Yes."

"Probably U.S. Coast Guard looking for drug smugglers or illegal immigrants," Congo suggested.

"Or they may want to board and check your paperwork and safety equipment to make sure you're in compliance," Banger proposed.

"Nah. These guys know me. They've checked me before. Shouldn't be a problem," Congo surmised as he cut back the engines.

He was right. After moving closer to *Mis Fortune*, the Coast Guard flooded it with a bright light that swept her deck.

"We didn't know it was you, Congo," one of the officers called as the ships moved up and down with the swells.

"Just taking these boys out fishing," Congo shouted as he waved his hand toward Banger and Moore.

"A bit rough for fishing!"

"I'm sure she'll quiet down in a bit," Congo answered.

"You be safe. Got some squalls out tonight."

"Yeah. We just went through one. We're fine," Congo shouted back as the Coast Guard vessel gathered speed and pulled away.

Turning to Moore, Congo said, "I told you it would be no problem. Won't be so easy if we get stopped by the Cubans, though."

Congo shoved the throttle forward and they continued their trip to Cuba.

Banger pulled Moore aside. "I've got a few tips for you about Cuba."

"I'm all ears," Moore said as he focused on Banger.

"Internet connection in Cuba is spotty. It's down most of the time. Some of the larger hotels have internet in the lobby. There are also internet cafes around that you can use. But the Cuban Intelligence Service could be monitoring internet use, so I'd suggest not using it. You're going to want to keep your profile low, especially when you're up in the mountains and can be more easily spotted as an outsider."

"Got it."

"And don't use a phone unless it's an absolute emergency," Banger warned.

"Why?"

"There are 1,500 Russians manning a listening post about twelve miles south of Havana in Lourdes. It's directed at the U.S. and they eavesdrop on our calls as well as calls made from within Cuba. They could pick you up in a heartbeat," Banger cautioned.

"Thanks for the warning."

"Don't be surprised if Cubans identify you as being a

visitor. They'll shout 'my friend' and want to know where you're from."

"I'll just tell them I'm from Key West. But why do they do that?" Moore asked perplexed.

"Cubans aren't allowed to travel. When they spot a foreigner, they like to know about the country they come from. And remember that Cubans drink straight rum. If you ask for a mix, they'll spot you as a visitor."

A few hours later, the boat was slowly trolling within calmer Cuban waters near Santiago on the southeastern coast. They had trolled within six miles of the shore when *Mis Fortune* was bathed in the floodlights of a fast-approaching Cuban patrol boat.

The patrol boat's captain had spotted the *Mis Fortune* and approached within a few hundred yards before switching on its light, hoping to find the boat filled with Cubans fleeing the island. Instead, he saw two men on board. One man was seated in the fighting chair in the stern as another stood by.

The patrol boat slowed and moved up to Congo's vessel. Two crew members jumped aboard and tied the two craft together. As they did, the Cuban captain jumped aboard and confronted the two men.

"Let me see your papers. You know you're in Cuban territorial waters, don't you?" he asked in English.

"Oh my. I didn't realize that we had drifted in that far. My radar is on the fritz," Congo replied, knowing that the reason it wasn't working was due to him disconnecting one of the lead wires. A little subterfuge never hurt anything.

"You are within six miles of our coast," the captain said indignantly. "Papers," he demanded as Congo and Banger, who was seated in the fighting chair, produced their passports.

"Only you two on board?" the captain asked.

"Yes," Congo replied.

"Any drugs on board?"

"No."

"Then you wouldn't mind if we searched your boat?"

"No, go right ahead. Make yourself at home," Congo urged as the captain motioned for his two crew members to search the boat. Within a few minutes, they returned from their search and indicated that there were no problems.

"You will have to move this vessel outside our territorial limits immediately and fish out there," the captain ordered. "We will escort you to make sure you comply."

"Sure. Sure Captain," Congo said as he walked to the pilothouse and the Cubans returned to their patrol boat. Banger tossed them their lines and the *Mis Fortune* picked up speed with the patrol boat following.

Banger returned to the stern where he squinted his eyes as he looked toward shore. He thought he saw a dark smudge against the water. It could be Moore. "Good luck," he said silently to Moore.

Two miles offshore, Moore was seated in a small Zodiac. Its 25-horsepower outboard was taking him toward the shore. He had seen the floodlights from the Cuban patrol boat and was glad that Congo had launched him overboard when he did. Meier's Operation Immaculate Deception may be working, Moore thought to himself. He didn't think that the Cuban Coast Guard had any idea that one of *Mis Fortune's* passengers had prematurely disembarked.

Moore turned around and peered at the approaching shoreline. He planned a landing at Playa Bueycabon, a beach community about a twenty-five minute ride west of Santiago. Once he beached the Zodiac, he planned to hide it nearby and hitch a ride into town.

Moore was dressed in off-white pants and a very well-worn t-shirt. He still hadn't shaved his beard and was hoping with his dark tan to blend in easily with the Cuban populace. He had left the wig behind and didn't apply the birthmark to his cheek. He didn't see any need to continue those parts of his disguise. He had a medium-sized duffel bag with his shaving kit and a few extra clothes at his feet.

CHAPTER 15

Later That Morning
Santiago, Cuba

Cuba's second-largest city was wedged upon hills between the looming Sierra Maestra mountain range and the aquamarine Caribbean Sea. This hot and humid seaport city fronted a pouch-shaped bay on the island's southeastern side.

Santiago had an interesting history. It was Cuba's original capital city before the capital was moved to Havana. Santiago also was where Spanish troops faced their main defeat at San Juan Hill, east of the city, on July 1, 1898 in a battle charge led by Teddy Roosevelt during the Spanish-American War. The Cuban Revolution began there on July 26, 1953 as Fidel Castro led his rebels from the surrounding mountains to attack Santiago's Moncada Barracks. When Castro died in 2016 following more than 52 years as Cuba's ruler, his ashes were buried in Santiago's Santa Ifigenia Cemetery.

Known as Cuba's cultural capital, Santiago was situated closer to Haiti and the Dominican Republic than to Havana. This caused its identity to be steeped in Afro-Caribbean influences and the area gave birth to salsa and conga music, including that of the well-known bandleader and actor Desi Arnaz.

After catching a couple of hours of sleep, Moore was able to hitch a ride in the back of an old Ford pickup truck that was headed into Santiago. The truck, which was filled with produce, drove east along a blacktopped, two-lane road that ran parallel with the Caribbean Sea. Its water was a number of shades of blue and green, but more turquoise near shore. It was a clear and cloudless day.

As they approached the outskirts of Santiago, the road changed to wide tree-lined boulevards with views of the mountains where heavy, dark clouds were hanging overhead. Moore hoped that the dark clouds were not foreboding.

Moore saw a number of bikes, motorcycles and motorbikes. Some of the two-wheeled vehicles carried two riders or goods headed for market. Driving along the palm-lined street in front of low, one-story homes, Moore took in the blooming flowers. They were just gorgeous. He smiled when he saw an old red Willys Jeep and a blue 1958 Plymouth Fury with its high tailfins. If he wasn't so focused on his mission, he'd enjoy exploring the city.

Santiago was a blend of the old and new as horse drawn carriages and wagons acting as taxis competed with the iconic 1950s classic cars for passengers. There were large trucks converted to buses. They had canopy-covered beds which were lined with seats. At the rear, an attached staircase allowed the passengers to climb aboard or exit. There were also large and air-conditioned buses like the modern buses you'd see in any American city.

Many of Santiago's streets were narrow and lined with tall buildings painted in a variety of pastel colors. They often opened onto large plazas in front of historic buildings where musicians entertained passersby. Sidewalk vendors were selling a variety of merchandise and food and doing a brisk business.

As the pickup truck entered a street close to one of the markets, it stopped to allow Moore to jump off. Moore paid the driver for the ride with Cuban currency that Meier had provided earlier.

Carrying his duffel bag, Moore walked past a number of locals sitting in the midmorning shade behind a long line of tables where they played chess or dominoes. Moore was hungry and wanted to grab breakfast before checking into a room to get some shuteye.

Moore smiled as he walked past several restaurants and bars. It was a festive atmosphere as salsa music poured through their open doors. He saw patrons and wait staff breaking out in dance moves. It was an energetic and fun-filled environment with pictures of Castro and Che Guevara on the walls.

Moore spotted a round red sign with black lettering and a coffee cup in black. It read Rumba Café. He entered the cozy café and opted to sit under an awning in the open patio area where the blue-painted tables and chairs contrasted energetically with the orange-painted walls. A nearby pedestal fan provided some relief from the midmorning heat.

After reviewing the menu, Moore elected to go with a traditional Cuban breakfast and strong Cuban coffee. He ordered his coffee and the server was back within a minute, placing his order on the table. It was served with a mug of warmed milk and a small metal carafe of hot coffee. Moore poured the coffee into the warmed milk and added sugar before he sipped it. It tasted great, he thought.

He ordered a tostada that consisted of a sliced, grilled and buttered Cuban bread served in a basket. He planned on doing as the Cubans did and dipped the tostada in his *café con leche*. He also ordered a fried egg and a fruit bowl filled with melons, papaya, mango and mamey. He was hungry.

After eating his delicious breakfast, Moore walked a couple of blocks and found a *casa particular* offering rooms. These were private homes where the owners rented rooms, very similar to a bed and breakfast. He wanted to avoid the larger hotels where staff would ask too many questions and request to see a passport upon guest check-in.

Moore paid the lodging owner twenty dollars and offered an additional five for a home-cooked dinner. He relaxed for the rest of the day and kept a low profile as he planned to catch a bus for Santa Lucha the next morning. He was pleased with his mission so far. It didn't appear to him that he had raised any alarms.

Flight

CHAPTER 16

The Next Morning
Santiago Bus Station

After an early breakfast at the *casa*, Moore caught a taxi to the central bus terminal where he purchased a ticket for the ride to Santa Lucha. He was hoping that the ride would be in one of the modern-looking, air-conditioned buses. When it was time to depart, however, he saw that his wish wasn't coming to fruition. There was a faded blue bus that had seen much better days. If it was in the U.S., the bus would be resting comfortably in a junk yard, Moore thought to himself.

Moore carried his duffel bag as he walked by the bus, peeking at the thin tread left on the tires. He wasn't pleased when he saw how worn some of the tires appeared, and he knew the bus would be driving on winding mountain roads with sheer drop-offs —a very dangerous drive.

He somewhat reluctantly climbed aboard the bus. To his chagrin, Moore found it already packed half-full with passengers. He observed many of them were carrying food that filled the air with a rich, spicy aroma that permeated the interior of the bus and mixed with an abundance of unwashed body odors. Moore was disappointed to hear one of the passengers comment that the air conditioning was out of order. It promised to be a warm ride to Santa Lucha.

Some of the passengers also held small cages with live chickens that added their clucking to the bus ride experience. An evil-eyed goat was wandering freely up and down the aisle as if it owned the bus. Moore laughed quietly when he heard one of the passengers swear at the goat when it crapped in the aisle next to his seat. The goat's owner hurried back and cleaned up the mess as the man's swearing continued.

All they needed were a few more animals and Moore thought riding in this bus would be a cross between a circus animal car and Noah's ark.

Moore grabbed one of the vacant window seats and gasped for fresh air. Between the noise from the passengers, goat and chickens, it promised to be a din-filled, ten-hour ride. It made Moore rethink his decision of not hiring a taxi to take him to Santa Lucha, but he had a concern that he'd stand out more if he arrived there in a taxi. He'd also heard that the last ten kilometers of the road presented a serious challenge to drivers who were unfamiliar with the route. Taxis were also known to take curves too fast on that stretch of road and uncontrollably careen down the side of the mountain.

Soon the bus was packed with people standing in the aisles for the long ride. A gray-haired, overweight woman had plopped in the seat next to Moore. She was odorous. Moore wasn't sure which was worse—her onion breath or her body odor. Moore smiled at her and she returned the smile. When she opened her mouth, he could see she was missing several of her lower teeth. He scooted closer to the window and noted the increased noise overhead that suggested some people chose to ride on top of the bus in the fresh air and hot sun.

Finally, the driver boarded the bus. Moore looked toward the front as the driver sat behind the wheel. He intently watched as the driver reached down along the left side of his seat and lifted a small, dark bottle. He raised it to his lips and took a long drink before placing it back on the floor.

Moore grimaced with concern. He hoped that it wasn't rum and, if it was, that the driver wouldn't be taking too many swigs as he navigated the dangerous mountain curves ahead.

The wayward driver started the bus and placed it in gear so it could ease its way out of the bus station. A hint of a breeze made its way into the bus through the open windows. It helped wash away the odors including the cigarette and cigar smoke from several passengers who had decided to light one up.

The bus had proceeded eleven kilometers east of Santiago along the coastal road when Moore noted they passed a turnoff to Parque Nacional de la Gran Piedra. It went inland and led to a steep, curving road to some of the most accessible peaks in the mountain range and the home of la Gran Piedra, the highest peak above Santiago and a favorite tourist spot.

Two hours later, the bus slowed and turned inland, arriving at a small gas station where most passengers hurried into the nearby foliage to relieve themselves. Some instead waited in line for the two restrooms. Moore joined those in the foliage before buying a cold bottled water and rice and beans from one of the nearby food stands.

Twenty minutes later, the driver tooted the bus horn as a signal that it was time to reboard. There weren't as many passengers now since a few had reached their intended destination.

When Moore reboarded and walked by the seated driver, he again saw the driver taking another sip out of his bottle.

Moore could tell now it was a rum bottle and wondered how often the man drank some during the trip.

As Moore walked down the narrow aisle, he was disappointed to see that the chickens and the goat remained onboard. He grabbed a different window seat and was joined by an old man who used a walking stick. Moore nodded at him and turned to look out the open window.

Grinding the gears, the driver eased the bus into a slow ascent up the winding mountain road. Moore, who was seated on the right side of the bus, quickly saw that there were no barriers between the road and the edge of the drop off. One false turn would send the bus plummeting into the rough ravines below.

The bus continued precariously up the mountain, which was lush and green due to its subtropical climate and smothered with towering palms. Moore was amazed by the number of palms he saw, not knowing that Cuba had the world's highest density of palm trees.

The bus followed the winding road with stunning views of cliffs, waterfalls, coves and beaches that seemed to stretch to infinity. The lower slopes were a patchwork of grasslands and jungles that gave way at the higher altitude to dense forests. Clouds formed, hung and were dispersed around the range's mountainous peaks.

Two hours later, the bus stopped as it had reached its first destination, a poor village named San Pedro. There was a small combination grocery store-gas station that acted as the center of the village. Next to it stood a wooden church with a white painted cross above the front entrance. The village contained a number of small wooden huts where grunting pigs, squawking chickens and gobbling turkeys freely roamed.

To Moore's relief, most of the poorly-dressed passengers,

including the ones with the goat and the chickens, exited the bus at this stop. He had his seat to himself and stretched appreciatively. Several passengers who had been riding on the bus's roof scrambled to find seats inside.

The bus soon resumed its journey to Santa Lucha, the village in the clouds. About halfway there, the incline steeped and the roadbed changed to concrete with horizontal corrugations for traction. That's not all that was changing. Moore noticed the vegetation was changing from tropical palms to firs and pine trees as they ascended. He continued to enjoy the view of water cascading over a number of waterfalls which they passed.

Overhead, a passing thunderstorm unleashed a torrent of rainfall as passengers worked quickly to close the bus windows. The downside was that the cigarette and cigar smoke and all of the other odors now were trapped inside the bus. Moore hoped the storm would be brief and he was thankful when it quickly passed. He then joined the other passengers in reopening the bus windows to breathe in the fresh mountain air.

As the bus neared Santa Lucha, Moore noticed the roadside huts gradually gave way to much nicer homes. Not only that, but the roadbed was upgraded as they neared the town. As the bus rounded a curve, Moore was stunned to see a beautiful town in front of them. It was surrounded by lush mountains and dramatic, untamed greenery. The buildings were two and three stories high and much more modern. There were street lights and people seemed more well off than what he had viewed at the lower elevations.

Santa Lucha was a small town of 8,000 Cubans tucked away on the side of the mountain. It covered about seven square miles up and down the mountainside. There was one main street through town and a number of narrow side streets.

The town was easily walkable on foot with most of the banks, stores, restaurants and one large hotel clustered on the main street named Calle Baudin. Calle Trejo, which ran parallel to the main street, had several *casas particulares*.

Halfway down Calle Baudin, the street opened into a broad plaza that was overlooked by several restaurants and a large Catholic church. The plaza acted as a central marketplace for the locals and people who lived south of town.

There was one supermarket in town and, unlike other supermarkets in Cuba, was well stocked with goods thanks to Baudin. Hiking trails were available south of town, but north of town there were warning signs that trespassing was not permitted. It was part of Baudin's private land holdings.

Most of the townspeople worked in some capacity for El Patrón, either within his compound or on his surrounding property, including the marijuana fields and the cocaine processing center.

The bus soon passed a police vehicle that was parked so its occupants could watch approaching traffic. Moore also noted several security cameras affixed to nearby buildings with their lenses pointed along the mountain road. Someone wanted to know who was entering and exiting the town, Moore thought.

When the bus finally pulled up in front of a large hotel, it stopped to unload its road-weary passengers. Moore stood and noticed that the old man had left his walking stick when he departed the bus at San Pedro. Seeing an opportunity, Moore grabbed the walking stick and his duffel bag and began to walk with a limp, thinking that it would throw off any observers.

As he limped off the bus, Moore stood on the sidewalk and quickly surveyed the town for a place to stay. He looked at the hotel in front of him and saw a man wearing a yellow cap, standing nonchalantly on its porch, but he was carefully watching people exiting the bus. Moore surmised that he was one of the observers that Meier and Banger had warned him about.

Moore eyed the hotel in front of him. It was named Hotel Santa Lucha and had 74 guest rooms, a restaurant and bar that offered musical entertainment at night. It looked busy and too formal for Moore. They would be sure to ask for his passport, and he was traveling without one.

Moore instead walked across the street to the parallel street. He remembered from his previous online research that it was lined with a number of *casas particulares*. He elected to get a room there rather than the hotel where too many questions could be asked by the front desk staff. He also wanted to see what Mr. Yellow Cap would do.

Using his walking stick, Moore hobbled across the street and walked into one of the *casas particulares* on the next street over. It was named Casa Felicia. Before he entered, he cast a quick glance over his shoulder and saw that Mr. Yellow Cap was following him at a discreet distance. Turning back to the entryway, Moore limped inside where he was warmly greeted.

"Welcome to beautiful Casa Felicia. Can I help you on this fine day?" the owner, Luis Marrero, asked Moore.

"I'd like to rent a room for a few nights," Moore replied.

They negotiated his room rate as the owner had Moore sign in on the registration book. While Moore reached into his pocket for cash, Marrero turned the registration book around and looked at the name Moore signed.

"Señor Manny Elias, again I say welcome to my *casa*," the owner beamed. "And what brings you to Santa Lucha?" Marrero asked as Moore counted out the cash to pay for his room.

"Exploring. Just exploring the beautiful countryside. I enjoy hiking," Moore answered. There was no way he was going to tell Marrero that his real purpose was to investigate Baudin.

"We have many wonderful hiking trails below Santa Lucha." Marrero answered as he looked at Moore's walking stick.

"I plan to check them out and I'll look for some additional trails farther up the mountain," Moore offered, as he awaited Marrero's reaction.

Marrero shook his head. "I'd be careful about going up the mountain farther," Marrero warned. "It's private property. The owner does not like trespassers."

"Oh," Moore frowned as he feigned disappointment.

"But the hiking below town is so beautiful. There are many waterfalls and rock outcroppings to enjoy along the trails," Marrero added as he tried to redirect his guest's focus.

"Thanks for letting me know," Moore said as he turned to go to his room. He wasn't surprised at all by Marrero's comments. He turned back and asked, "What happens if I do go up there?"

Marrero's eyes narrowed as he stared at Moore. "That would not be a good idea, Señor. The area is well-guarded and there are roving patrols. Not a good thing," he said as he shook his head from side to side. "Some people have been roughed up. Not worth it."

"Thank you for the advice," Moore said as he headed to his room. He was pleased that Marrero hadn't asked to see his passport.

He opened the door and noticed that the room had definitely seen better days. The single bed had a thin mattress and threadbare blanket. A decrepit wooden chair was next to the bed. A well-worn, two-drawer dresser stood against one of the light-green painted walls. A lamp without a shade stood on top of the dresser next to a small crucifix. A solitary oscillating fan turned its blades from where it was set on a nightstand below the room's open window. A slight breeze caused the light blue curtains to billow.

Moore placed his duffel bag on the bed. It seemed so strange to Moore to be without his cell phone and laptop. It was a bit disconcerting to be so isolated, but again he realized that the circumstances dictated this approach.

He decided to scope out the town to get its layout. Grabbing his walking stick, he limped out of the *casa* and headed to the marketplace in the middle of town. As he hobbled on his way, he looked over his shoulder and saw Mr. Yellow Cap behind him, bobbing and weaving amongst the townspeople to keep him in sight. Moore hatched a plan to confront his tail.

A narrow alley led off to the side and connected to several other alleys through a maze of buildings. The eaves of their tiled roofs were nearly touching, forming a near perfect canopy that allowed only thin shafts of sunlight to penetrate the deep shadows.

Moore turned into the alley and broke into a run. His eyes searched the dark recesses in front of him for a place to hide and lie in wait. Rounding a corner, he tripped over his feet and fell, dropping his walking stick. He grabbed the stick and scrambled upright only to hear the sharp staccato echo of heavy footsteps from the direction he had come.

Stepping inside the archway of a building, Moore pressed his back against the carved wooden door. He could barely hear the approaching steps over his labored breathing. As his pursuer ran past, Moore launched himself from his hiding place and knocked the man to the ground. The man's head struck the corner of the concrete curb. His body went limp as he lost consciousness to Moore's dismay. He wanted to question the man to see why he was following him.

Moore quickly looked around to see if there were any others in pursuit. When he didn't see anyone, he went through the man's pockets, but didn't find anything of value. He did take the small .22 caliber pistol he found tucked in the waistband of the man's trousers. Standing, Moore stuck the weapon in the waistband of his trousers and under his shirttail.

Breathing a sigh of relief, Moore walked to the end of the alley and emerged hobbling onto the busy street. He felt more secure that he had the .22. Now he was no longer unarmed and that pleased him.

Stopping several times to look over his shoulder, Moore quickened his pace as he limped faster. He was eager to return to the *casa* a few blocks away. It was getting late.

When he entered the *casa*, Moore joined Marrero, his wife and young son for a dinner of Cuban-style fried chicken. Afterwards, Moore wandered down the street to a corner café named Patio del Decimista. He took a chair in the shadows and sipped a cup of coffee as he watched people walking by and an occasional vehicle motoring down the street. He looked for Mr. Yellow Cap, but didn't see him.

Moore wondered if his cover was broken. Why had Mr. Yellow Cap been following him? Was it normal to tail anyone new who exited the bus? Or was it just a common criminal studying Moore as a potential target? Moore wasn't sure as he allowed the questions to race through his mind.

An hour later, Moore left the café and returned to the *casa*. Once again, he looked over his shoulder, but didn't see anyone tailing him. It had been a long day. He tossed his duffel bag on the floor and laid on his bed where he fell fast asleep.

The next morning, Moore showered and shaved. When he walked into the dining area for breakfast, Marrero greeted him.

"Come. Come sit down," he said as he pointed to the table that had a variety of fruits. "We picked these this morning. We have papaya, plantains, mangoes, limes, guava, mandarins, oranges and chirimoya," Marrero spoke proudly.

"Looks healthy and delicious," Moore replied as he sat and Marrero's wife appeared with coffee, pouring a cup for Moore.

Afterward, Moore decided to continue exploring Santa Lucha and headed for the marketplace again. He needed to buy a camera and he knew where he could get one. Madame Seres in Key West had given him her cousin's name and address after sharing that her cousin ran a small store near the marketplace.

As Moore limped along with his walking stick, he stopped several times to see if anyone was following him. He saw no one and relaxed. Maybe Mr. Yellow Cap was just a street criminal targeting Moore as a victim.

He located the small store and walked out of the morning sunlight into the store. The store's interior was painted a bright blue and was filled with a variety of new and used items from clothes to cell phone accessories. It reminded Moore of a pawn shop.

A dark-haired man in his fifties walked out of the back of the store to greet Moore. He was wearing a beige guayabera shirt with four front pockets. The shirt had a dark stain on one of the two closely-spaced pleats that covered the front and back of the shirt. The man was sweating even though the morning mountain air was still cool.

"Te puedo ayudar?" (Can I help you?) the man asked.

Moore responded in his limited Spanish, *"Es usted Carlos Mendoza?"* (Are you Carlos Mendoza?)

"Si." (Yes.)

"I'm a friend of your cousin, Madame Seres," Moore explained in English.

Mendoza flashed a quick smile as he switched to English. "Good. And how is she doing?"

"I venture to say that she has a very profitable business," Moore replied.

"She and her fortune telling," Mendoza chuckled. "You're American?" Mendoza asked as he straightened a pile of folded shirts.

"Yes."

"And what brings you to our little town? We don't get many visitors here."

"I was in Santiago and heard about how nice your town was. The hiking is good. So, I decided to check it out."

"Very quiet around here. There's hardly any trouble," Mendoza added.

"Good. I'm hoping to hike up the mountain," Moore said, seeing if he'd get the same reaction from Mendoza as he did previously from Marrero.

Mendoza's face clouded over at the comment. "I will tell you as a friend of my cousin. Do not go up the mountain. It's private property and they don't like visitors," he warned. "Explore all you want below Santa Lucha."

"Oh. Who owns the property up there?" Moore asked as he played dumb.

"Very wealthy man. He takes care of this town and its people," he answered.

It was obvious to Moore that the man was somewhat nervous in saying too much, but he pressed. "Why doesn't he allow people to hike on his property?"

Mendoza carefully eyed the American. "You know how it goes with rich people. They want to be left alone," he said as he sidestepped Moore's probe.

Moore continued. "Does he have something there that he doesn't want outsiders to know about?"

Mendoza was quiet. He cast his eyes downward to avoid Moore's stare.

Moore pushed. "He must have. You're afraid."

Mendoza didn't respond at first, then replied, "I am and so should you be, too. I tell you this since you are a friend of my cousin. Do not go up there. Bad things will happen to you."

Mendoza glanced nervously toward the entrance and the large storefront window to see if anyone was watching him talk to his visitor.

"What kind of bad things?" Moore wasn't letting go.

Mendoza shook his head as he looked down and then back up at Moore. "Sometimes people just disappear," he said softly.

"Because they saw something they shouldn't have?" Moore asked persistently.

"Maybe. Who knows? Just trust me on this."

"Listen, I won't say anything. Your cousin said I could trust you and go to you if I need help. Can I trust you, Carlos?"

Mendoza shifted his weight from one foot to the other as he thought about his response. "I wouldn't trust anyone in this town. This town has many eyes and ears. Everything gets back to El Patrón."

"But can I trust you as your cousin implied?" Moore asked again.

Mendoza hesitated. "I don't need any trouble. I have a good life," Mendoza offered.

"That wasn't my question," Moore pushed. "Can I trust you?"

"Can't you go talk to someone else?" Mendoza asked, slightly irritated at Moore's persistence.

"No. I don't have any other connections here," Moore said. He next threw out a question to see how Mendoza would respond. "Is there a drug operation up there?"

Mendoza's eyes widened in surprise at hearing this from Moore. "What are you? Are you an undercover agent for the United States?" he asked with growing fear. He was not happy where this conversation was going.

"No, I'm not." Moore decided to halfway level with Mendoza and take a chance that he could trust him. "I'm a reporter. I'm doing a story on El Patrón and his operations. I know that I can't talk to anyone else in town. I just need some insight from someone I can trust."

"No. No. No," Mendoza said while shaking his head from side to side. "I don't want to be involved. If they suspect me, my life will become difficult. I could end up dead for talking to you, especially since you are a reporter!"

"I won't say anything to anyone about you helping me," Moore assured Mendoza.

Taking a deep breath as he leaned against a shelving unit,

Mendoza looked at Moore. "If I answer a couple of your questions, will you go away and stay away from me and my shop?"

"I will," Moore agreed quickly.

Mendoza sighed. "Ask."

"Is there a drug processing lab up there?"

"Yes."

"Is it in the compound?"

"No. It's before you get to the compound. There's a road that veers off the main road. It goes to the lab."

"How do you know?" Moore asked.

"People in town talk amongst themselves. They work there. Sometimes I overhear things." Mendoza was becoming more nervous. "That's all I can say. I've said too much," he added, as he looked again toward the doorway for any prying eyes.

"Thank you for what you shared with me. It gives me a start," Moore said.

"You go now. And do me a favor."

"What's that?" Moore asked, hoping he could help the shop owner.

"Don't come back," Mendoza said in a very serious tone.

"Wait," Moore said. "I need a camera. Do you have any cameras?"

"What kind are you looking for?" Mendoza was obviously distraught, but willing to make a sale.

"I'm looking for a small digital camera."

"Step over here," he said as he walked to a shelf that had three digital cameras in a glass display case. "These are the only ones I have."

Moore's eyes took in the small selection. "I'll take that Canon."

The two dickered back and forth on the price and Moore paid with local currency. He slipped the small camera in his pocket.

"Thank you for the purchase," Mendoza said appreciatively as Moore turned to walk out of the store. "If I talk to my cousin, who should I say stopped by to see me?"

"Manny Elias," Moore said. "Please give her my best regards."

"I will do that." Mendoza agreed as he followed Moore to the doorway.

As Moore limped out with his walking stick, he looked around. He didn't see anything that would signal that he was being followed or watched.

Mendoza picked up a broom and under the pretense of sweeping the sidewalk in front of the store, looked around nervously to see if anyone had been watching. He didn't see anyone either and breathed a sigh of relief as he returned inside. He walked to the back of the store and pulled out a bottle of rum that he kept in a cabinet. He poured himself a double shot and downed it quickly.

Mendoza and Moore weren't as savvy as they thought they were. They both missed a watcher who had been tailing Moore since he left his *casa*. He was very skilled at doing surveillance work. He should be. He had worked for Cuban Intelligence for years before El Patrón recruited him into his organization. He reached for his cell phone and called to set up the next step in watching Moore.

Nearing the marketplace in the central plaza, Moore saw several older men sitting in the shade and playing dominoes, a game that Moore was intrigued by and wanted to learn one day. Moore wandered through the marketplace and enjoyed the feel and aromas filling the air.

The vendors were offering an assortment of food and merchandise for sale in their stalls. There were booths offering leather bags, fresh bread, Havana Club rum, Cohiba cigars, churros, sesame sticks, black beans and rice, mojo chicken, herbs, eggs, holy water, wooden carvings, ceramic bowls, jewelry and clothing. It looked like a giant flea market to Moore.

As he neared the other side of the market, he noticed a very attractive dark-haired woman in white shorts and a short-sleeved blouse walking by. He wasn't the only one who noticed her. Three youths eyed her and whispered amongst themselves before breaking into a run after her. Two of them ran past her and turned to ask her a question while the third stopped behind her. As she was distracted by the two boys, the third one reached out and sliced the shoulder strap of her purse.

Grabbing the purse, the youth turned and ran two steps when he received a strong blow to his head. Moore was close enough to launch his walking stick like a spear. The boy shook his head as he fell to the ground, momentarily dazed. He dropped the purse and Moore's walking stick clattered to the ground next to him.

Forgetting to limp, Moore ran over to the boy, but the boy jumped to his feet and ran like a frightened deer around the corner where his two fellow thieves had retreated.

Moore bent over and picked up the purse and his walking stick. He turned to the woman and smiled as he said, "I believe this is yours."

Moore froze when he observed her radiant beauty. Her deep brown eyes were like dark chocolate and tastefully inviting. Long, jet-black hair hung well past her shoulders, caressing a soft, cream-colored face that reminded Moore of the softness of peaches in July.

Her lips were full and appeared as two voluptuous rosebuds flush with bright crimson in a summer afternoon rain. Her wide, gleaming smile was set perfectly against the backdrop of daylight. She wore very little make-up. She looked fresh and clean. He was dumbstruck.

Her lips were moving, but Moore wasn't comprehending. He broke out of his trance and heard her finish expressing her gratitude.

"Oh, you are quite welcome," he said as his senses came back down to earth.

"You're an American," she intimated.

"Yes. And it sounds like you may be, also?" Moore inquired.

"I am." She stuck out her hand. "I'm Lorna Babbit, but my friends call me Peaches," she replied with a touch of a southern drawl. "My daddy started it."

"I'm Manny Elias," Moore said as he shook her hand.

"Hello Manny. Thank you again for rescuing me," she said demurely.

"It was nothing. I hadn't rescued any damsels in distress this morning. So, you were my first."

"I see." She laughed softly as Moore was drawn to her full lips and deep eyes.

"Where are you from?"

"Atlanta. And you?" she asked.

Moore hesitated for a second before answering. "Key West."

"I've always wanted to visit Key West."

"It's a great place to visit. I love living there," Moore said. Spotting a café nearby, Moore asked, "Hey, would you like to grab a *café con leche?*" He didn't want her to get away from him.

"Sure."

The two walked over and took a seat on the sidewalk patio and ordered their drinks. While they waited, they continued to chat.

"What brings you to Santa Lucha?" Moore asked the woman who was about five-foot-six-inches tall.

"My brother," she answered with a touch of anxiety in her voice.

"He lives here?" Moore asked.

"No. He came here for a visit and disappeared. I'm trying to find him," she said. The tone of her voice echoed her deep concern. "I've gone to the hotel where he stayed, but they told me that he just disappeared one day, and they haven't seen him since. They gave me his suitcase with his belongings."

"Have you gone to the police?"

"I did and it was a waste of my time. They said people disappear in the mountains all of the time. Fall off cliffs. They were no help at all," she lamented.

The server returned with their coffee and milk. They mixed the two and sipped the strong brew as they continued their discussion.

Moore wrinkled his brow. "Why did you brother come here?"

"I told you. He came here to visit," she said, slightly irritated that she had to repeat herself.

Moore pushed. "I know. But why here? Did he like to hike in the mountains?"

Babbit lowered her head and scooted closer to Moore. "My brother was a DEA agent. He was working undercover," she revealed.

"And he told you? I didn't think they were allowed to tell you," Moore countered.

"He didn't usually, but he was worried about this assignment and wanted me to know," she explained.

Moore did his best to hide his reaction. Based on what he heard about the life expectancy of DEA agents in Cuba, he figured her brother was dead. But it could also be an opportunity to learn more about El Patrón.

"And he told you that he was coming here to do undercover work?" Moore inquired.

"He did."

"I'm surprised. I thought those guys kept things close to the vest."

"He and I were very close. We told each other almost everything," she confided.

"Did you contact the DEA?"

"I've contacted everyone, including our senators. No one wanted to help. So, I came down here on my own to see what I could find out."

"How many days have you been here?"

"Two."

"Any luck?"

"None at all."

"Maybe I can help."

"Why? Are you DEA, too?"

Moore chuckled. "No. Did your brother tell you who he was investigating?"

"Yes. Some guy called El Patrón. He's supposed to run a drug cartel here. That's all I know."

Moore stared at her intently as he tried to make up his mind whether he could trust her. He decided to take the risk.

"Would it surprise you to know that I'm investigating him, too?" he asked.

Her eyes widened. "You are?"

Moore nodded.

"What are you if you're not DEA?" she asked excitedly, thinking that the man next to her was some sort of law enforcement agent.

"I'm an investigative reporter," Moore replied.

"Oh," she commented. It was obvious that she was disappointed.

"I'm doing a story on his illegal drug activities," Moore confided in her.

"Do you have much?"

"I do as far as his operations in Key West, but I want to see what I can add from here. Maybe scope out his drug processing operations and sneak into his compound."

"Sounds dangerous."

"It is," Moore agreed.

"Maybe you'll find my brother." She reached into her purse and withdrew a photo of a man. "This is my brother."

Moore took the photo from her and examined it. "I'll be sure to keep an eye out for him," Moore assured her, although he felt the odds were against it.

"I can make it easier on you," she offered.

"How's that?"

"I'll come with you," she volunteered.

Handing the photo back to her, Moore protested. "No way. Like you said, it's going to be dangerous." He really didn't want her in the way if something bad happened. It was going to be dangerous enough for him, let alone having her tag along.

"I won't be any trouble," she professed.

"No. I can't do this with you coming with me."

She turned away from him as her eyes filled with emotion. Her disappointment was palpable. He didn't like to see her downcast.

Moore thought a moment. "I'll tell you what I'll do. I'll meet you here tomorrow at the same time and I'll let you know what I discovered, especially if I see anything that would help in finding your brother," Moore suggested.

She pouted as she turned back to him. "I really want to come with you."

"Like I said, no way," Moore said firmly.

"Okay, then. I'll meet you here, tomorrow," she stormed quietly.

Seeing the check on the table, Moore reached into his pocket and pulled out a few bills. He threw them on the table for the server and reached for his walking stick. Moore stood and she did the same.

"I've got some things I need to do today before I go out tonight, Peaches." He reached out his hand and she shook it.

"It was nice meeting you, Manny," she said as her eyes worked their magic on Moore.

"Same here," he said as he reluctantly pulled himself away from the beautiful woman. She could easily be a pleasurable distraction, Moore surmised.

Suddenly he stopped and asked her, "Hey Peaches, where are you staying?"

She smiled and replied, "Hotel Santa Lucha. Why?"

"In case we don't connect tomorrow, I know where to find you," Moore grinned as he turned. He hobbled away and she went in the opposite direction.

Moore finished off the day with exploring the town and talking to people about living there. There were no surprises and many of the people talked about the Baudin family and how much the Baudins supported the town. No one discussed any illegal activities, and Moore was hesitant to bring it up as it could reveal what he was really after.

He returned to the *casa* and rested. After dinner there, he dressed in a dark, long-sleeved polo shirt and dark trousers. He placed the .22 in his waistband and silently crept out of the house soon after sunset.

Keeping in the dark shadows of the night, he made his way to the north side of town and began walking toward his intended destination. He kept to the side of the road to Baudin's compound in case unexpected traffic would necessitate him jumping into the forest. He had learned that it would be a mile walk to where the road ended at a steel gate that blocked the entrance to Baudin's property.

It was a moonless night and with heavy cloud cover, making it even darker. Moore was glad. He had barely walked a quarter of a mile when he heard a sound behind him.

Turning quickly, he saw something dart into the forest. He wasn't sure if it was an animal or a human. Carefully, he stepped into the foliage along the road and waited.

Two minutes had elapsed before he saw a dark-clothed figure furtively walking along the roadside. Moore waited until the person was parallel with him before jumping out of the foliage and tackling the person.

He quickly subdued and pinned the stranger to the ground.

With his flashlight raised overhead in preparation to strike, Moore demanded, "Who are you and why are you following me?"

"I wanted to go with you," a familiar, soft voice beckoned.

Moore recognized the voice. "Peaches! You can't go with me," he said quietly as he eased his body off of hers.

"With you or without you, I'm going up there. I need to find my brother," she insisted firmly. She was not going to be dissuaded.

Sighing and realizing he was stuck with her, Moore commented, "Okay. You can come with me, but you have to do what I tell you. I don't want you getting hurt or getting us captured. Understand?" Moore's serious tone underscored the danger of their intrusion.

"I understand," she acknowledged eagerly. She looked closely at Moore. "Where's your cane? You're not limping!"

Moore realized that his sham was up. "Quick healer," he said weakly.

She looked at him skeptically and shared, "I heard there's a gatehouse there and they have a dog and cameras."

"Doesn't surprise me. And I bet he has armed patrols on the property. We're going to need to be very careful and alert."

"Right," she agreed.

"Follow me. We're going to go over the edge of the mountain and sneak around that gate."

The two moved forward along the road for another quarter-mile before going over the side of the mountain. They skirted through the forest and gave the gate area a wide berth before emerging on the other side of the gate, a half-mile farther up the mountain.

When they reached a secondary road that turned off the main road, they paused.

"I bet that leads to the cocaine processing lab," Moore guessed. Suddenly, they heard the sound of an approaching vehicle.

"In there. Quick," Moore whispered urgently as he led her into the brush next to the road. They crouched as a Jeep Wrangler drove by with two armed men. They appeared to be on patrol.

"I don't think they saw us," she said in a low voice.

"I think we're good," he agreed as he led her back onto the road. They wandered down the mountainside road until they saw lights illuminating a number of buildings.

"Must be his cocaine processing lab," Moore suggested.

"Nothing like being out in the open," she said as they looked at people scurrying around.

"It certainly is easy when you've got the government in your back pocket," Moore added. Spotting a bus parked next to one of the buildings, Moore commented, "That must be how they transport their workers from the town to here."

She nodded her head in agreement as Moore withdrew a small camera and began snapping photos.

"See any signs of your brother?"

"Not yet," she replied.

"Let's get in closer."

The two made their way through the forest shadows to a better viewpoint.

He took a couple more pictures then asked her, "Do you know how they make cocaine?"

"No, I don't have the slightest idea," she answered.

"It starts with the coca plant. Baudin probably has a large

number of coca fields on the mountain. They pick the leaves by hand and soak them in large drums filled with gasoline and some other chemicals. Then they extract the coca base and pour it into brick molds. They press the water out and let the bricks dry into hard blocks before packaging them for shipment."

"Sounds simple," she said as they looked at the open-air buildings that were stacked high with drums that contained gasoline and processing chemicals. Wooden walkways connected the buildings so that the manufacturing process could be done easily.

"I bet he either trucks the bricks down the mountain or flies them out from his compound," Moore said as he eyed a number of large trucks parked near the warehouse area. "I heard that he has several helicopters at his compound."

"Then where would they go?" she asked as she continued to look for any sign of her brother.

"I'd guess the helicopters would take the bricks to one of the marinas so they could load them on Baudin's ships or go-fast boats. Then off to the good ole U.S.A.," Moore offered. He laid his hand on her arm. "You stay here. I'm going in for a closer look."

"I'll come with you," she said firmly.

"No. If something goes wrong, I need you to go for help," Moore cautioned. In the light that was reflected from the lab below, Moore could see that she wasn't pleased with his instructions. "Peaches, I really need you to do this for me."

Reluctantly, she agreed.

Moore turned and began his descent to the processing lab, pausing every so often to take pictures. He couldn't get in as close as he wanted as there were about forty people working at the various processing points. He was frustrated that he couldn't see into any of the closed buildings or the offices that were inside. It was just too risky.

After an hour, Moore made his way back up the mountainside where Babbit waited impatiently.

"Did you see my brother?" she asked.

"No. Nowhere. He may be up at the main compound."

"Okay, let's go check it out," she said as she stood.

"No. No. No. We can't just go barging in there. Baudin's smart enough to have it more heavily protected than here. We better be sure that we can make it safely back to town, then we can figure out what our next step will be."

"I guess you're right," she said resigned to the fact that he wouldn't go anywhere near the main compound that night.

The two stealthily made their way back up the side road to the main road and worked their way around the main gate and guardhouse as they did when they entered. They walked down the road back to town, two black silhouettes against the dark sky.

"So, what did we accomplish?" an exasperated Babbit asked.

"I have some good pictures of Baudin's operations for my story," Moore replied.

"But no sign of my brother," she said frustrated.

"No, and that could be good. I'd say he's being held in the compound," Moore replied, although he thought otherwise, but didn't want to share the thought.

"I shouldn't have stayed back when you moved in closer. I was wrong. I should have gone with you to see for myself if my brother was there." She was irritated.

"No, it was better for you to stay back," Moore countered.

"Didn't you think it was odd that we didn't see more

armed guards?" she asked.

"Not really. I'm sure that Baudin feels secure here. He's not worried because he has the Cuban government bribed up," Moore explained.

"What's next?" she asked. "Are you going to have some DEA paramilitary team swoop in here and kidnap Baudin? Then they can look for my brother."

Moore shook his head. "No can do. Cuba wouldn't permit it. That would create a real political problem. Violating a country's sovereignty is bad stuff."

"Again, what's next?" she prodded.

"Don't know. I'll think on it today," he said as they neared the edge of town. "We better split up so no one sees us together coming down the road. It's almost dawn," he added as the rosy fingers of the sun began creeping over the horizon.

The two went their separate ways and Moore reached his lodging without any problems. He did look over his shoulder a few times to see if anyone was following him. And he was happy that he didn't see anyone. It seemed lately that he was looking over his shoulder quite a bit.

CHAPTER 17

Later That Morning
El Patrón's Compound

After a steep ascent, the main road emptied through an archway into the compound's parking area. Access was past a guarded gate with a concrete lookout tower that gave the guards a good view of the surrounding countryside. Two cameras were aimed at the road and the gate area.

The parking lot contained three white Chevy Suburban SUVs and two pickup trucks. It was next to a large helipad which contained two workhorse helicopters and one sleek, fast-flying helicopter.

There were several buildings within the compound which had walls adorned with mosaics and bright paintings of flowers, animals and birds. A gardener with a machete and pruning tools tended the grounds, which were filled with lush colorful plantings.

Next to the main house was a three-car garage. Its doors were open and displayed a white BMW, a bright red Alfa Romeo convertible and a green Land Rover.

The main house had Romanesque arches and was painted pale blue. A walkway led through the open entryway and past

BOB ADAMOV

a rock waterfall to a large swimming pool in the terrace that overlooked the other side of the mountain. In the distance, one could see the bright blue of the Caribbean Sea and the lights of Haiti at night. The front of the house overlooked the valleys past Santiago to the eastern mountains and Pico Turquino, the highest mountain peak in the Sierra Maestra mountains at 6,560 feet. It was a majestic setting for a drug lord.

Women were flown in by helicopter from Santiago several times a week for drug and alcohol-fueled parties that Baudin hosted poolside.

The master bathroom had a jacuzzi tub that could hold four bathers. The entire room spoke extravagance from the gold-plated faucets to the gold-rimmed mirrors.

The space in front of the sink was filled by the broad frame of a man. He splashed cold water on his freshly-shaven face, then reached for a plush green towel to remove the splotches of shaving cream that were left behind. He ran a comb through his thick black hair. He was a tall man with a broad chest and narrow waist, in his late forties. A waxed mustache hung down the sides of his mouth. There was a sinister aura to the man as he gazed at his reflection in the mirror.

"Patrón," an approaching voice called as Henri Baudin replaced his towel on the gold towel rack.

"Yes?" he said as he turned.

In front of Baudin stood a tough-looking six-foot tall man. His name was Noe Cruz. His face was a skull wrapped in chocolate-colored skin. His black hair was slicked back. His eyes were two dark darts set deep in his eye sockets. He had massive hands that had seen their share of brutality.

"We had activity on the cameras last night."

"The man and the woman?" Baudin asked.

"Yes."

"As we expected."

"Yes," Cruz agreed.

"And you didn't stop them, did you?"

"No. You said you didn't want us to," Cruz explained.

"That's right. What did they do?"

"The man took pictures. She stayed back. We have it all on camera if you want to see any of it," Cruz offered.

"Not necessary. Have someone get his camera right away, but don't cause a scene. Do it quietly," Baudin said in a serious tone. "No sense in allowing any pictures of our operations to get out."

"I'll get right on it," Cruz said as he turned to leave the bathroom.

"Where are they now?"

"They're back in town. We got a call from one of our watchers."

"Are they sharing a room?"

"No. At least not yet," Cruz said as he hurried out of the room.

Baudin turned back to the sink and reached for a bottle of cologne. As he applied it liberally to his face, he smiled. "You've done very well so far, Manny Elias. From Key West to here. Right where I want you. We have a score to settle for killing my people in Key West."

Taking one last look in the mirror, Baudin left the bathroom and headed to his dining room where breakfast waited. After breakfast, Baudin went downstairs into the thick-walled basement. There were several soundproofed rooms there with doors that locked from the outside.

Grabbing the handle of one of the doors, he twisted it and walked inside.

"Any progress?" Baudin asked Socas, one of his rugged henchmen.

"Not yet," Socas replied as he looked from Baudin to a man tied in a chair. The man was badly beaten. One eye was swollen shut from being battered.

Walking casually across the room, Baudin stopped in front of the man who was suspected of stealing from the money-counting operation in the compound. He was caught by one of the room's surveillance cameras.

Baudin's helicopters made daily flights from the marinas, which were used by Baudin's fleet of boats. They flew back the bags of money that were collected when the go-fast boats and ships delivered the cocaine bricks. The money was taken to one of the compound's buildings where it was counted and bundled. The money then was flown and deposited into banks in Haiti and the Dominican Republic as part of his money laundering scheme.

Leaning toward the captive, Baudin asked in a malevolent tone, "Why did you think you could get away with stealing from me?"

The man could barely raise his head off of his chest.

"Oh, come now, you can answer me." Baudin's eyes stared evilly at the man.

"Maybe you need a little pick-me-up to help you talk," Baudin suggested as he looked over to Socas. He motioned to Socas to pour some of the gasoline from a gas can on a nearby table into a small container.

The pungent smell of gasoline filled the area as Socas handed the container to Baudin.

Baudin held the container close to the man's face. "Can you smell this?"

The man's response was a groan.

"Progress," Baudin grinned. "He can speak."

Again, Baudin shoved the container under the man's nose. "Smell this?"

The man moaned again.

"I bet you can. Maybe I should dump it on your good eye."

In reaction to the comment, the man jerked his head to his right, trying to create distance from his tormentor.

"Do you know how much damage gasoline in your eye can cause?"

The man moaned.

"But I'm not going to start there." Baudin surprised the man by dumping half of the container's contents onto the man's shoes and pant legs.

"I could start here and throw a lighted match on you. But no, I have something else planned." Baudin paused to allow his fiendish words to momentarily linger in the man's mind. He was bent on instilling uncontrollable fear in his victim.

Having said that, Baudin poured the remaining gasoline onto the man's crotch. "I think I'll start by throwing the match there," Baudin said as he withdrew a cigarette from his shirt pocket and placed it in his mouth. He then withdrew a matchbook and broke off a match that he used to light the cigarette. He held the burning match close to the man's face before he threw it to the concrete floor and stepped on it.

"No!" the man screamed.

Baudin was taking his time as he used this tortuous method. "But I'm still not done. Maybe first we will take what's left of you outside and, in front of the people you worked with, tie you upside down from a tree and use you as a human piñata! After that, we shall set you on fire. What do you think?"

The man moaned again.

Baudin knew how to keep people in check by using fear. It would be a lesson to them all not to think for a moment about stealing from his operations.

"Are you ready to talk?"

The man's face was contorted with fear. "Yes. Yes."

"Why did you try to steal from me?" Baudin asked as he exhaled a puff of cigarette smoke.

"There was so much. I didn't think you'd mind," the man responded quietly.

"But you knew the money was mine?"

"Yes."

"And you still wanted to take what was mine?"

"I wasn't thinking clearly. I made a mistake," the man replied earnestly.

"You made a deadly mistake."

"But El Patrón," the man pleaded.

"And now I'm your Patrón. What was I when you decided to steal from me? I was nothing. That's what you thought. I was nothing! You should have thought more clearly before you stole from me," Baudin said as he casually flipped his burning cigarette into the man's lap. The man was immediately consumed in flames and emitted shrieks of pain from Baudin's barbarous abuse.

Baudin turned to Socas. "You can douse the flames. Then take him out into the courtyard like I said and treat him like a piñata in front of the money counters."

"As you say," Socas agreed.

"It will be a lesson to them all." Baudin turned and quietly walked away.

CHAPTER 18

Early Afternoon
Santa Lucha

Yawning, Moore rolled over in his bed and reached for his watch. No wonder his stomach was rumbling like a pair of tennis shoes in the dryer. It was past lunchtime and he hadn't eaten breakfast.

He sat up in the bed and swung his legs over the side. He felt rested. He stood and grabbed his shaving gear, then headed for his morning shave and shower. When he returned, he changed into a blue denim shirt and khaki shorts. He also tucked the .22 in his waistband.

Locking the door behind him, he left his room and walked past the owner, Marrero.

"Slept in?" Marrero asked, as Moore walked through the house.

"Yes. Heading out for a bite to eat, Luis."

"We have fresh fruit if you'd like some," Marrero offered.

"No. I'd like something more substantial," Moore said as he walked outside.

"You're not limping!" Marrero acknowledged, as he

realized that Moore was walking normally and didn't have his walking stick.

Moore laughed. "It's amazing. I woke up today and didn't have any problems."

"The Virgin Mary has certainly blessed you," Marrero said as he crossed himself.

Moore grinned as he left the *casa* and walked the short distance to Babbit's hotel. He continued to stop and look over his shoulder to see if he was being followed. They had agreed to meet for dinner, and he was looking forward to getting to know her better. He looked overhead and saw dark clouds moving in. It was going to rain.

Approaching the hotel, Moore saw Babbit sitting on one of the chairs on the front porch. She looked stunning. Her dark hair hung down past her shoulders. Her eyes were alluring. She was dressed in a white linen shirt and khaki slacks. A navy-blue sweater was draped over her shoulders to use as the evening air cooled.

"Hello gorgeous," Moore greeted her as he stepped up to the porch.

She smiled at the compliment. "Did you get your rest?"

"Yes."

"I did, too."

"Hungry?" he asked.

"Famished."

"Great," he said as she stood and hooked her arm with his, surprising Moore.

"I found a little restaurant that looked interesting," she suggested.

"Sure. I'm game," he said agreeably.

The two chatted as they walked three blocks to the

restaurant. It was called La Bodega. The low, one story-building was painted yellow with a red-tiled roof. The interior walls were painted orange and soft pink. Wooden tables with bright yellow tablecloths dotted the interior, where a duo played Cuban music.

"Let's sit outside," Babbit suggested when they entered the restaurant. "It will be easier to talk."

"Sure," Moore replied as the hostess guided them outside and seated them in a far corner of the outdoor patio.

A server appeared and took their drink orders.

"A mojito for me," Babbit said.

"Rum and Seven-Up please," Moore requested as he looked out toward the street to see if anyone looked suspicious to him. He was still alert to being followed and watched.

"Looking for someone?" Babbit asked, as she noticed Moore's eyes searching the street.

"Yes, but I'm not sure who it is," Moore said quizzically, as his face turned back to Babbit.

"What do you mean?"

"Sometimes I sense I'm being followed."

"I frequently have men following me and trying to hook up with me," she teased.

"I bet," he smiled. "I wish I had women following me and that's all it was. But I'm not sure."

"Why do you say that?"

Moore explained what had transpired the day he encountered Mr. Yellow Cap.

"You killed him?" Babbit asked wide-eyed.

"I don't think so. I think he was knocked unconscious when his head hit the street, but I did take his .22," Moore said.

Babbit was stunned by his story and asked, "You always carry a gun?"

"No, but I just haven't felt safe here. That's why I have it," Moore explained.

"I haven't had any problems here," Babbit countered.

"Yes, you did. Remember how we met. The purse snatching?" Moore reminded her.

She smiled, "That's right. I did forget and I haven't even started drinking."

Their server appeared with their drink order and they each made their dinner selection.

Babbit raised her mojito in a toast to Moore. *"Salud, amor y dinero,"* she said in wishing Moore health, love and money.

Moore raised his drink, returning the toast. *"A usted también."*

"Who do you think is following you?" she asked after taking a sip.

"My only guess is Baudin's men. But I don't know what tipped him off to me."

"You are a stranger in his town," she remarked.

"I know, and so are you. Have you been followed?"

She had a surprised look on her face. "I don't know. I never gave it a thought."

"Have you been asking questions in town about your brother?" Moore probed.

"I have," she nodded her head.

Moore frowned. "That could have alerted Baudin. Then if they saw me with you, they could have thought I was with you," Moore proposed.

"I never gave it a thought," she said. "I am so sorry Manny if I've caused trouble for you."

"That's not a problem. We'll just have to be careful," Moore warned.

"All I ever wanted to do was to find my brother," she said remorsefully before taking another sip of her drink. "And I will find him," she said with determination.

Over a dinner of salad, bread and mayo, rice with chicken and mango for dessert, the two talked about their lives. Moore was careful on how much he revealed. As far as she knew, he was an investigative reporter from Key West and he was going to leave it at that.

As the evening passed and two more rounds of drinks, it became obvious they were developing a romantic attraction for each other. The music from inside floated out to their ears and suddenly became mixed with a few rumbles of thunder from the darkening sky.

"We probably should go or we're going to get drenched," Moore suggested.

"You're probably right," she agreed as Moore summoned the server and settled their bill.

The two walked out of the restaurant and were heading down the street when the low-hanging clouds seemed to drop down on the town, covering it in a drenching rain. It hammered like bullets on the metal-clad and red-tiled roofs.

They were caught in the initial deluge and laughed as they ran into a doorway to seek shelter. Their bodies were close. In the flickering light she looked like a beautiful shadow to Moore.

As Babbit looked up to Moore, she said, "This has been a fun evening."

"It has," Moore admitted as he thought momentarily about the amount of alcohol he had consumed.

"You know, you're not like other men I've met."

"I'm not?"

"You're the most honest guy I've met," she said.

"I don't know about that." Moore felt guilty. He hadn't revealed his real identity to her.

"I do. You rescued me from the purse snatchers and let me go with you to the lab, too," she said as she placed the palm of her hand lightly on his beard-covered cheek. She leaned up to him with her lips slightly parted and touched them to his lips.

Her slightly quivering lips and tongue were on fire as she and Moore engaged in a long, passionate kiss and his arms wrapped around her waist. She moaned in enjoyment of their kiss. He bent back and kissed her forehead, her cheeks and her neck. He then took her small hands in his and kissed each fingertip as she laid her head against his chest and listened to his strong heartbeat.

After a few moments, she pulled back and looked into Moore's eyes. "That was very nice," she said sweetly.

"I'll say," Moore admitted honestly.

"Manny?"

"Yes?"

"The men in my life have always done small favors for me. Do your friends do favors for you?" she asked in a somewhat suggestive tone.

"Yes," Moore answered, not sure where the conversation was heading.

"I'm your friend, right?"

"Right."

"So, would you do a favor for me?" She asked as she met his gaze in the semi-darkness.

"If I can," he answered. She was going to be a hard one to say no to, he thought as he looked at how alluring she was.

"I want you to take me to the main compound and help me find my brother," she said in an enticing tone that hinted at a passionate reward in return.

Moore really didn't want to take her into the compound. It would be too dangerous for her, let alone for himself.

"Listen Peaches. You know I can't do that. It's too dangerous."

"But I need to find my brother. He's probably up there and Baudin is holding him captive," she pleaded.

Moore had an idea to buy time. "Let me think about it. There could be a safer way to find out if your brother is there."

"What way?" she asked, frustrated by his refusal.

"I don't know. Promise me that you won't do anything rash until I can figure out what to do," Moore urged.

"I don't want to wait any longer," she wavered with a look of despair.

"You need to be patient with me," Moore said.

"It's difficult. It's my brother," she retorted tearfully. "No one seems to care about him," she added as she wiped the tears from her eyes. She was not usually the crying type.

"Will you be patient?" Moore asked, noting that she seemed edgy. She appeared troubled.

"I'll do my best," she replied, although a plan was hatching in the back of her mind. Placing both hands on his chest, she said, "Just don't make me wait too long." She smiled seductively.

It wasn't lost on Moore that she was giving him a silent promise of better things to come.

"I won't," he assured her. "Are you angry with me?"

"No," she smiled, although she felt otherwise. "I just want to be able to trust you."

"You can," Moore insisted as he realized that the storm had passed. The rain was replaced by the light from an emerging full moon. It bathed her with a soft light, highlighting her beauty.

"We should probably go. The rain stopped," Moore said despite himself.

"You're right," she conceded as they stepped out of the doorway and she relinked her arm with his for the short walk back to her hotel.

When they reached the entrance to the lobby, they stopped.

"Thank you for a wonderful evening," Moore said.

"I hope it's just the first of many," she teased. She kissed him lightly on his lips before entering the hotel's lobby. Her breath was hot and scented with rum.

Moore watched her walk away when suddenly she stopped and yelled, "Hey Manny."

"Yes?"

"There's something that I've been meaning to tell you."

"What's that?" Moore asked.

"You have a nice butt," she grinned and winked at him as she turned.

Was that a subtle invitation or was he misreading her, Moore wondered. Should he follow or not? He elected not to pursue her. He instead watched intently as she disappeared into the elevator, then he turned and walked outside.

He felt more relaxed with the knowledge that she wouldn't do anything rash. He just hoped he was right. Moore knew that she was irritated when he wouldn't agree to her request to take her to the compound.

He didn't want to see anything happen to her. Besides, he admitted to himself, he was growing very fond of her.

Flight

Moore left her hotel and walked a hundred feet away. He climbed the steps to a terrace that overlooked her hotel. He was hoping her room was on this side of the building. Suddenly, the light in one room flicked on and Moore saw her enter the room. He settled back, leaning against the wall in the near distance and watched her.

The shutters to her room were open and a white gauze curtain billowed in the wind. He watched as she walked over to the open window and lit a cigarette. She inhaled and watched as the smoke spiraled skyward. It looked to Moore as if she was in deep thought. Within a few minutes, she had finished her cigarette and threw the butt out the window.

She then walked over to her bed where she stretched. Moore watched as she unbuttoned her blouse and tossed it on a chair. She then slipped off her slacks and threw them on the same chair. Moore felt guilty in watching her disrobe, but he wanted to see if there was anything suspicious about her. He saw her enter the bathroom and close the door behind her. Ten minutes later, she emerged with a bath towel wrapped around her curvy figure.

She turned to face the light switch, dropping the towel as she flicked off the light. Seeing nothing suspicious but more than he expected to see of her, Moore headed back to his *casa*. He was ready to call it a night.

When Moore returned to the *casa*, he walked into the doorway. A very nervous Marrero looked up at him as he entered and nodded. He looked upset as Moore watched Marrero walk to the rear courtyard.

When Moore opened the door to his room, he was stunned by what he saw. His room was a mess. The contents of his duffel bag were strewn around the room. The drawers to the small chest were thrown on the floor and the mattress was halfway off the bed. Someone had been searching for something.

Moore quickly took inventory of the room's contents as he picked up everything. Only two things were missing. The first made Moore chuckle as he saw that the thief had stolen the box of condoms that Meier had given him.

The second missing item made Moore's chuckle disappear as he realized his camera with the photos from the previous night was gone. He mentally kicked himself for not taking the camera with him when he went to dinner. He was glad that he had taken the .22 that was tucked in the back of his waistband. Otherwise, it probably would have been stolen.

Leaving his room, Moore tracked down Marrero in the courtyard.

"Luis, someone trashed my room and stole my camera. Did you see or hear anything?" Moore asked.

Marrero shrugged his shoulders. "I didn't see anything. Sometimes a thief will break into places and steal valuables, especially if they spot a tourist. You should keep your valuables with you, always."

It was obvious that Marrero didn't want to talk about the theft.

"Should I report it to the police?" Moore asked.

"You can, but this type of thing can happen. There's not much they can do," Marrero said as he tried to discourage Moore.

Moore was very frustrated as he returned to his room and sat. He lost his pictures from the previous night's work and now wouldn't have the evidence for his exposé. He decided to return to Mendoza's store the next morning and purchase another camera. Then maybe he could return to the cocaine lab and take more pictures to replace the ones that were in the stolen camera.

CHAPTER 19

The Next Day
Santa Lucha

Sunlight poured into his bedroom window and sweat poured off Moore's body. Yawning, he rolled over in his bed and glanced at the watch on his nightstand. Nine o'clock. He jumped out of the bed, shaved, showered and grabbed a light breakfast before heading back to Madame Seres' cousin's store to buy another camera.

As Moore neared the store, he was puzzled to see that the "Closed" sign hung in the window. The store should have been open for two hours. Moore placed his face against the glass in the front window and peered inside. He didn't like what he saw. He reached into the back of his trousers and pulled out his .22.

Moving quickly, he reached for the front door and turned the handle. Finding it locked, Moore stepped back and delivered a strong kick to the door with his right foot. It broke the lock and the door forcibly swung open.

At the back of the store, two evil-looking men were standing over the badly beaten store owner, Carlos Mendoza.

"What's going on here?" Moore bellowed as he strode through the store.

The two men replied by raising their .45s and firing off a few rounds at Moore who dove behind a display table. Crawling along the floor, Moore made his way to the other end of the table, then snapped off a round at the men. The first shot missed. Moore's .22 coughed again and his second shot struck one of the assailants.

A hole appeared above the assailant's right eye and disappeared into the darkness of his brain matter as he tumbled to the floor.

The other assailant fired twice more, then disappeared out the rear door. Cautiously, Moore stood and approached the rear of the store. He stepped over the body of the dead assailant and ran to the back door where he cautiously opened the door and stuck his head out. He looked up and down the alley, but didn't see anyone. He quickly walked back to Mendoza's side and knelt on the floor.

"Carlos, it's your cousin's friend, Manny. Are you okay?" he asked, although he could see the badly bruised man was severely injured. The man had been violently pistol-whipped.

"You go before the police get here," Mendoza mumbled weakly.

"No, I'll stay with you," Moore replied, not wanting to leave the battered store owner.

"You can't. Too many problems for you. They are watching you," the man murmured.

"Who's watching me? The police?" Moore asked, now concerned.

Mendoza didn't answer. He had lost consciousness.

Moore heard the sirens of approaching police cars, responding to the sound of the gunshots. He looked around the store and wondered if he should wait for the police to enter. He instead decided to take the store owner's advice. He stood and exited out the rear door. Moore walked quickly down the alley and stopped in the doorway of an adjoining building.

He then realized that he was still holding the .22 in his right hand. He tucked the gun back into the waistband of his trousers and looked down at his hands. They were calm, not trembling.

His stomach, on the other hand, felt strange. It was knotted and tense. He took a deep breath and started walking away, trying to figure out why Mendoza had been beaten. It was apparently connected to him since Mendoza had said that they were watching him. And who were they? Was it the police or was Baudin already on to him? Moore was confused. Not the way he had planned to start his day.

Moore spent the next hour walking around the town and contemplating possible solutions. He stopped occasionally to see if he was being followed, but couldn't spot anyone. If he was being followed, they were pretty good at it, he thought—whoever they were.

As Moore neared the central marketplace, he saw a man turning a hog on a spit. The man's wife was slicing off pieces of meat and offering it to people walking nearby. Moore stopped and bought a plateful with a soft taco and a can of pop. He then found a chair in the shade and plopped into it.

Within seconds he was enjoying the tasty pork and thinking about the events from the prior evening and the morning. As he ate, he allowed his eyes to gaze over the activities in the market plaza.

After a few minutes, he saw a bus round the corner and stop at the edge of the plaza. It looked familiar, but he couldn't place it. As he watched it unload its weary passengers and load up another group, he remembered why it looked familiar.

It was one of the buses he saw next to the cocaine processing labs. Must be a shift change. Or it could be workers for the coca growing plantations on the mountain sides, Moore thought to himself. He wasn't sure.

He looked down at the can of pop next to him and picked it up. As he was drinking, he almost spit out the liquid he was ingesting. He saw a dark-haired woman running to board the bus. It was Peaches Babbit. Moore stood and looked at the bus as its gears made a grinding noise and it began moving.

It drove past him and he saw her sitting alone in a seat next to the window. She was staring straight ahead and didn't see him as he shouted several times and waved his arms to get her attention. He couldn't believe his eyes. She was going to try to mix in with the workers and find her brother at Baudin's compound.

Moore was dumbfounded by her action. She was acting stubborn and being reckless. He dropped back into his chair and mulled over what he could do next. Nothing during the daylight for sure.

Moore's mind was filled with ideas for a next step, but none of them seemed practical. He decided to return to the *casa*. When he walked in, he saw Marrero emerge from the rear courtyard.

"Luis."

"Yes, Manny?" the owner asked.

"I just saw a bus drop off and pick up people in the plaza."

Marrero's calm demeanor changed. He appeared to become agitated. "Yes."

"Do you know where it goes?"

Marrero paused. It was obvious that he was uncomfortable in answering. "It goes up the mountain."

"Where?" Moore probed.

"It takes workers to El Patrón's property."

"To his house?"

"It depends on who is on the bus. Some work at the house, some work on his plantation. Others work in his other businesses."

Moore was confident that Babbit was going to the main compound to see if she could find her brother.

After pausing again, Marrero asked, "Why do you ask me?"

"I was just curious. I was in the plaza and saw the bus. I knew it wasn't the same bus line that brought me to Santa Lucha," Moore said.

"You don't want to make a mistake and get on the wrong bus," Marrero warned.

"Why?"

"The passengers are checked at the entrance to the property to make sure they work there," Marrero answered.

Moore's heart skipped a beat. He realized that Babbit would be caught at the checkpoint. Why did she think she could easily penetrate the grounds? "What happens to people who don't belong on that bus?"

Marrero averted his eyes. He didn't want to talk about the bus any more.

Moore pushed. "Come on, Luis. You can tell me."

"I don't know," he replied quietly.

Moore scrutinized Marrero's face. He was confident that Marrero did know. "I'm not going to say anything to anyone."

Marrero looked around before replying. "I hear that some people come back beaten up. Others just disappear."

Moore was afraid that would be the answer. "Thank you, Luis. Like I said, that's between you and me."

Moore returned to his room where he laid on the bed. He spent the next hour thinking about different ways to go after Babbit and rescue her. He soon fell into a fitful nap.

After dinner, he changed into his dark clothes and prepared for the evening's intrusion. As the evening darkened, Moore quietly slipped out of his room and entered the dimly lit street.

He headed for Babbit's hotel. Upon his arrival, Moore entered the lobby and noticed its distinct odor of stale cigarette smoke and burnt coffee. Its stuffed chairs needed to be replaced as they were well-worn and covered with a gaudy fabric. Salsa music drifted out of the bar where a group played to its half-full interior.

He walked up to the front desk where he discovered a balding, overweight desk clerk chowing down a plate partially filled with rice and beans.

"Excuse me," Moore started as he interrupted the man's snack.

"Yes?" the man asked as he wiped his grimy hands on his shirttail.

"Could you tell me if Peaches Babbit is back?"

The clerk tilted his head to the side. "Yeah. She's out on the back porch."

"Thanks," Moore said in surprise as the clerk ignored him and started eating again.

Now Moore was really confused. How had she been able to get through the guards at Baudin's front gate and make it back safely? Moore walked through the lobby and out the rear door to the porch. He looked for Babbit, but didn't see her.

He did notice a white Chevy Suburban parked behind the hotel. The driver's door opened and the rugged-looking driver stepped out. He began to approach Moore.

At the same time, another tough-looking man walked around the edge of the porch. "You're coming with us," the man said as he withdrew a pistol and pointed it at Moore.

"I don't think so," Moore said as he withdrew his .22 and realized that the front desk clerk had lied to him.

Before any shots could be exchanged, Moore's world went black. He didn't see another thug approach behind him and use the handle of his weapon to knock Moore unconscious.

They dragged his limp body to the vehicle where they tossed it in the rear. Then they tied his hands behind him with a plastic tie. The three men entered the vehicle and drove off with Moore.

CHAPTER 20

Forty Minutes Later
El Patrón's Compound

Moaning as he regained consciousness, Moore slowly opened his eyes and saw that he was in a basement room. He sat slumped in a simple wooden chair in the center of the room. Across from him sat a man.

"Awake now?" the man asked as he took an expensive Cuban cigar from his coat pocket and lit it. He inhaled and enjoyed the flavor of its rich leaves. Then he exhaled a puff of blue white smoke that curled upward in the light from a single bulb overhead. He took a second draw and exhaled toward Moore's face.

Moore winced at the pungent odor from the cigar. He shifted position in the chair to angle his body away from the cigar smoke that was drifting in his face.

"Do you know who I am?"

"I can guess that you're Henri Baudin, better known as El Patrón."

Baudin smiled. "Very good, but you're not as smart as you think you are, Manny Elias."

Moore grinned inwardly since Baudin hadn't discovered who he really was. "How do you know my name?"

"It's my business to know strangers in Santa Lucha," he responded firmly.

"Can you untie me?"

"Not quite yet."

"My arms are sore from being behind my back," Moore explained.

"We will see how well you cooperate with me," Baudin said in a deadly tone. "Then I'll see about freeing your hands."

"Cooperate about what?"

Baudin ignored Moore's question. "Why are you in Santa Lucha?"

"I'm on vacation. I'm just a hiker. I came here to hike these beautiful mountains," Moore volunteered.

Holding up Moore's .22, Baudin asked, "And why does a tourist walk around with a .22?"

"For protection."

"Protection from what? Cuba is safe. Santa Lucha is safe."

"Not as safe as you think. People have been tailing me. Someone took a shot at me the other day and someone broke into my room and stole my camera," Moore retorted.

Baudin ignored the comment about the exchange of gunfire. He reached into his pocket and pulled out a digital camera. "Is this your camera?"

The camera was close enough for Moore to recognize it. "Yes. That's it. Why did you take it?"

"I didn't take it. It was given to me. And what were you going to do with these pictures?"

"You had someone steal my camera?" Moore asked with feigned disbelief. He suspected that Baudin was behind everything that had happened to him.

"What were you going to do with these pictures? Answer my question. I don't like to ask twice," Baudin said as he nodded to Cruz who was standing in the shadow slightly behind Moore.

Cruz stepped forward and struck Moore in the rib cage with a rubber truncheon. Moore didn't see it coming and jerked to the side in pain from the sharp blow.

"What were you going to do with the pictures?" Baudin asked as he leaned in closer to Moore.

Moore didn't respond. He just stared at Baudin.

"Who do you work for? DEA? Some other United States government agency perhaps?"

Moore was silent.

"Oh well," Baudin murmured as he stood. "You'll talk. They all do, don't they Noe?" Baudin asked Cruz who was preparing to question Moore further.

"I will see you soon, Mr. Manny Elias," Baudin said nonchalantly as he walked across the room and placed his hand on the doorknob to leave.

"Where's Peaches Babbit?"

A thin smile crossed Baudin's lips as he turned to peer at Moore. "You are not in a position to ask me any questions. But I will tell you that yes, we have her," he sneered.

"You need to let her go. I'll report you to the U.S. embassy," Moore said bravely.

Baudin snickered. "Will you? Careful what you say. You realize that you've entered Cuba illegally. You have no passport. At least there wasn't one in your room or on you when you came in here tonight. There's no record of you being here from what my sources tell me. Technically you're not here; you do not exist in my country. And in my way of thinking, you're going to vanish into thin air or should I say dark soil if you don't cooperate." Baudin laughed sinisterly as he nodded once again at Cruz and left the room.

Cruz stepped in front of Moore while Socas paced the floor behind Moore. Moore tightened his stomach muscles and took a deep breath to prepare for the pain. This was not going to be pleasant.

For the next several hours, the two men took turns beating and questioning Moore. They took a few breaks, and when it appeared that Moore was drifting into unconsciousness, they'd douse him with a pail of cold water.

The door to the room opened and Baudin walked in.

"How is it going?" he asked Cruz in the perspiration-filled room.

"We haven't let him sleep. He is weak and exhausted, but he doesn't fear us. He has said very little since we started."

"Did he say anything new?"

"No."

Baudin scowled and motioned for Cruz and Socas to leave the room.

Moore raised his head from his chest and gazed at Baudin through tired, bloodshot eyes that bulged. Dried blood trickled down his battered face. His chest heaved and his body ached from the repeated blows to which he was subjected. A pool of urine had collected on the cement floor directly below him.

Dropping into the chair across from Moore, Baudin carefully eyed him. "Why are you being so difficult? You're only suffering more." Baudin's body leaned toward Moore. "Tell us who you really are, Señor Elias, and who you work for," Baudin stormed quietly.

Moore slowly raised his head and looked across the small wooden table at his nemesis. Even though he was bruised and battered, Moore maintained his calm and unflappable self-assurance. "I've told you. You can continue beating me, but my story isn't going to change. I'm on a hiking vacation," Moore muttered firmly through his cracked lips.

Despite himself, Baudin admired Moore's inner toughness. Baudin stood and walked behind Moore to a table. He picked up a .45 and returned to sit on the edge of the chair. He pointed the .45 at Moore's knee.

"I know of ways to make people talk. I could start by shooting a round into your right knee and then your left knee. I doubt that you'd ever walk again."

"Or, I could start a little higher," Baudin said as he raised the barrel of the .45 and pointed at Moore's genitals. "I could make sure that you'd never enjoy lovemaking again."

Moore's face broke out in a sweat at the threats, but he was determined not to break. "I've told you everything. I don't work for any agency." Moore's voice was calm as he responded.

Baudin lowered the weapon and stood. "I don't believe you. You are more than what you say you are. Death seems to follow you. I lost several of my people in Key West, including our mutual friend Newton. You killed one of my men in Santa Lucha at Mendoza's store."

Moore's eyes widened at Baudin's revelations. "Newton worked for you?"

"Many people work for me. At least the smart ones do. Are you smart?" Baudin's face was sinister-looking.

"Smarter than you will ever realize," Moore countered bravely.

"Then you should realize how wise it is for you to tell me who you really work for. Maybe, you need some time to think over the consequences of not being truthful with me."

Baudin returned the .45 to the table behind Moore and walked over to the door. Opening it, he beckoned Cruz and Socas to enter the room. He was going to change their approach for getting Moore to talk.

"Yes?" Cruz asked.

"Get him cleaned up. Let him shower. Get him some fresh clothes and lock him in one of the other basement rooms. And make sure he has a good meal."

"Right," Cruz acknowledged the instructions he had been given.

Moore was stunned by what he heard, but it would only last a few seconds as Baudin turned back to face Moore.

"You'll find a comfy bed in the room so you can relax, but I want you to think about the different ways that we get people to talk. Noe, tell him."

"We have very sharp knives that we can use to slowly cause you pain as we skin you alive or dismember you. Or we can attach electrodes to you and run electrical current through your body. Or we can take a sledge hammer and demolish your feet, knees, elbows and hands. There are all kind of ways that we can make you talk your crazy head off," Cruz said with an evil look of glee.

Moore's countenance did not change. He was determined not to show fear and looked forward to this welcome respite from pain. He understood that they were going to give him the heaven and hell interrogation method. He needed to buy time and recover enough to break free and rescue himself and Babbit.

"Well done, Noe," Baudin said as he left the room.

Cruz and Socas walked over to Moore and helped him to his feet. Moore would have fallen if they hadn't been there to hold him. They walked and half-carried him out of the room and down a hallway that ended in a large bathroom.

Cruz produced a knife and cut the plastic tie that bound Moore's arms behind him. "Strip," Cruz ordered.

Moore leaned against the vanity for support for his wobbly legs and shook his arms in front of him to relieve some of the soreness. Then he removed his clothes and stepped into the shower, pulling the curtain closed behind him. The warm water cascading over his body refreshed him as he stood still.

After a couple of minutes, he reached for a bar of soap and began washing himself, carefully scrubbing the blood off his face. His lip and nose were sensitive to touch. When he finished washing his body, he reached for the shampoo and washed his hair. Then he turned the water to cold and let it refresh and numb his sore body.

"You done yet?" Cruz's voice interrupted the pleasure of the water easing Moore's pain.

"Yes," Moore said as he turned off the shower and pulled aside the curtain. He grabbed a towel and slowly dried himself before stepping out of the shower.

He saw a pair of socks, boxer shorts and light tan, cotton short-sleeve shirt and pants on the vanity, which Socas had brought. Moore slipped them on and pulled on his shoes.

"This way," Cruz said as he led Moore out of the bathroom and down the hall. Moore shuffled along slowly as Socas followed with a loaded .45 in his hand.

Moore felt better, but still wobbled a bit and had to catch himself a couple of times when he stumbled. When Cruz led him into a windowless room, Moore was pleased to see a single bed awaiting him. His natural instinct was to head to the bed and crash, but Cruz stopped him.

"There's food for you there," Cruz said as he pointed to a small table with a single chair next to it. On the table was a plate filled with rice, beans and some tortillas. There was also a bottle of spring water next to the plate.

"Thank you," Moore said as he walked to the table and sat. Before taking his first bite, Moore asked, "Noe, can you tell me anything about Peaches Babbit? Is she in one of these rooms?"

Cruz answered by silently walking out of the room and locking the door from the outside.

Moore turned to the food and quickly devoured it. He washed it down with a long swig of the water, then turned to examine the sparse room. Next to the bed was a small stand that held a lamp providing light for the room. Moore spotted a bucket in the corner with a roll of toilet paper on the floor. He guessed he wouldn't be allowed to walk down the hall to use the bathroom.

Moore stood and walked over to the door. He pressed his ear to the door and listened. Not hearing anything, he reached for the door handle and turned it. It was locked, as he guessed. He positioned his face near the edge of the door and called out into the hallway.

"Peaches. Are you there?"

Silence answered his call.

Moore turned and shuffled over to the bed. He plopped down and enjoyed the comfort of the flimsy mattress. Tired, he reached for the lamp. He turned it off and fell into a deep sleep. It wouldn't last long. Maybe an hour.

Suddenly a bright overhead light flicked on and the door was flung open. Cruz and Socas entered the room, yelling at the top of their lungs to wake up Moore.

Trying to ignore them, Moore moaned and buried his head under his pillow—but to no avail. They pulled the blanket off of Moore and dragged him to his feet.

"Time for more interrogation, Manny!" Cruz screamed as they made him walk toward the door.

Moore's brain and body screamed for rest. He wasn't ready for this.

Just as they neared the door, the two men let go of Moore, allowing him to drop to the floor.

"Not quite yet. Maybe next time or the time after that. You can live with that fear," Cruz cackled sinisterly as the two men exited the room, locking the door behind them.

The light overhead switched off, leaving Moore in sweet darkness again. He crawled across the concrete floor and up onto the bed where he immediately fell into a deep sleep.

Over the next three hours, Cruz and Socas repeated the mental harassment twice before finally leaving Moore in an agitated peace.

That peace was interrupted the next morning when the overhead light switched on. Cruz and Socas unlocked the door and reentered the room.

"Wake up," Cruz said as he walked over to the bed, leaving Socas standing in the doorway.

Moore rolled over and groaned. He wasn't ready to get up.

Cruz grabbed the blanket and threw it back. "Up on your feet. You should be able to walk by yourself."

Moore slowly sat up on the edge of his bed, then just as slowly stood. He felt much better and alert although his body ached from the beatings.

Cruz put his hand on Moore's shoulder and gave him a hard shove. Moore allowed the momentum to take him into the doorway where Socas stepped aside. Abruptly Moore pulled the door shut and it locked. Cruz was stuck in the room.

Socas roared as Moore bull rushed him and knocked him to the floor. Then he turned and sprinted, despite his pain, for the exit door at the end of the hallway.

While he did, Socas swore and jumped to his feet. He unlocked the door to let a very angry Cruz out of the room. The two took off after Moore.

Moore ran up a flight of stairs and out through a door that connected the house to the large garage. When he entered the garage, he saw a mechanic leaning against one of the vehicles. He was talking to a guard, who upon seeing Moore, began to lift his .45.

Moore pivoted to his right and started to run out the open garage door. Instead he ran into another guard who was just entering the garage. The two wrestled as they fell to the ground. As they fought, the guard was able to pull a knife from its sheath and attempted to leverage control on Moore so that he could stab him.

Moore wrestled the knife away and with one swift thrust to the man's jugular vein, Moore pushed the knife in deep and his perpetrator fell away dead.

The second guard by now had reached Moore and begun to attack Moore, who struggled to free himself. As he twisted about, Moore abruptly turned and thrust the knife into the guard's chest cavity below the rib cage where it penetrated his heart. Two attackers now were dead.

Moore heaved a sigh of relief, gasping heavily to catch his breath. As he began to get to his feet, the mechanic had crept behind Moore and swung a wrench through the air, striking Moore's head. The intrepid reporter instantly slumped to the floor unconscious, but still alive.

When Moore awoke later, he was once again sitting in the interrogation room and his hands were secured behind his back with a plastic tie. Sitting across from him was Baudin, who was furious at Moore's attempted escape.

"You killed two of my men," Baudin raged.

"Self-defense," Moore countered.

Baudin reached into his pocket and pulled out a small pillbox. He opened it and withdrew a white capsule.

"Open his mouth," Baudin ordered Cruz and Socas, who were standing on each side of Moore. The two men pried open Moore's mouth and Baudin walked over. He popped the capsule inside.

"This should slow you down," he said as he stepped back.

"What did you give me?" Moore asked as the men stepped away.

"Just a little something to take you on a trip," Baudin chuckled wickedly. "Only thing is that it will fill your mind with nightmares. Or maybe it's something like cyanide and you're on your way to meet your maker. One never knows."

"Tell me this, Baudin. If it is cyanide, what are you going to do with the Babbit woman? You can tell me now. It's not going to matter."

"Wouldn't you like to know?" Baudin smiled with evil glee. "Sweet dreams, Señor Elias."

The three men left the room in partial darkness with the door ajar. The light from the open door cast a ray of light about ten feet into the room.

Moore spit out the pill onto the floor. He then used the

heel of his right boot to grind it into the floor. He cocked his head toward the door and could hear the men talking in the hallway. Socas was asking to take a turn with Moore. His voice reflected the anger he felt in allowing Moore to escape.

If there was ever another good time to escape, it was now, Moore thought. He slowly stood and eased his arms up the back of the chair. He then squatted on the floor and brought his arms to his feet and over them so that his arms were now in front of him. He quickly sat back down on the chair and brought his hands to his face. He remembered the technique that his friend Mad Dog Adams taught him some time ago.

Using his teeth, he positioned the plastic zip tie so that the locking bar was on top and in the space between his two hands. Then in one fluid motion, he raised his arms and brought them down quickly while trying to have his shoulder blades touch each other. The zip tie broke and he was free.

Standing again, Moore moved to the table behind him and grabbed one of the knives that they were going to use to torture him. Looking around the room, he noticed that the best hiding spot was in the girders overhead.

He moved the chair to the wall close to the entrance door and used it to stand on. He reached up and painfully pulled himself up among the girders, then quietly positioned himself over the doorway.

The three men were wrapping up their conversation with Baudin instructing Cruz to accompany him and warning Socas not to start any torture until they returned. Moore heard the two walking away. Then he heard a match being struck and soon after smelled cigarette smoke. He guessed it was Socas having a smoke before he returned to the room.

Within a couple of minutes, Moore heard Socas stamp out his cigarette on the floor and his approaching footsteps.

The door opened wide and Socas entered the room. He froze when he saw that Moore and the chair had disappeared. He cautiously looked in the room and saw the chair against the wall, then he looked upwards.

"Looking for me?" Moore asked as he dropped from the open girder and landed on Socas' shoulders.

Socas grunted and cursed as he tried to shake himself free. Moore rode him down to the floor and began stabbing him. He was able to stab Socas several times in the ribs as they fought.

Suddenly, Socas rolled free and jumped to his feet to stand over Moore. His chest was pocked with puncture wounds. Streams of blood crisscrossed his chest and dripped to the floor. Bubbles of blood leaked out between his lips. Socas' eyes swelled and his lips curled back in a snarl. He toppled to his right and rolled onto his back. The pupils in his eyes dilated.

Moore bent over Socas and took his .45. Then he walked over to the doorway and listened. He heard nothing and slowly eased himself out into the hallway. Quickly he ran down the hallway, stopping to open each door as he looked into each locked room for Babbit. He was disappointed because each room was empty.

He ran for the stairway that he had used to escape before and went up to the landing. He slowly opened the door to the garage and looked around for the mechanic. The garage was empty.

Cautiously, Moore entered the garage. As he began to walk by a rear window, he stopped in his tracks and was shocked by what he saw. The window overlooked the pool where Baudin and Cruz were standing under a blue and white-striped awning. They were drinking coffee and chatting with a third person who was sitting in a poolside lounge chair.

Peaches Babbit looked stunning in her skimpy bikini, but why was she there enjoying a cool drink and chatting away with the Cuban drug lord and his henchman?

Moore's heart sunk at the realization that she may have betrayed him and intentionally set him up. How stupid he felt. Moore was extremely disappointed as he now realized that Babbit probably worked for Baudin. He wondered if the purse snatching also was a set up to draw him to her. He hadn't seen this one coming and wondered how long he had been under surveillance.

Knowing that he didn't have time to waste, Moore looked around the garage. For a fleeting moment, he thought about stealing one of the vehicles and crashing through the gate, but quickly discarded the idea. Since there was only one road down to Santiago and it ran through Santa Lucha, which Baudin owned, it wouldn't be practical. Baudin could just call down and have him stopped or chase him from the air in one of his helicopters.

Moore decided to get lost in the mountains. After all, Moore thought, Castro had hidden there for years without being found.

Moore raced across the back of the garage to a side door. A man shouting in the compound drew Moore's attention. He hid behind the Land Rover and looked out into the compound where he saw men carting bundles wrapped in plastic from a building to one of the helicopters on the helipad. He watched for a moment as they heaved the last bundle aboard and heard the man shout at the pilot.

"You're clear. Off to the bank."

Moore watched the men return to the building, which he figured was the money-counting room. The helicopter's engines fired up and its blades began whirling as it lifted off and headed southeast to Haiti.

Moore turned back to the door next to him. He eased it open and carefully peered outside. Seeing no one, he sprinted through the shrubs to the compound's wall, where he was able to climb atop it. He dropped down the other side and disappeared into the thick coniferous forest with its skyscraper pines.

Twenty minutes later, Cruz wandered down the hallway to the room to start the next phase of Moore's interrogation. He walked through the open doorway and stopped. His jaw dropped as he saw Socas laying dead on the floor.

Withdrawing his .45, he looked around the room to confirm his initial thoughts. Moore indeed had escaped. He ran into the hallway and checked each room, but each was empty. He hurried up the stairs and onto the patio. He knew that Baudin was not going to be happy.

"Henri," he called as he emerged on the patio.

Baudin stopped talking to Babbit and turned to face Cruz. "Yes?"

"Socas is dead and Elias has escaped." The words tumbled out in a torrent.

"What?" Baudin asked as he threw his beverage glass to the ground, breaking it before erupting into a string of expletives. "I want him found now! Are any of the vehicles gone?" Baudin asked in case Moore had stolen one.

"I don't know."

"Check the garage! Have the compound checked and see if he's stupid enough to hide here. And alert the gate," Baudin bellowed.

"I told you that you should have killed him right away," Babbitt said as she watched the angry scene unfold in front of her eyes.

"Shut up!" Baudin screamed as he turned and raced into the main house. He stormed into his office and called to one of his assistants.

"Download a picture of that guy who we saw on the video the other night, down by the labs."

Baudin reached for his cell phone and dialed Eduardo Fuentes, the chief of the Intelligence Directorate in Havana. It was Cuba's version of the C.I.A.

"Hello, Henri," Fuentes answered. "And how is your day going?" he asked as he sat behind his expansive desk.

Baudin's reply was profanity-laced as he asked for help in finding Manny Elias.

"Do you have a picture of this Manny Elias?" Fuentes asked.

"Yes. I'll have it sent over right away."

"Good. We will check him out and see what our records tell us about him. Do you want me to send a team up from Santiago?"

"Not yet, but keep them on standby. We're searching the grounds to see if he is hiding here. But check him out for me, Eduardo, and get back to me as soon as you can. He might be DEA."

"We'll find out who he works for," Fuentes said as they ended the call.

When the picture arrived on the fax, Fuentes had his staff scan it into their computers and began running searches to identify Manny Elias.

Within fifteen minutes, Cruz returned to Baudin's office.

"He's not here," Cruz said. "We've searched everywhere."

Baudin's eyes glowed like red coals as a blind rage swept over him like a fire. He began swearing again with the force of a hurricane.

Cruz had never seen Baudin this vehemently angry in the past. He stood and did his best to weather the verbal storm.

Fuming, Baudin turned and looked through his massive office window at the thick forest covering the mountainside down to the tropical jungle. It looked as impregnable as Gibraltar. On the horizon, he could see the blue of the Caribbean.

"It will be tough finding him in the forest," Cruz offered.

"Tell me something I don't know," Baudin lashed out at Cruz as he turned back to face him.

In the face of Baudin's overwhelming fury, Cruz thought quickly. "I know where we could start looking for him."

"Where?" Baudin seethed.

"The cocaine processing lab," Cruz suggested.

Baudin's brow furrowed as he evaluated Cruz's idea. "You may have something there, Noe."

Cruz felt some of the tension leave his body as his boss liked his suggestion.

"What better way for him to strike back at me than to damage that lab?" Baudin wondered aloud. "I want you to bus the workers out. You take two of our best men and hide yourselves in the lab. When Elias decides to strike, you'll have him."

Cruz nodded. "We'll get him."

"Take him alive if you can. I have something special planned for him when you bring him back." A fiendish look filled Baudin's face.

"We'll get him," Cruz assured Baudin as he left the office to put Baudin's plan into motion.

Baudin's cell phone rang. He looked at it and saw that it was Fuentes calling back.

"Hello Eduardo."

"Henri, your visitor is not Manny Elias. His real name is Emerson Moore. He's an investigative reporter for *The Washington Post*."

"A reporter? I don't think so. He must be working for one of the agencies. A reporter wouldn't be as well-trained as he is. No, he must work for one of the agencies. Dig more." Baudin was very dissatisfied with Fuentes' information.

"We'll continue to dig, but this guy is different than typical reporters. He trained with a former Special Forces expert in Florida. That's where he got his skills."

"I don't believe it. Dig more."

"We will," Fuentes assured Baudin. "It looks like this guy has been in some tough scrapes and has survived them."

"Well, he hasn't run into anyone like me."

"You remember the other day that you had us check all possible ports of entry to see if we had a Manny Elias entering the country?"

"Yes."

"We went back and checked to see if there were any records for an Emerson Moore and there were none."

"Like I said, this guy is very skilled. That's why I think he works for DEA or CIA," Baudin boiled.

"We're checking our contacts in the United States to see what we can find," Fuentes added.

"We're setting a trap for him and we should have him tonight." Baudin gloated. "But just in case, I want you to be sure he can't leave the country."

"Consider it done."

The two men ended the call and Baudin turned once again to stare out of his office window at the impenetrable forest below.

Meanwhile, Moore was working his way down the mountain slope toward the cocaine processing lab—just as Cruz predicted. When he left the compound, he had to decide whether to make his way down the mountain or delay his escape and blow up the lab in retribution for what Baudin had done to him. He also thought it would slow down the cocaine processing and hurt Baudin financially.

Moore worked through the thick foliage to get near the lab and find a hiding spot for the day. He stayed away from the road to the lab, remembering that Baudin had surveillance cameras along the road.

He was near enough to the road that he heard one vehicle descending it to the lab. Moore had no way of knowing that Cruz had arrived before him and was setting a trap for Moore.

Occasionally, Moore would fall and slither down the mountainside on his way to the lab. Then he'd lay on the ground and listen for any pursuers coming down after him. He was pleased when he didn't hear any.

Finally, he reached a vantage point that offered him a view of the lab. It was also a good place for Moore to rest his battered body and recuperate a bit. He watched as workers went about their duties. He also noticed a Jeep that was parked by the compound and thought he saw Cruz's head in one of the office windows.

While he waited, he thought back to seeing Babbit at the pool with Baudin. There was no doubt in his mind that she worked for Baudin. How stupid of him to fall into a honey trap, he thought. Women! Was he ever going to find one who was the real deal, he wondered?

Shortly before nightfall, Moore was surprised when all of the workers lined up and boarded the bus that he had seen in town. They were evacuating the lab and leaving no one but

Cruz and a couple of armed men behind. Moore smelled a trap. He knew that they were waiting for him.

He withdrew the stolen .45 and ejected the magazine. After checking to see that it was full, he slipped it back into the weapon. If they wanted to play cat and mouse, he'd play their game—but with his rules.

He watched as the fully loaded bus ground its gears and began to ascend the mountain slope to the compound's gate and the town below. Then he turned his attention back to the lab where Cruz was assigning his two armed guards to hiding places. Moore smiled as he watched each one move to their assigned locations. This was going to be too easy, he thought as the day turned into night.

Moore laid back to relax and wait. It was nearly dawn when he decided to make his move. He figured that the men below would be tiring after their long vigilance.

Slowly he eased down the mountainside and made his way to the edge of the forest. He remained just inside the forest as he worked his way to where he had seen one of the armed guards station himself.

The guard was near the coca leaf drying area and hiding behind a stack of wooden pallets while smoking a cigarette. Leaving the protection of the woods, Moore moved like a ghost as he carefully approached the guard. He crept up on his unsuspecting target. The man never heard Moore coming as Moore swung up his .45 and brought it down sharply on the man's head, instantly knocking him unconscious.

Quickly, Moore went through the man's pockets and found the pack of cigarettes and matches. They would come in handy for what he was planning. Moore used the man's belt to tie his arms behind him and took his 9 MM Uzi submachine gun. It would be handy as it included a 32-round magazine.

Quietly running crouched over, Moore moved to the area where the cocaine was mixed with the gasoline. He had seen the second guard hide in the building's shadows. Moore moved silently closer to the man.

As he neared him, Moore called out in Spanish, *"Un momento!"*

The guard hesitated as he swung around to face who he thought was the first guard. That hesitation allowed Moore time to rapidly close the distance between the two. Moore knocked the guard to the ground and the two grappled. The guard was able to roll free, recover his own Uzi and jump back to his feet.

Turning, he pointed it at Moore. Before he could fire, Moore fired directly into the man's chest, lifting him off his feet and backwards to the ground. The man was dead.

Any plans Moore had to quietly surprise Cruz evaporated with the gunshots. Cruz would be fully alerted.

In the wooden storage building that housed the bricks of cocaine awaiting shipment, Cruz picked up his radio and radioed the second guard. "Did you get him?" he asked.

"No, he didn't get me," Moore answered as he held the dead guard's radio in his hand. "I'm coming for you now," Moore said confidently as he dropped the radio and moved back into the dark coverage the forest provided.

As he flicked on all of the lights for the lab, Cruz thought for a moment about calling Baudin, but dismissed the thought. He didn't want to suffer the ire of his boss. Instead he smiled at the thought of personally killing Moore and presenting the dead American's body to his boss.

He opened the door to the storage building as an invitation for Moore to enter, then hid where he had a clear view of the open doorway. When Moore entered, Cruz would have an easy shot at him.

Meanwhile, Moore was emerging from the underbrush when he tripped over a tree root and stumbled forward just as a bullet whistled through the air, narrowly missing him. Moore rolled and looked in the direction that the bullet had come from. There he saw the first guard who had regained consciousness and freed himself. He was advancing with his .45 in front of him.

Moore fired twice. The first bullet shattered the guard's jaw. The second bullet hit him in the chest, quickly killing him.

Inside the storage building, Cruz heard the shots. He thought about leaving his hiding place, but decided to wait. He was so focused on the open door to the building that he didn't hear the side door open. Moore slipped silently into the building. The noise from two circulating fans overhead masked any sound that Moore could have made.

He paused and looked around. He saw the back of Cruz. He was leaning against a large stack of cocaine bricks with his Uzi pointed at the doorway. Noiselessly, he crept up to Cruz and stuck the muzzle of his weapon against the back of Cruz's skull.

"I'm here," Moore whispered in a dangerous tone. "Push your weapon over the bricks."

Reluctantly Cruz complied and shoved his Uzi forward. It clattered on the wooden floor.

Moore carefully reached into Cruz's holster and pulled out his .45, then threw it to the floor where the Uzi was.

"Do as I say and you'll have a chance to live," Moore warned.

"What are you going to do?" Cruz asked as he continued to lean with his stomach pressed against the cocaine bricks.

"You're going to help me blow up this operation," Moore explained.

Cruz's radio crackled, causing Moore to look at it where it sat on top of the bricks.

Baudin's voice could be heard. "I've been hearing gunshots. Did you get him?"

Sensing that Moore's attention was distracted, Cruz swung around and grabbed Moore's shoulder. Moore spun around and used his elbow to strike Cruz's ribs, splintering three of them. Then he delivered a punch to Cruz's right kidney causing excruciating pain that dropped Cruz to one knee.

The radio crackled again as Baudin asked, "Noe, did you get Moore? Answer me." It was readily apparent that Baudin was irritated by the lack of response to his question.

Slowly, Cruz got to his feet.

"It doesn't have to end like this," Moore cautioned as he held his weapon leveled at Cruz.

Cruz stood still for a long moment, staring at Moore and then threw his head back and laughed before charging forward. He looked angry with his teeth wolfishly bared as he reached out to grab Moore's Uzi.

Before he could grab the barrel, Moore fired several shots into Cruz's chest, killing him.

Then Moore turned to the radio. He picked it up and mumbled a response. "Not yet," he mumbled, hoping to disguise his voice.

"Let me know when you do," Baudin responded.

Moore placed the radio on the cocaine bricks and went outside. He walked over to the barrels of gasoline and began working feverishly. He rolled three barrels up to the wooden building that housed the cocaine bricks.

He found two empty beer bottles and filled them with gasoline to make a Molotov cocktail. He stuffed pieces of cotton from a torn shirt down the necks of each bottle, leaving about six inches exposed.

He placed one bottle on the ground next to the three barrels by the wooden building. He set the other bottle on the ground in front of the remaining twenty barrels of gasoline. Pulling the matches from his pocket, he lit the first bottle, then ran over to light the second bottle before retreating to the protection of the forest.

From the forest edge, Moore aimed the Uzi at the three barrels. He shot off a short burst of rounds that placed holes in the barrels, allowing gasoline to pour out over the ground. He repeated the process by shooting holes in several of the other barrels. In both locations, the gasoline poured out on the ground where the beer bottles were placed.

Moore aimed at the first beer bottle and fired off a few rounds, breaking the bottle, allowing the burning cotton cloth to drop into the gasoline. The result was a loud explosion as the gasoline ignited and the wooden building caught on fire, destroying the cocaine bricks inside.

Then Moore fired at the other beer bottle. When its flame connected with gasoline, the barrels exploded scattering chunks of metal, wood and burning debris around the demolished compound. It was a scene from hell with flames everywhere. The steel drum explosions sent reverberations off the side of the adjoining mountainside and down into the valley.

Satisfied with completing the first step in his night's work, Moore began making his way through the forest. He was returning to the compound for the second step in his quickly-devised plan, one that would infuriate Baudin even more.

Hearing the first explosion below, Baudin hurried to the other side of his house and peered down the side of the mountain. He was just in time to see the brilliance from the second explosion light up the night sky.

Baudin was furious as he called over and over on his radio to Cruz. Getting no response and expecting the worst, he hustled down to the compound where he ordered three of his men to accompany him to the lab site.

They jumped into one of the Suburbans and sped out of the compound. When they reached the access road to the lab, the vehicle careened into the turn and went as fast as it could down the mountainside.

Reaching the site, the driver stopped the vehicle as the men poured out to survey the damage. The fire was still burning, its flickering flames dancing on the shadows of the forest. Little remained of the lab operations. It was a complete loss.

One of the men spotted two burned corpses and alerted Baudin, who walked over to see them. His rage seethed as he looked toward the forest.

"I will make you pay dearly, Emerson Moore," Baudin vowed. "Where's Cruz? Anyone seen Cruz?" Baudin asked his men, who scurried off to search for their number-two-in-command.

The Santa Lucha fire truck that Baudin had bought for the town arrived and the crew began hosing down the burning remains. Later, Baudin would find Cruz's body in the debris from the storage building for the cocaine bricks.

Baudin reached into his pocket and pulled out his cell phone. He called Fuentes. The phone rang three times before it was answered.

"Henri, isn't it a bit early to be calling?" Fuentes asked as he rolled over in bed and saw that the clock showed five o'clock in the morning.

Baudin's anger got the best of him as he blasted Fuentes with a stream of obscenities as he explained what happened.

"Easy. Easy," Fuentes replied. "I can help, but it's going to be difficult finding anyone in those mountains."

"I don't need excuses. I need results," Baudin fumed.

"I'll get some helicopters up and we'll use thermal imaging to find Moore as we fly through the mountains."

"Start here by the lab and work out from there," Baudin instructed.

"Okay. I'll make some calls and get them in the air."

"And lock down the airports and marinas. I don't want him leaving Cuba," Baudin steamed.

"You can count on us to do our best," Fuentes assured.

"I don't need your best. I need results!" Baudin huffed angrily as they ended the call.

Baudin returned to the Suburban and had the driver take him back to the compound.

Meanwhile, Moore had worked his way up the mountain to the compound. On his way, he heard vehicles leaving the compound to go to the lab. Baudin's men would be helping extinguish the smoldering fire and cleaning up the remains. El Patrón was not going to lose any time in getting his lab up and running again.

Moore hoped that the compound would be lightly guarded—and it was. There were only three guards on site— two at the entrance and one in the house.

Scaling the compound's wall, Moore dropped on the other side and crouched. He had two objectives: hurt Baudin by destroying his money-counting operation which he suspected was on site, and secondly, finding Peaches Babbit. He didn't have much time.

Keeping in the shadows, Moore made his way to the first building in the compound. It was near the gate. He found the door unlocked and slipped quietly inside. The room was windowless, so Moore switched on a light.

In front of him was a room that was used for administrative purposes. Moore didn't know it, but this was where Baudin's accountant worked. There were several desks with laptop computers.

Moore strode across the room to an office which had a desk and executive style swivel chair behind it. Moore figured someone important worked in this office. Flicking on the light switch, Moore stepped to the desk and looked for anything that would give him a clue. He found nothing, but a metal door drew his attention. He walked over to it and tried the handle. It was locked.

Returning to the desk, Moore began opening drawers as he searched for a key to the door. No luck. He dropped to his knees and looked under the desk to see if a key was hanging there. Nothing.

Turning to the swivel chair, he reached underneath and felt around. His fingers made contact with metal. It was a key. He was in luck.

Against Baudin's warnings, the accountant had made a copy of the key in case he lost the one he kept on his keychain. He didn't want to incur the wrath of Baudin if he lost his key and had to ask Baudin for a replacement. Hiding it under the chair had been his idea. He thought that no one would ever look there. He was wrong.

Moore withdrew his hand with the key firmly in his grip. He ran across the office to the door where he tried the key. It worked.

He opened the door and switched on the lights. There

in front of him was the windowless, money-counting room. There were several tables with money-counting machines. Garbage bags filled with cash were on the floor, waiting to be counted. Next to the door, Moore saw stacks of money that had been counted and wrapped in plastic, awaiting transport to the banks in Haiti or the Dominican Republic.

Moore's mind raced as to how he could destroy the room's contents. He turned and made his way out of the building. He remembered seeing a stack of propane tanks next to the garage when he had tried to escape the first time. He cautiously walked over to the garage, while keeping an eye out for the two guards at the entrance gate. He didn't have to worry since they were standing outside the gate and staring down the mountainside in the direction of the lab fire.

Seeing a wheelbarrow in the corner of the garage, Moore grabbed it and placed four propane tanks in the barrow. He saw a half-pack of cigarettes on the workbench and stuffed them and a lighter in his pocket.

He looked through one of the Suburbans and found two flares in an emergency kit under the front seat. He threw them in the barrow and looked out of the garage for the guards. He saw them in the distance still watching the lab fire.

As Moore wheeled the barrow down to the money-counting building, his mind raced with ideas for improvising an explosive device. When he reached the building, he unloaded the wheelbarrow and hid it around the corner. Then he quickly carried the four propane tanks into the money-counting room. He placed a tank in each corner of the room and opened the valves, allowing propane to begin filling the room.

After removing the caps from the two flares, he set them on the floor near the door. Then he lit a cigarette and laid it on the floor next to the igniting end of the first flare. He repeated the process with a second cigarette and the second flare. When the cigarettes burned down far enough, they'd ignite the flares which would the cause the propane in the room to explode, destroying the room's contents and causing a huge financial loss for Baudin.

Moore took one last look around before exiting the room and locking the door behind him. He put the key in his pocket and walked out of the office, turning off the light as he left. When he reached the main door to the room, he switched off all of the lights and carefully opened the door. He had little time left in which to find Babbit.

Cautiously peering out of the slightly opened door, he looked outside. He heard voices coming across the courtyard from the direction of the garage. He looked in that direction and saw that the lights were on in the garage.

A guard was talking to Babbit, who had settled in the seat of the Alfa Romeo with the engine running. The top was down, giving Moore a clear view of her. She and the guard were arguing, but Moore couldn't make it out.

Suddenly, the Alfa Romeo accelerated in reverse out of the garage and into the courtyard. Babbit shifted gears and the sports car roared out of the courtyard and through the gate toward Santa Lucha.

Moore was disappointed. He had planned on finding her in the main house and confronting her. There was no way that was going to happen now.

Moore looked over his shoulder toward the money-counting room. His time was running out, but he couldn't leave the building until the guard in the garage went back inside the main house. Moore looked again at the guard who was still staring in the direction that Babbit had driven. After a minute, the guard finally walked back into the house.

Losing no time, Moore raced out of the building and made for the far wall. He scaled the wall and dropped over the side facing Haiti. He needed to put some distance between himself and the compound as he raced downhill as fast as he could through the dense forest. He was thankful that the early morning dawn was giving him faint light so that he could move faster and undetected.

He chose to make his way down the mountain to the sea. He moved as quickly as he could because he expected Baudin to be in hot pursuit. Knowing the success that Castro and his band of guerillas once had in not being found in the thick woods and jungles of the Sierra Maestra mountains, Moore counted on duplicating their feat.

Two minutes later, the compound was filled with the sound of an explosion as one of the cigarettes ignited a flare, which in turn lit up the propane-filled room. Everything was destroyed in the ensuing, raging inferno.

Halfway up the road from the lab to the compound, Baudin was seething as the driver returned him to the compound. He heard the explosion and wondered what Moore had done. Baudin vowed to make Moore pay and make him pay dearly.

When Baudin drove through the unguarded gate, he became angrier. His rage skyrocketed when he saw the two gate guards standing outside of the money-counting building. Smoke was billowing out through the building's open door and through the metal roof which had been blown apart in several places. The metal door inside, that had secured access to the money-counting room, was askew on one hinge and twisted by the explosion.

Swearing at his men, he directed them to get hoses and start working on putting out the fire. In a profanity-laced tirade, he directed his driver to get the town fire truck to leave the lab fire and put the fire out here before it could spread.

Seeing the guard run out of the house and noticing that the Alfa Romeo was gone, Baudin yelled, "Where's the Alfa?" He suspected that Moore stole it and was driving down the mountain.

"Babbitt took it," the guard responded.

"What do you mean Babbit took it?" he growled, furious that she had abandoned him and suspicious that Moore was with her. "Who's with her?"

"She left by herself," the guard replied quickly, wishing he was somewhere else.

"I'll take care of her later. Did you see anyone else in the compound? Anyone who shouldn't be here?" Baudin snapped.

"No. No one."

"Help them," Baudin said enraged. He was livid at the thought that Babbit might have gone to help Moore escape. He reached for his cell phone and called the police department in Santa Lucha. He asked for Perez, the chief.

"Hello?" Perez answered.

"It's Baudin."

Perez sat up straight in his chair. He could tell from the opening tone that it was not going to be a pleasant call.

"Yes, how can I help you, El Patrón?" he asked.

"You know about the explosions?"

"I know about the first two. The fire department told me. I heard a third explosion from near your compound, but I don't know anything about it."

"It's that Manny Elias–Emerson Moore guy. He's behind all of this," Baudin fumed. "I want you all to help catch him if he shows up in town. I think he's smart enough not to go through town, but you never know."

"I'll alert everyone. We'll set up a roadblock. We'll do as you wish," Perez quickly assured Baudin.

"I'll send you a picture of him."

"That would be helpful," Perez replied.

"And find Babbit for me. She took off a while ago in the Alfa."

"She's already gone through town. I saw her while I finished breakfast at one of the cafes," Perez said. "She was driving very fast."

"Was there anyone in the car with her?"

"No. She was by herself."

"Good! Call down to Santiago and make sure they detain her. I want her brought back here so I can deal with her."

"What has she done?"

"I'm not sure, but her leaving as quickly as she did is suspicious," Baudin replied. "She may be involved somehow with the explosions here."

"I'll call Santiago and have them put up roadblocks and I'll send some of the men after her, too."

They ended the call and Baudin began planning to catch Moore.

CHAPTER 21

One Hour Later
El Patrón's Compound

Wasting little time, Baudin was standing in his compound in front of the men that were assembled there. He glanced at the firemen who were dousing the flames of the money-counting building as the smoke mixed with the early morning fog that had crept into the mountain tops. He was dressed in jungle fatigues and heavily armed as were the three dozen men standing nearby, awaiting instructions to hunt down Moore.

Baudin barked out orders to the two helicopter pilots to begin an aerial search for Moore as soon as the fog lifted. He then assigned the waiting men with sections of the mountain to scour. Armed with a rifle and a .45, Baudin led his men out of the compound to search for Moore. The farther down the mountain they went, the farther apart from each other they would spread.

In response to an earlier call from Baudin, one of his foremen in Santa Lucha was contacting the lab workers and others to join his search team. Although they wouldn't be as heavily armed as Baudin's men, they would assist.

Meanwhile, Moore had scrambled in a southeastern direction downward and around the mountainside. Several times in the morning mist he had tripped and fell. Every time as he stood to his feet, he was grateful that he had not injured himself. Any serious injury would slow his escape and now that could be fatal. He knew that it would be too dangerous to head back to Santa Lucha or in that direction. If he was sighted, he'd be at risk of being turned over to Baudin.

After a grueling morning downward trek, Moore was pleased when he found the remnants of a wide path through the forest. The trees along the path were not as old as the ones towering overhead. Moore looked up, expecting to see power transmission lines, but there were none. Strange, he thought to himself.

He decided to follow it downward since it offered easier going than what he had experienced to that point. An hour later, he stopped when the trail ended. He was stunned by what he saw in front of him. It was the crumpled carcass of a plane that was partially covered with undergrowth. It looked like flames had consumed the tail section of the plane, leaving skeletal remains.

Moore's curiosity made him stop to examine the aluminum-skinned plane more closely. As he walked to the side, he saw the large overhead wing. It was bent backwards and an engine with a misshapen propeller dangled from it. A wheel strut was crushed against a tree.

Moore recognized the plane as a Ford Trimotor. He thought back to the missing trimotor from 1928 and wondered if this was it. He also knew that it could be the remains of another trimotor that had crashed. Maybe this was just a plane that was heading to Santiago and got lost in the mountains on its way there. Moore wasn't sure.

It looked like the plane's nose struck first and plowed chunks of rock, trees and soil upon impact. Its nose section with its prominent engine was hanging over the edge of a cliff. There were shards of glass scattered on the stony ground from the impact.

Moore cautiously entered the plane through the twisted midsection. He saw the partially burnt remains of a couple of wooden chests. He bent over to examine them and saw that their contents had been removed. He also noticed several rusty padlocks on the plane's floor. Someone had used bolt cutters to cut them open.

Slowly he made his way up into the nose of the plane and its shattered windshield. He saw that the pilot and co-pilot's seats were occupied by two skeletons, strapped into their seats with their seatbelts and still dressed in what they were wearing when they crashed.

Moore examined their tattered clothes. The co-pilot grabbed Moore's attention since he wasn't dressed in typical pilot attire. He had the remains of a long overcoat or raincoat. Moore remembered that the Pinkerton agent who took off during the hurricane may have been wearing rainwear like this.

He wanted to edge closer, but was concerned about the strength of the floor which was missing sections. He could see through the gaps in the rusty floor to the towering pines which grew from the cliff bottom below. The pines with their cushiony boughs seemed nearly close enough to touch.

Hesitatingly, he placed a foot on the floor between the pilot and co-pilot seat. It was very flimsy and much too dangerous to stand on.

Laying his Uzi on the floor, Moore cautiously reached around to the co-pilot's chest. He withdrew his hand quickly when a large, black and furry spider ran across it and then dropped to the floor. A shiver ran up Moore's spine at the thought of a poisonous spider being hidden there.

Moore slowly repeated the action and found a worn leather wallet. He withdrew it and stepped back a foot or two. He opened it. The first thing he saw was a Pinkerton badge. His eyes widened at his discovery. He examined the wallet more closely and found the identification of the Pinkerton agent. His name was Joshua Van Duzer. He was the missing Pinkerton!

A feeling of excitement rose within Moore as he realized he had found the missing Ford trimotor. He couldn't wait to report it went he returned home as another puzzling mystery resolved.

Suddenly, he heard three taps of metal against metal. Moore quickly turned to look toward the source of the sound. It was coming from the area where he had entered the plane. He was greeted with the sight of a .45. It was aimed at his chest.

"I thought I might find you here," Baudin gloated diabolically.

"How's that? I didn't even know that I'd end up here."

"Obvious. If you were coming around the mountain, you would have come across the easiest way to descend this part of the mountain. I took a wild guess that I'd find you here, Señor Moore."

"You've been here before?" Moore asked as he noted Baudin's use of his real name.

Baudin snickered. "You might say that. This is where our wealth started. It just dropped into my family's lap," he chuckled.

"What do you mean?" Moore asked.

Since he had the upper hand, Baudin decided to humor Moore and tell him. "My grandfather found the plane a short time after it had crashed in the late 1920s. He had heard the stories from Key West about the train that had derailed and its empty armor car. He also heard about the Ford trimotor that was chasing the plane and its disappearance."

"This is the missing plane," Moore confirmed.

"Yes. And you know the story about the missing treasure?" Baudin asked.

"Yes. When they searched the armored train car, it was gone."

"That's quite right. The treasure was never loaded in that armored car. It was misdirection," he laughed. It was an evil laugh.

"What?" Moore asked. "How?"

"There were people who had their eyes on stealing that treasure. That's why the Pinkertons created the misdirection. The treasure was in the plane and my grandfather found it."

"What was the treasure?" Moore asked.

"Gold bars. Probably worth $300 million today."

"That's where your wealth came from?" Moore asked.

"Exactly," Baudin replied with a smirk on his face. "A very good deduction. That Pinkerton in the co-pilot seat was in on it."

"What? How do you know that?" Moore asked in surprise.

"The plane stopped in Havana to refuel before heading to Haiti. Apparently, she ran into engine problems and crashed here."

"But how do you know about Haiti and the Pinkerton agent being in on the deal?" Moore asked.

"My grandfather didn't know at first. My family had roots in Haiti ..."

Moore interrupted, "And your family probably was one of the first sugar plantation owners to flee during their slave revolt."

Baudin tilted his head toward Moore in approval. "Very good. You have done your homework, Mr. Moore. I am very impressed."

"I try to."

"There were some powerful figures in Haiti that had connections to Flagler. When they learned about Flagler's treasure train, they were able to buy off that Pinkerton."

"How did your family know all of this?"

"When the plane disappeared, a couple of the Haitians came to Cuba. They went all over the island, asking people if they had seen the plane. They even had a picture of a trimotor like this one. My grandfather was one of the people they showed the picture to. It turned out that my grandfather knew the guy they worked for and contacted him."

"To tell him he found the treasure?"

"No, he asked if there was a finder's fee because he offered to search the mountains for him."

Nodding his head, Moore commented, "And the whole time he had the treasure."

"Right," Baudin chuckled quietly. "My grandfather played his friend and got more information out of him. That's how he knew about the Pinkerton being bought off. Apparently, the guy was having financial difficulties. So, it was easy for him to be approached."

Baudin continued. "My grandfather had a narrow path cut from our first home on the mountaintop through the forest to the plane. Then he had a couple of trusted workers help him transport the treasure on the backs of donkeys to the compound."

"And your family started bribing whoever was leading Cuba," Moore suggested.

"That was a very good deduction, Moore. Yes, from that time on, the Baudin family could operate in any business we wanted, legal or illegal, and we didn't have to worry about any police interference. We were above the law."

Just then, Baudin's radio crackled, distracting his attention. That's all Moore needed as he grabbed his .45 from the waistband in the back of his pants and took a shot at Baudin.

Out of the corner of his eye, Baudin saw Moore's action and turned slightly. The bullet missed him, but hit the radio, destroying it as Baudin allowed it to drop to the plane's floor.

Baudin fired and the bullet tugged at Moore's left shoulder. As Baudin moved for his second shot, he stumbled over the charred remains of one of the treasure boxes and the bullet missed Moore, ripping overhead into the plane's fuselage.

Moore knew that he was trapped in the nose of the plane. He only had one choice to make. He jumped to the weak area between the two pilot seats and the rotting floor gave way, letting Moore fall twenty feet below to the tops of the towering pines.

As he crashed another thirty feet through the thick pine branches, he was thankful that the branches helped break his fall. His bruised and battered body hit the ground with a thud as he screamed. His right side below the rib was pierced by a broken branch that had been on the ground. It had broken off one of the nearby deciduous trees.

Moore carefully eased himself off the sharp-pointed end of the branch and looked at his wound. It was bleeding. So was the wound to his left shoulder. He saw that the shoulder wound was just a graze, so he wasn't as concerned about it.

Moore looked around and found some moss which he used as a poultice and held it to his side. He knew that moss was a natural iodine and was used for dressing wounds in World War I. Moore found some large leaves which he placed over the moss and then took his belt and tied it just below his rib cage to hold the poultice in place.

Grimacing in pain, he looked for his .45. He had dropped it when he fell through the pine branches, but couldn't locate it. He decided not to waste any time. He pointed himself down the mountainside and started moving.

Within twenty-five feet, he realized that he was weak from his loss of blood and might need a walking stick to help support his weight. He spotted an eight-foot long fallen branch. It was about two inches in diameter and one end was jagged. Moored propped the branch between two rocks and stepped on it, breaking off about two feet.

He picked up the six-foot section and pulled off some small branches that dangled from it. Hefting it, he thought that it would serve him well in supporting his weight and the sharp end could act as a spear that he could use to defend himself. He had no choice and no other weapon. Looking around for imminent danger, Moore turned and continued his downward trek.

Meanwhile, Baudin moved to the gaping hole in the plane's open floor that Moore had made. He peered through the hole with his .45 extended, hoping to get a shot at Moore. He couldn't see anything because of the thickness of the forest. He swore as he looked at the steep cliffsides. It would take some time to climb down as he would have to find a portion of the cliff that wasn't sheer.

Baudin's deadly voice thundered a warning below to Moore. "I'm coming for you, Moore."

Baudin turned and exited the plane. He thought for a moment to go for help since his radio was damaged, but decided against it. He didn't want to lose Moore.

Forty minutes later, Baudin had worked his way down a less sheer area of the cliff and located the spot where Moore had fallen. He smiled to himself when he found Moore's .45 and tucked it into his belt. As he searched the area under the trees, he was surprised when he found fresh blood on the ground.

He inspected the area more closely and saw blood on the end of a sharp branch that was pointed upright. Moore must be hurt, Baudin grinned at his good fortune. He began to quickly make his way through the forest down the mountainside as he hunted Moore.

Two hours later, Moore reached the edge of a clearing and again stopped. The burning pain in his side overwhelmed all other feelings. Gingerly, he reached under the poultice and gently touched his wound with his left hand, then brought his hand up to his eyes. It was not red with blood which meant the bleeding had stopped. He was relieved, but felt weak from the loss of blood. He knew that he had to push himself forward or he'd likely die.

He looked across the clearing as he decided whether to risk being in the open. As he did, he listened for any noises from behind that would indicate a pursuer was near. He heard nothing and started to emerge from the forest when another noise caught his attention. It was the thumping sounds of helicopter blades.

Moore shrank back into the forest and watched as a Cuban Army helicopter flew low over the area. Baudin must have everyone under the sun looking for him, Moore thought.

Not wanting to risk being in the open after seeing the helicopter, Moore skirted the clearing and walked around the edge of the forest until he could continue heading downward. His frustration grew as he wasn't walking as fast as he wanted. The pain below his ribs was slowing him down.

An hour later, Moore emerged from the forest into another clearing with grass four feet high. He was trying to decide whether to again risk crossing an open clearing when he swatted away a bee, then another and another. He turned to look behind him and shuddered at what he saw.

It was a massive bee hive. He guessed it was seven feet in length and two feet wide. It was attached to a tree close to where he had emerged from the forest. It was swarming with bees, perhaps thousands of bees and more than he had ever seen in his life.

Moore recalled his research on poisonous life in the mountains and jungles of Cuba. He had read several articles about killer bees with up to 800,000 bees living in a hive that size. They were known to be very aggressive and could become easily enraged. If the hive was disturbed, the entire colony would attack their target relentlessly.

The killer bees would leave their stingers in their target's skin with the venom sac still attached. The sac would continue to pump venom into the victim and cause a toxic reaction. The victim could have difficulty in breathing, swelling, nausea, diarrhea and vomiting as well as unconsciousness and a heart attack. For those allergic to bee stings, it could also cause instant death. In any event, immediate medical attention would be warranted.

Moore turned away and began walking slowly across the clearing. He was eager to get away from the bees. He had walked forty feet when a voice froze him in his tracks.

"Got you, Moore."

Moore turned to see Baudin walk out of the edge of the forest. He held his .45 at waist level and pointed it at Moore. His rifle was slung over his shoulder.

Moore leaned on his walking stick. "I thought I lost you."

"Not that easy. And I'm going to enjoy taking you out," Baudin glared as he looked over Moore.

"I have to admit I'm surprised you got as far as you did with the bullet wound to your shoulder and the wound that you got when you jumped from the cliff. I saw your blood on the ground. Is it still bleeding, Moore?" Baudin asked with feigned concern.

"No. But some pain killer would help," Moore replied.

Moore's reply made Baudin smile as he casually swatted away a bee with his left hand. "I have just the right painkiller for you," he chuckled as he raised his weapon up and down.

"Before you kill me, I have a question," Moore said.

"Go ahead," Baudin smiled. He was curious as to what Moore wanted to know.

"What does Peaches Babbit do for you?"

"Anything I ask," Baudin grinned.

"I'm serious," Moore retorted.

"So am I," Baudin countered before adding, "She's more than she lets on to be. She runs cocaine in the U.S. for me. She's also very good at deceiving people, as you found out. She said you were a real pushover."

"My weakness. Seeing a damsel in distress syndrome," Moore agreed, disappointed at hearing the truth.

"You were set up so easy with the purse snatching. We figured you'd jump in. A honey trap, yes? From then on it was so easy to find out more about you, although you had us going with that Manny Elias alias. But we soon uncovered who you really were, Emerson Moore," Baudin boasted. He was enjoying verbally toying with his prey before he killed it.

Moore shrugged his shoulders, then winced in pain from the shoulder wound.

"Tell me, Moore, before you leave this earth. Who do you really work for?"

"I'm just an investigative reporter," Moore answered truthfully. "From Key West."

"No, you're with a newspaper in Washington. Right? Tell me the truth," Baudin urged.

"I did." Moore decided to be a bit difficult.

"You know Moore, I can make this very painful for you. I can kill you slowly until you talk and tell me who you really work for," Baudin warned in a dangerous tone.

Moore knew that Baudin was right.

"Will you give me a sporting chance?" Moore asked as an idea crossed his mind. There was one way that he could avoid certain death if Baudin would agree.

"What do you mean?"

Moore straightened his stance and lifted his walking stick. He groaned from pain as he hefted the stick like a spear.

"You give me one chance to take you out."

Baudin's laughter echoed off the trees and across the field.

"With that? That's not even a good spear. You think you can kill me with that?" Baudin asked with disbelief.

"I do. It's a Hail Mary, I admit," Moore confessed.

Baudin scoffed at the absurdity of Moore's request. "I thought you were smarter than that, Moore." He paused. "And if I allow you to try and you don't kill me, what's in it for me?" Baudin asked, thinking what a fool Moore was.

"I'll tell you who I really work for and then you can kill me," Moore answered.

"Okay. But you are very foolish. Take your best shot," Baudin said confidently. He planned to adeptly step aside if Moore's spear came close to him.

Moore stood with his left side facing Baudin and, with all of the strength he had left in his weakened body, launched his spear. In the process of heaving the spear, he reopened the wound in his side. It started bleeding again. He grimaced in pain.

Baudin roared with laughter as the spear soared over his head, missing him.

"You're dumber than I thought, Moore. Now, who do you work for?" Baudin asked as he raised his .45 to shoulder height and aimed it at Moore's chest.

"Not as dumb as you think," Moore said triumphantly as he looked toward the edge of the forest. "Think again!"

"What do you mean?" Baudin asked, not comprehending why Moore was responding in that manner.

"Look behind you, Pilgrim." Moore nodded behind Baudin.

Baudin turned and saw that Moore's spear was stuck in the bee hive and the disturbed and angry bees were swarming toward Baudin. When Baudin turned to shoot, Moore had disappeared.

The bees aggressively attacked Baudin, burying their stingers all over his body. The swarm covered him as his screams of agony filled the air. He tried to run back into the forest, but he couldn't move. He looked like a walking bee hive as the colony shrouded his body.

Within minutes, Baudin's suffering ended in a tormenting

death. His heart ceased to pump life through his toxic-filled carcass as he fell to the ground.

When Baudin turned his head to see where Moore had nodded, Moore had dropped into the tall grass to hide from Baudin and the bees. He quickly and painfully crawled away as he heard Baudin's cries of anguish. He had hoped the bees would go for Baudin who was nearer to them and his plan had worked. It was a well-deserved death, Moore thought.

Reaching the other side of the clearing, Moore slowly stood as the pain wracked his body. He looked back. He didn't see any bees and turned to reenter the forest. Walking slowly, he found some more moss and made another poultice that he used to replace the original. He retied his belt to hold the new poultice in place as he continued his descent through the ravines and valleys. He stopped to find a new walking stick and to drink water from nearby streams.

As day changed into night, Moore found a rocky outcropping that would serve as his hideout for the night. He dragged some broken pine boughs to his hideout. He leaned some of them upright to create a wall while he pulled the others over him to keep warm in the cool mountain night. He hoped that the rocky ledge would help hide his heat signature from any helicopters using thermal imaging tools to try to spot him at night.

Moore had a difficult time falling asleep and it wasn't because of the pain from his wounds. It was a different pain. He couldn't stop thinking about Peaches Babbit and how she had deceived him. Over and over like a broken record, his mind replayed his interactions with her and reminded him how stupid he had been. Exhausted physically and mentally, he finally fell asleep.

He tossed and turned all night with the pain wracking his side and shoulder and from the bruises he incurred during the fall from the plane wreckage. When he awoke the next morning, he slowly emerged from his hiding spot and surveyed his surroundings for danger. Seeing and hearing nothing of concern, he continued his escape.

As he walked, he wondered if anyone had found Baudin's body. He thought that Baudin's failure to respond to any calls on his radio could send his people to find him. That could give Moore some breathing room, at least until they found Baudin's body.

If they found the radio in the plane, then they'd probably start searching for their El Patrón, but they'd narrow the search to the area below the plane and that part of the mountain. That could be bad for Moore, because it would help their search become more focused. Finding Baudin dead from bee stings and not from Moore's hand could help confuse them as to his location. There were so many "what ifs." Moore's only hope was that it would take them time to locate the radio and Baudin, then he could make it to his objective.

As he walked slowly, he spotted a bohio—a thatched hut with palm fronds. Moore took cover behind a tree and watched it for twenty minutes. When he didn't see any activity, he carefully approached it. As he neared it, his head moved from side to side for any signs of danger—and he was grateful that he didn't see any.

When he reached the open doorway, he peered inside— hoping not to be greeted by a wild boar. It was empty. It looked like it hadn't been inhabited for some time. There was a stool and an overturned wooden table. In the far corner, he saw a sleeping mat on the floor.

The hut was so simple that it made an Amish home look

like the Ritz Carlton. Moore searched through the hut, but found nothing more than an old knife. He stuck it in his waistband and exited the hut.

Surveying his surroundings, he decided to continue his trek to the rainforest below. In the distance he could see the sky darkening and heard thunder like the beat of a drum. It was a storm blowing in from Haiti and the Dominican Republic.

In a few hours, Moore was sweating and weakening as he stumbled his way down the steep slopes of the jungle that he had entered. It was hot and humid in the shaded jungle of palms and ferns. He stopped several times when he heard helicopters pass overhead and to drink from the swift-moving creeks where water cascaded over boulders and rocks. Moss and begonias lined the water's edge and sprawled across the rocks.

The rain had been threatening most of the day and finally unleashed its fury. It came down with a rush. Lightning flickered overhead and the thunder rumbled, too. The rain increased into a solid drenching downpour. Moore was concerned that the rain would slow his downward trek, but he also recognized it would ground the helicopters that were searching for him and slow his pursuers.

Moving as quickly as he could in his weakened state, Moore grabbed fallen palm fronds and tried to shelter himself from the torrential rain. He spent the rest of the day and night huddled in his makeshift shelter. It wasn't long before he developed a fever and endured a restless night of terrifying dreams.

When he awoke in the morning, he was barely conscious as another hot and humid day greeted him in the rainforest. He eased his head up and listened for any noises that would betray anyone hunting for him.

The foliage was alive with noises—hums, clicks and other sounds. A swarm of gnats surrounded him, plunging into his ear canals and nostrils. Flies settled at the corner of his mouth where they drank from his drool. Attacking his scalp and his underarms, mosquitoes swooped up from the ferns and wet areas and swarmed in clouds. He didn't have a chance as they attacked him in his weakened state.

His shirt was torn and stained. His trousers were in tatters. His eyes opened and he saw the dense canopy overhead. He was on his back, but he felt agony in his back and shoulders. Moore painfully turned his head to one side, then another. He was still alone. He crawled out from under the palm fronds.

A movement out of the corner of his eye caught his attention. He turned to look and saw a hutia, a tree-dwelling rodent. It looked tasty, but Moore didn't have any means of catching it.

As Moore placed his left arm on the ground in preparation to stand, he felt a sharp pain in his arm. He quickly looked down in time to see a small scorpion scurry away into the underbrush. Moore let out a sigh. It was going to be one of those days, he thought, although he was thankful that it wasn't a larger scorpion. He expected that the pain would eventually subside, as would any swelling from the sting.

His stomach noises distracted him, reminding him that he had not eaten in two days. He looked around and spotted a bush with red berries. He crawled over to it and plucked some of the berries. He was so hungry that he decided to take a chance and eat some.

After a few handfuls, he mashed some of them into a paste in the palm of his hand. He then applied the paste to his face to see if that would help protect him from the bugs. Moore was desperate. When he saw that it worked, he grabbed more berries and made more of the paste. He applied it to his exposed skin. Not only did it provide relief from the bugs, it felt like a healing salve on his skin, especially on his scorpion sting.

As he moved to a sitting position, he looked around. Rainwater droplets were dripping off the ends of the palm fronds. They would be evaporating in the morning heat. He gathered several fronds and folded them in half, then allowed the water to flow into his mouth when he lifted the fronds to it.

He observed a large tarantula scurry by and shivered. He didn't like tarantulas and wouldn't want a bite from one. He spotted an eight-inch long centipede on a nearby twig. He thought for a moment about catching the centipede and eating it, but decided against it. He wasn't that hungry.

He listened to the sounds around him again. He could hear the rustle of the palm fronds in the warm breeze. He spotted several snails crawling on the ground. They were green, yellow and red. He thought about eating them, but couldn't bring himself to give it a try.

Slowly standing to his feet, Moore began moving downhill again. He was walking noticeably slower than the previous day. He did his best to avoid the thick underbrush of the jungle and decided to walk along the rocks next to the creek. The pain in his side throbbed as he staggered through the rock-strewn creek bed.

About an hour later, the rain returned and continued for the whole day. Moore found refuge under an overhanging ledge near the stream and he sat there shivering. He became nauseous from the scorpion sting and then began throwing up the red berries that he had recently consumed for breakfast.

Moore's mind was becoming clouded. He was cold and he shivered in the shelter without any covering to ward off the chill from the cold rain. He was exhausted from the loss of blood, lack of food and the trek downward.

Physically drained, Moore prayed for strength. He didn't finish his prayer. Instead he fell asleep.

When Moore awoke the next morning from a fitful sleep, he was very frail. A movement in the undergrowth caught his attention. He watched as a jungle-chicken emerged and began pecking the ground.

Slowly Moore crawled the short distance to the undergrowth and began to search it. His effort paid off as he found the chicken's nest. It held two eggs. Carefully Moore picked up the two eggs and broke them open. He downed the gooey contents for breakfast. It wasn't much, but it provided some nourishment.

It was time to go. He used his makeshift walking stick to help him stand and he nearly fell over. His weakened condition caused him to wobble on his legs. He knew that he couldn't continue walking and he saw his chances for survival were disappearing.

His attention was drawn to the creek, which had changed in flow from a slow-moving stream to a raging millrace. He saw several logs floating with the current downstream and decided that would be his ticket out of the mountains. His strength was too spent to think that he could complete his escape by walking out. He felt that he had no choice but to ride the water to safety.

As he walked toward a nearby log, he stopped when he heard a noise in the jungle. He turned and saw a Cuban parrot with its colorful plumage. Scanning the tree line, he also saw one of the pygmy owls that Cuba was known for. He jumped suddenly and almost fell when something ran across his foot. It was an iguana. He smiled weakly as he watched it move across the rocks and back into the jungle.

Trying to focus on the task at hand, Moore pushed the log to the edge of the creek. Removing his belt, he loosely tied it around the log so that he could stick his right arm through the loop, then pushed himself into the stream.

Upon entering the creek, the force of the current knocked Moore off his feet and he was dragged with the log downstream. He ignored the excruciating pain when his side made contact with the log. It was an arduous and pain-filled journey as the log and Moore ricocheted off of boulders and other debris in the creek where more water rushed in from adjoining creeks.

The creek dumped into a small river and Moore floated with it. The current was quick and the depth of the water increased as he rapidly descended the mountain. Because of the increased water depth, Moore and his log stopped bumping into boulders, and he was carried quickly down the river.

It was a tiring experience for Moore. He felt half-drowned and the cold water was sapping away more energy from his already debilitated body. He was nearly lifeless. An hour passed and Moore's log stopped abruptly as it smashed up against other debris that had piled up against a wire fence trapping the flow of debris under a bridge.

The water, however, overflowed the bridge due to heavy rain and swept across the roadway into the first of several fences guarding a security perimeter. A sign in Spanish warned that trespassing was prohibited. It was the United States Naval Base at Guantanamo Bay.

The base is located at the foot of the Sierra Maestra mountains on the southeast side of Cuba. It encompasses forty-five square miles of land and water as it straddles the entrance to the bay on two points, Leeward and Windward, about forty-three miles southeast of Santiago. The city of Guantanamo is eighteen miles up the bay from the base.

Just as Europe had its Iron Curtain, Cuba had its Cactus Curtain. The Cubans planted an eight-mile long barrier of opuntia cactus along the desert-like northeastern section of the seventeen-mile perimeter fence surrounding the base. It was in addition to the minefield they placed along their side of the entire fence in an effort to stop Cubans from fleeing to the U.S. Both sides of the fence contained guard towers from which American Marines and Cuban soldiers stared at each other daily.

Moore had been swept along the Guantanamo River and under the Cuban fence to the American perimeter fence. His plan to reach "Gitmo" had succeeded, but his survival remained questionable.

With agonizing pain decimating his body, Moore tried to disengage his arm from his life-saving log, but was too weak to make the final push out of the debris-clogged river. His body had been tormented enough and Moore lost consciousness.

From one of the guard towers, a Marine raised his binoculars and casually swept the field of his sector. He slowed as he carefully eyed the area where the river entered the base. With widening eyes, he refocused the binoculars as he saw an arm on a log in the river where the debris had collected. He took a second glance to make sure his eyes weren't playing tricks on him.

Quickly he reached for his radio and contacted the base Marine Corps Tactical Operations Center.

"TOC. This is sector seven."

"Go ahead sector seven."

"I may have a body in the river. You want to send over one of the Hueys?"

"Roger that. One Huey on the way," the dispatcher responded as he turned to direct a chopper into the area.

Within a few minutes, a low flying Huey approached the area. It dropped altitude and flew slowly over the river to get a bird's-eye view before making a hard-banking turn.

"We've got a body in the water," the chopper pilot radioed the TOC. "We're going to pop smoke and deploy a rescue swimmer for a snatch and grab."

"That's a go," TOC radioed back.

The Huey descended to ten feet and flew over the body. As the rescue swimmer was lowered from the chopper in a rescue basket, he threw out a couple of smoke flares to hide what they were doing from the prying eyes of the Cuban tower guards.

When the basket touched the water, the swimmer rolled out of it and headed for Moore with the basket in tow. When he reached Moore, he saw that the fallen reporter was not responsive and that his arm was strapped to the log. Working quickly to release the arm, the swimmer began heaving Moore's body into the rescue basket. He then looked up and gave a thumbs-up for him to be hauled into the chopper.

When Moore reached the chopper, he was lifted out of the basket which was then dropped back down to retrieve the swimmer. A flight medic began checking Moore's vitals.

"Is he alive?" the pilot asked.

"Barely."

"Yeah. Looks like he was trying to get on the base," the pilot guessed. "Came down the river. If he was trying to flee Cuba, good thing he came down the river and missed the minefield the Cubans have laid on their side of the fence," he said.

Once the rescue swimmer was aboard, the chopper regained altitude and air speed as it flew toward the base hospital.

Moore's blood pressure was low. His heartbeat was irregular and difficult to detect. His breathing was labored. He was suffering from dehydration and hypothermia.

His paled skin and limbs were cool when the flight medic touched him. His skin was turning a bluish purple, signaling that blood circulation was poor—a sign also that his blood was being drawn to the vital organs. Death was near.

The medic quickly gave him an IV and oxygen and started to treat him for shock. When he examined Moore's eyes for a response, they had an empty, dark look about them. His pupils were non-responsive and dilated.

"Come on, buddy. Stay with us," the medic said urgently to Moore before radioing the results of his examination to the emergency room staff. Who knew what type of bacteria Moore had picked up in that swollen river filled with a variety of dangerous microorganisms?

The chopper landed at the base hospital. It was a low, two-story concrete building painted white with aqua shutters. It was staffed with two hundred fifty personnel, providing full medical support to base personnel and their families.

Emergency room personnel rushed out with a gurney and transported Moore inside.

Twenty minutes later, a red-haired monster of a man pushed his way into the emergency room. "Where's Moore?" he stormed.

"We don't have anyone here named Moore."

"What about that guy who was just brought in from the river?"

"He doesn't have any identification," the staff nurse responded.

"Mind if I take a look? He might be the guy we've been looking for," Chuck Meier asked as he toned down his voice.

"No. Go ahead," she said, knowing how difficult and headstrong these contractor warrior types could be in a crisis. She could always spot them, she thought as she escorted him into the emergency room.

As they entered the room, there was a flurry of activity and a number of doctors and medical staff were working feverishly on one patient.

Pointing to that patient, the nurse said, "That's him."

Meier walked over to the gurney and peered at the patient's face. He recognized Moore immediately and turned to the nurse.

"That's my bro. His name is Emerson Moore—American civilian," he said as they began to walk away. "It looks like he's in pretty bad shape."

"He is," the nurse agreed.

"Is he going to make it?"

"They're not optimistic."

To Be Continued

Coming Soon
The Next EMERSON MOORE Adventure
Assateague Dark